The Tarshis Family Endowment

of The Library Foundation

THE Library FOUNDATION

Enhancing the work of our library
libraryfoundation.org

WEDDING BUSH ROAD

WEDDING
BUSH ROAD

A NOVEL

DAVID FRANCIS

COUNTERPOINT

BERKELEY

Library of Congress Cataloging-in-Publication Data

Names: Francis, David, 1958- author.
Title: Wedding Bush Road : a novel / David Francis.
Description: Berkeley : Counterpoint Press, [2016]
Identifiers: LCCN 2016020224 | ISBN 9781619027879 (hardcover)
Subjects: LCSH: Families—Australia—Fiction. | Interpersonal
  relations—Fiction. | Domestic fiction. | BISAC: FICTION / Literary.
Classification: LCC PR9619.4.F73 W43 2016 | DDC 823/.92—dc23
LC record available at https://lccn.loc.gov/2016020224

Cover design by Kelly Winton
Interior design by Domini Dragoone

COUNTERPOINT
2560 Ninth Street, Suite 318
Berkeley, CA 94710
www.counterpointpress.com

Printed in the United States of America
Distributed by Publishers Group West

10 9 8 7 6 5 4 3 2 1

For Judy Francis
(1923–2008)

And I hear the far-off fields say things
I cannot bear without a friend.

—Rilke

FRIDAY

✦———◇———✦

hat are you humming, my love?
W Water pours down the louvers, blurring the last of the afternoon. The bridge at the bottom of this wild ivy garden, the creek that flows down Wonderland. A street that morphs into the riverbed it once was; the paved-over streams of the Hollywood Hills unfurling down the blacktop. This rain will disappear and it'll be dripping and dark, silent but for the sound of water on leaves and the whisper of raccoons. And you'll be alone here, Isabel.

You kneel on the hearth with your lips slightly parted, sewing popcorn on a string to loop around our homemade Christmas tree. Fashioned from wire and tape, elegant and fine-boned as you. Four months since you flew across country to study reflexology when I knew it was really for us. The way the amber refracts in your eyes, the dark caterpillars of your Venezuelan brows.

As I pack this pile of clothes you've folded on the bed, you turn the switch and the branches illuminate. Fairy lights wreathed with white blossoms. "What do you *reckon*?" you ask, imitating my accent, yours still laced with your mother's singsong.

It could be a garland of miniature gardenias but for the smell of popcorn in the air, dancing with smoke as it curls from your incense. Those kundalini yoga classes you take every morning, down the hill at Golden Bridge.

"Will you be safe from those guys in linen and scarves?" I ask.

You touch the opal I bought for a pendant, now set in a big hoop earring. It's supposed to change color with your mood but it always stays that peacock feather blue-green. "We'll see," you say and smile, your bleached teeth glistening, the one in the front that wants to overlap. Your hair in the firelight, you crouching barefoot in your low-cut jersey dress, almost molten. It drapes without clinging as you hang those tiny wooden ornaments. I've only managed to toss in my shaver and toothbrush; my body has the handbrake on. Images of the ornate bathrooms back on the farm, cobwebbed and paint-peeling, Victorian.

You come over and rest your face in the nape of my neck. "Come on," you whisper, "we can do this." Pairing socks from the heap, you roll them, taking care of me in ways I'm not used to. Coming out here to master the vagaries of the nervous system at some shonky-looking woo-woo school. I want to tell you not to worry, there'll be socks stashed in my wardrobe in the Senator's Room, but you're already folding short-sleeved shirts, the pink and green with the Penguin insignia. I wouldn't be seen in that down there.

"I'll be back by New Year's," I say.

EIGHT THOUSAND MILES and two days lost to the blazing Australian summer, when I'd promised myself I'd ask her to marry me before year's end. A promise eclipsed by last week's telephone call. "Family's first," said Isabel. But why is that? Why not this? She folds my boxer shorts with strange precision, too many pairs, like origami, packing for who I am when I'm here. I'll miss her rose perfume. A six-foot tree made from nothing but coat-hanger wire and tape, lit up as if it's real. The glow of occasional car lights, the dull squish of tires. This guesthouse attached to the slope with rogue ivy, the great shadow of the stringy-bark outside the window, perpetually shedding. The water pulling at every-thing. Isabel rolling my seersucker shorts—imagine what Old Nev would say if I donned those, if the Genoni brothers saw me in the town.

"We need to hit the road," I say. My mother told me she thought she was dying. *Dead as Dickens by the end of the year*, she forecast, pretending not to be scared. "So much for Christmas," I say, clasping my Samsonite case. Lunch reservations at Providence, our plan to drive up the coast to Santa Barbara, a night at the San Ysidro Ranch. My plan to be all romantic, kneel with a ring and ask her. A dream swept aside by a phone conversation. "We'll have a lifetime of Christmases," says Isabel, but her tone feels tenuous.

We both stare up at the collage of photos arranged on the wall she painted blue to surprise me. Me on a small white pony by the pond. The house through the long angular shadows of the cypress trunks. My mother playing polo as a girl.

"What if I don't go?" I say.

If I leave this new life, even for a short while, will it keep and still be waiting?

Isabel pushes a sheaf of dark hair from her eyes, secures it back with a band. The light timpani of rain on the roof now, softening. "You'd never forgive yourself," she says.

"What if the plane gets hijacked?"

She ties a tartan hair ribbon to the suitcase handle. "You've already been hijacked."

THE TOO-LOUD SOUND of my suitcase wheeling across the wet bricks drowns out the hum of chanting, our landlady's group in her drawing room. The candlelit shapes of them fondling their beads, raising their eyes to the newfallen dark.

"You're not driving in this weather," I tell Isabel, but still she puts on her tortoiseshell glasses as if I need a copilot. I reach across and slam her in.

The Jeep hydroplanes down Lookout. "Must we go so fast?" she asks. I try to slow down, don't mean to scare her, but LAX will be a nightmare this time of year.

The marquee at the Sunset 5 and the avenue of lights all the way down Crescent Heights, shimmering south forever.

Green lights, all of them. What does it mean? "It's amazing after the rain," I say, but my smile feels forced. The knot in my gut releases then tightens at the prospect, maybe the longest flight there is, and my mother's voice so frail on the phone. My mother who avoids telephones, slurring the "D" in my name, more concerned about some old car on the farm set on fire than the fact that her left side isn't working right. *Maybe you had a stroke,* I said.

Maybe I've had a few, she answered, *but I'm not going to that hospital.*

Alone with her dog in that big old house, not answering the gong at the door. *I need you here,* she said, and she never says things like that. The fear of duty and losing her coursed through me all night. I'd cashed in all in my Qantas miles by morning.

Turning right at Beverly, Isabel smiles over at me, calm and cautious. "We should take La Cienega all the way." Her new command of the city amazes me, how proud she is, her chin raised high.

"Name dropper," I say. She tries to temper me, make me notice things—another avenue of lanterns unfolds, the streets gleaming, pristine, the miracle of rain these days, but I run another amber light and feel her cinch. She learned to drive out here in a week, the same way she lives, in rhythm with time. I'm the one always pressing the edges. I can't seem to help it, the image of LAX on the last Friday before Christmas.

I reach for her hand. "Speaking of all the way," I say. "When I get back can we talk about . . . you know? Getting hitched?"

"Hitched?" She stifles a laugh. "Is that your Australian way of asking?"

I stare at the taillights. Now would not be the time. "I'm just saying let's have the conversation when I get back."

"If I'm still here," she says.

Traffic slows. The city south of Pico seems suddenly nondescript. Another red light. The hunger in the men's eyes as they look at her from other cars and I'm heading away and back in time, the known world slipping out behind me like the clothes I should have left. I *parp* the horn to get things moving, make the light at Washington.

"You should come with me," I say as if that's even possible now. My disingenuousness laid between us like the grease-slicked water pooled on the road.

"Next time," she says. She wasn't ashamed of her mother's place in Queens. The pale sculpture of Jesus on crutches with rolled-up dollar bills around his hands, spotted plaster dogs licking at his feet.

Random oil derricks planted on the bare hills in the middle of the city shine in the dark like enormous praying mantises. "Make sure and call me when you land," she says.

Traffic backing up, a bottleneck all the way to La Tijera. "I will," I say, but I forgot to get roaming on my phone. "I may go with Mona to Esalen," she adds. Her new friend from those kundalini classes, my hands bunch on the wheel. "There's a Rumi and ecstatic dance retreat." She's looking out the window, into other cars. "It won't be the same as being with you, but it's something."

I'm not even sure what that means. "Be careful on that road," I say. "There are rock slides this time of year. Don't drive up at night." The idea of her smashed on the cliffs of the Pacific Coast Highway makes me want to turn this car around. And Mona, the heavily tattooed photographer she met at yoga. Nice enough but now I've suddenly gone off her, the idea of them on a trip of their own to some *woo-woo* retreat in Big Sur, while I'm taking care of what's left at the farm. It has me spinning the wheel and making my own lane, splashing along the rain-filled edge to pass the line of idling cars.

Isabel from the corner of my eye, her hands on the dash. "You can just let me out here."

I veer back into the flow without any indication, right before the light. Honking from behind, someone flashing high beams. "You know I love you but I really need to get there," I say.

She turns away. The opal dangling, reflecting in the red of the taillights, now somehow gray, not aquamarine. "No need to kill us," she says, "It's only a plane." She stares over at me, the amber alive in her eyes. "I bet your mother's a tough old bird," she says.

THE QANTAS A380 is silent through the air, especially with Isabel's plush earphones, the drinks trolley a mirage appearing down the aisle, an Australian film without the sound on—two pretty mothers falling in love in a beach town somewhere, maybe Queensland, the coast windswept with palm trees blowing. It makes me think of photos of New Guinea. My father in a safari suit. Now the chance of my mother dead, Isabel so Zen about the possibility when she doesn't know my mother at all. I told her my mother might be circling the drain, but she wouldn't go down it so easily.

Isabel didn't want to come inside the terminal, just asked that I park at the curb outside Departures. She came around to the driver's side and kissed me full on, but she didn't look back when she got in the car. She just drove away.

I settle in with a pillow and cover my head with the blanket for the long haul, enter the fugue state for traveling. But my mother's phone call keeps reconstructing itself in my mind, some need to make more sense of it. She's deaf as the night but an explosion woke her. I see her out of bed and on the veranda, a flicker of orange against the dark. "I thought it was the cottage," she said, a flame roping up at the edge of the bush. The field where she said those three big horses live. She knows how things begin and end in flames. The fire along Station Road all those years ago, the night my father was nowhere and I slipped inside that unlocked cottage somehow knowing, straight down the blackened hall. The childlike panic on his face as he sat up in bed beside his tenant, Elsie. In his dead mother's bed, uncovered by his teenage son, his hayfield burning like broom straw. My mother out fighting the flames alongside the firemen. The New Year's night she threw my father off his own farm.

This time my mother said she dialed the CFA even though she doesn't approve of involving outsiders. "A fire at the cottage on Wedding Bush Road." I imagine her moving through the paddocks in the dark, the way she knows the land by heart, the shapes of the concrete water troughs, the shadows of the rabbit warrens, the cattle as they balk. The distant flicker and a hint of smoke, a far-off siren wailing. I imagined it from above, the fire truck already on the highway and my mother breathless down by the windmill. I asked if she'd been okay before the fire but she ignored me, wanted me to hear the story. She didn't seem to know her speech was strange.

"It wasn't the cottage but a car in the back paddock up in flames." She talked about the shadows of the heavy horses circling, arched up with fear. She left the gate open as the cattle shuffled through it and away but the three big horses retreated and advanced, snorting as she flapped her coat. She told me how the car was furled in flames and the cottage on the rise a dark spectator. My mother who's too old for fighting fires in the dark the way she did the night she threw my father out.

On the phone she said she gave up swinging her coat at the burning grass when she noticed a piece of my grandmother's sideboard from the cottage, an ornate hacked-off corner, and then at the base of the flames a dining room chair, a bridge table tossed on the hood, sending sparks. My grandmother's furniture that had survived the passage from England eighty years ago, used as kindling.

She allowed as how the flames were blue and orange,

wrapping round a mahogany headboard, chopped in strips. The bed where my grandmother died with *The Book of Shrubs* on the pillow beside her, her small round specs on the still-open page.

I cover my head again with the blanket, try to get my feet warm, pulling on those awful nylon airline socks. I imagine my mother out in the night, wonder if she had on more than slippers. The fire engine rattling in over the cattle grid toward the burning furniture and car and my mother in a sweep of yellow headlights. "It was Bobby Genoni," she told me, shouting. Bobby Genoni who I played tennis with as a kid, when I was back from boarding school and hung out with the townies. Now they were unwinding canvas hoses. Gusts of high-pressure water on the windshield, a burning chair sent flying, charcoaled pieces of French-polished wood.

"Sharen," my mother shouting, pointing to the cottage, her voice no doubt trailing off in the wind, firemen yelling. The hissing of car seats and my absent father's burning heirlooms, sprung from the house he rented out regardless of my mother's warnings. He promised he'd keep an eye on them. "An eye on his new tenant," said my mother, rather than his valuables.

"Then I saw your rocking horse," my mother told me. "That was the last straw." I imagine its silver mane and leather bridle incinerated. My grandmother rocked me on it as a boy; hers as a child in England, the country she called the "Frightful Antipodes." The wooden horse now blackened, its paint blistered in the rubble. From under this blanket I see

Granny Rawson's delicate English face, her blue eye shadow. How she lay in the bed beside me.

My mother told me how she had wet soot on her hands, treading through the dark toward the cottage. She climbed the chicken-wire fence. "Your father cares less for his family treasures than a chance at a woman like Sharen." My mother pounding on the green-paneled door but the door wasn't locked. Sharen's outline through the frosted glass into the sitting room. I'd already heard about the smell of pot, adulterating rubbish, and now the fresh-split mahogany. There alone in bra and panties slouched in a modern rocker-recliner, a room bereft of my grandmother's things, the axe leaning up against the wall. My mother said she found Sharen in a kind of trance, staring out at the waning bonfire in the night, firemen in their yellow coats ranging about in the beams of the truck lights, the steaming remains framed by the window in the dark.

"I wanted to drag her out by her stringy blond hair."

But when Sharen Wells turned away from the window she was sobbing. "I'm so sorry, Ruthie," she said. "I couldn't help it." She got up from the recliner and hugged my mother. "It's not you, it's Earley. He's really got to me."

My father's name is Earley, a family name. My mother used to say "Better Earley than not at all," but she doesn't say that anymore. His middle name is Derrick, which she says is short for Derelict, of duty. She also calls him Gates sometimes, just as a reminder, so he might be more reliable and close the gates behind him. He lives five miles away in a sad-looking brick veneer in a coastal subdivision my mother christened Bitter Snug when it's really Blind Bight. Still, he attends the farm every morning as if he's a day laborer, lighting the wood boiler in time for my mother's shower, for hot water to groan through the pipes, to go out and feed wheelbarrowed hay to sixty horses. And though I transferred the title to the farm into my mother's name before I left, to shield it from his de factos, he believes he still owns the cottage at the edge of the bush because his little English mother died there. He's not much for legal concepts or fidelity. At seventy-six he still has his cheeky smile, his charms. Cocooning myself in this thin airline blanket, struggling for comfort, spearing through the sky toward him too.

* * *

SUNDAY

◆———◇———◆

T he sign on the gate droops only slightly. *Tooradin Estate.*
Driving up silent in a new-model Prius, past horses in
fields, some in fly veils under the dying cypresses, swishing
their tails, the cattle yards freshly creosoted, past the barn
that was once the shearing shed, the corrugated iron saddle
room, the ancient stables. Lucerne trees struggle to survive
in the dust. The chicken coop's fallen in a heap.

Twenty-four hours since I left LAX, with a five-hour
layover at Sydney, the flights on to Melbourne overbooked
for Christmas. I should have known I'd have low priority,
flying on miles. Exhausted, I park the Prius under the flowering gum, its boughs that drape to the earth. Walking up
to climb the stile by the woodshed, the rented car looks
akin to something from another galaxy. I take in the hot,
dry air, the view to the bush out the back. A distant black
shape in the field, the burned-up Mitsubishi, and behind
it my grandmother's cottage still there on the rise, its

bay-window eyes staring out at the Pakenham Hills as if watching for fires.

I get my bag and roll it along the bluestone path to the big house. The long veranda striped by the shadows of the cypress trunks in the late afternoon, the lawn all but dead save for capeweed, the garden thirsty but overgrown. This place that's so verdant in spring. No dog out here to greet me. Just the meat-safe and laundry, the ivy crawling, eating the bricks. The brindle cat spies out from under the bee plant, the bees already swarming.

Staring through the stained-glass kitchen door, I wonder why Isabel isn't with me to dilute this. I can hear a dog barking but it's not here at the door. The house unlocked as always, no wreath or signs of Christmas. A lump in my throat as I push the door open. The vague smell of compost and frantic yelping. A glimpse of my mother in the dining room, alive and mobile, armed with a broom and flyswatter. Her movements jerky, the same boys' jeans cinched tight but baggy now, legs thin as wires as she follows the dog deeper into the house. After seven years I'm afraid to see her face.

It's usually a bird they're hunting but as I enter the dining room, a brushtail possum scratches its way along the picture rail. It pisses with fright on the portrait of Aunt Emma Charlotte, then over the pastel of me as a boy. The innocent eyes that were never quite mine. My mother's face paler, so angular now, the wattles on her throat buttoned like vines into a high-collared shirt. Still she doesn't notice me, mesmerized by the leaping dog and the hiss of the possum as it plummets to a corner table, smashing plates, and hurtles out past me through the open doors and into the warm Gippsland evening, the dog a blur behind it.

My mother turns. "Hello, my boy," she says, as if knowing I was here all along. "How was your trip?" She hoists the broom over her shoulder like a rifle.

I give her a hug but her body stiffens as if she's afraid it's too American, so I retract my arms and rustle up a smile. "Hello, old girl."

"Did you get yourself an upgrade?" she asks, but doesn't wait for an answer, already involved in a project on a kitchen bench, as if I'm a ghost that often appears. Still, I wonder how she's heard of upgrades.

She's irrigating ants from a cupboard, wiping them up with an ant-speckled cloth. Her left arm moves awkwardly as though with a life of its own. Is she showing me how she can cope by herself? Wanting me here but showing she doesn't need me? Observing her in this strange silence, in the no-man's land between the kitchen and living room, back in this place that's been here all along. The faint rustle of wood ducks nesting in the chimney, cooing again now the house is still, the house that coos as if calling out. A place for the shelter of various species provided they keep themselves hidden.

"It's good to see you," I say.

She waves her good arm. "Nearly finished," she says. The slur is barely evident now. Maybe she was drunk on the phone, but I doubt it. She's never had more than a Bailey's after dinner.

A letter lies open on the kitchen table, the table already set for tomorrow's breakfast. Set for two. She remembered I'm coming. She's good at writing things down. But this writing is not hers; it's angled and childlike, addressed to *Those Whom Are Concerned,* signed at the top and the bottom, *Sharen W.*

My mother pretends not to watch as I pick up the heavy crayon paper. She guides a trail of golden ant poison along the ledge. My mother slaughters armies of them, shows off piles of the dead to occasional visitors. Magpies and noisy miners fly down these chimneys, seeking shade, the black and tan dog lying in wait to hunt them, to land them stunned and breathless on the hardwood floor.

I am not aware of how much you know but I can only assume you are naive in the field. That is of the situation of Earley and myself and I will not be harassed by Earley who is bulling me to leave. I pay the same for my horses being here as anyone else but I don't get the use of the faculties.

I glance up, my mother's eyes upon me. "She's illiterate," my mother says, "but no fool." Sharen Wells, whose rent checks provide my mother's shopping money. "Looks like he jilted her or she jilted him and now he wants her out." The way my father turns on women, except my mother who turned on him first.

I feel sorry for the fire but there is a stigma because of me and Earley. Also I have been attacked by those three black

Clydesdales. None of this is safe for me but I will not leave under these provisions. I will get my own soliciter. I will not be railroded.

"Hell hath no fury . . . " My mother trails off as she hands me a dustpan, a load of dead bees and ants, spoils of the sweetness she's left on the jam jars as lures.

I head outside and stand on the path beneath the lantern, empty the dead insects on a lavender bush, and watch the purple remains of the sky, the glint on the windows of the distant clapboard cottage, way out the back where the wedding bush grows. You can see it from Station Road on the way into town or from the window of the shearer's quarters, or from here, out across the Lagoon Paddock rise.

The brilliant band of the Milky Way stretching above me, a vivid skin across the sky, and near the horizon the Southern Cross rests on its side, marking its emu head on the lip of the night. Not like our view in LA as we walk up the top of the street to Lookout Mountain from where the city glitters as if the night is upside down.

I think of Isabel there in the guesthouse in the eucalyptus canyon, the lemon-scented gums that remind me of this place. But she's alone up that winding brick driveway, the call and response of coyotes and local dogs, the rustle of squirrels and raccoons in the leaves. The Christmas gift I slipped under her pillow. I already miss the feel of her, the vague smell of incense and the taste of her rose-scented skin.

The phone rings shrilly, summons me inside. My mother under her jigsaw lamp, leaning over a Wysocki puzzle. She's

always been sharp at cards and crosswords and puzzles—
she did a stint in the fifties with the War Office in London as
a cryptologist, deciphering codes. Now she has the television
on so loud it sounds as if a plane's about to land on the roof.
Oblivious, she gazes at her line of jigsaw edges, the bottom
of a lighthouse, as the black rotary phone on the desk goes
unanswered. A crackling message being left on the machine.
"Ruthie, it's Sharen. Are you okay? I need to talk."

"She grows marijuana out there," my mother lifts her
head, "in tubs in a horse float." She doesn't mention the fire,
returns to sorting pieces of sky. My mother, who dreads
the phone and resents others using it. The silver polo mug
of familiar pens and broken pencils, the "situation" with
Earley. I don't want to deal with this Sharen. Her number
fifth on a list tacked to the wall, after the fire brigade and
the vet, my father and Dr. Hopkins.

"Mum, do you want to talk about what's going on?" I ask.

"Not tonight," she says. "You must be so tired."

She doesn't ask about me, away in her Wysocki world,
staring at jigsaw pieces. I traveled eight thousand miles. But
she seems strangely detached, parting and closing her lips.

I pull my suitcase along the carpeted hall and let it rest
outside the good bathroom. The original tiles, the bath with
its iron-clawed feet. The same aqua toothbrush with the
pick waiting for me here in a small pewter goblet. I squeeze
the remains of my miniature Qantas toothpaste and regard
the jetlagged ghost of myself in the mirror.

Back in the living room, I replay the message, wondering what my father has done to this one. On the television

screen, the marsupial eyes of the new prime minister. Only the dog observes me from its roost in the cushions along the back of the couch.

I dial Isabel but the call goes straight to the service, her new-age music I try to find charming. I leave her a message, "*Lejana y sola,*" *away and alone*, quoting the Lorca poem she taught me. "The Song of the Horseman." I hang up and wish I'd not sounded glib, watch my mother who might just as well be on her own.

I call Sharen Wells from the list of numbers on the wall, a call that rings and rings and has me succumbing to an old desire to escape this house and find out what's going on, steal out like my father used to. *Through the meadow, through the wind, pitch-black pony, crimson moon.*

"Earley come, Earley go," my mother used to say, but at least he stayed local. I got lost in cities far away.

THE SILENT PRIUS glides through shadowy fields, scraping along the overgrown track down toward the windmill, rabbits scurrying in the unexpected spray of headlights. As I close the Lagoon Paddock gate behind me, a *whoop* above me, maybe an owl, then three dark horses emerge from the night, approach to sniff the soundless car. Heavy part-Clydesdales with wide chests and foreheads, broad appled rumps. The two with no white I don't quite recognize, but one has a blaze, probably the twin foal born hind legs first the year I left, grown into this giant mare with curious eyes. Dockweed stalks plume her forelock, sticking out like fragile antlers.

Back in the car, I press the shrill horn. The three raise their heads in unison, turn and trot stiffly away, one with its black tail high as a flag in the air. The familiar cacophony of crickets. I try to remember why I don't live here. The noise or all the silence. The whisper of horses moving through the grass. As if the past might fold in on itself and disappear.

Lights from the cottage, its bay windows beckon through trees, the bedroom where I lay with my grandmother, the book between us. Suddenly there was no more snoring and I could sleep. I didn't know she'd gone to be with her Jesus. The same bed where Elsie slept and my parents' marriage ended.

A dark hump appears in the gray beams, the blackened frame of Sharen's car hunkered among the charred remains. Steel and ash and wood. Thirty yards beyond it, the garden fence, the yard that was once tidy, now a carnival of corrugated iron, engine parts, and overgrowth, a rusted clothesline moaning. My grandmother grew hibiscus here, black-eyed peas and black-eyed Susan, a seven-foot passion fruit vine.

I park under a gum tree near the garden gate and wend my way on foot past an old metal wheelbarrow, rusted fenders, and a sunken laundry trough, to the sagging carport. Gingerly, I knock on the brown waterlogged door, unsure why I'm here. My father's mess is not my business. Then I remember my mother's voice on the phone, how she told me the rocking horse burned. And now that I'm here she doesn't want to talk.

A shout from inside and then footsteps. The door opens a crack, a woman's face—sun-worn, creased smoker's cheeks and bright turquoise eyes, her hair a tangled sun-bleached nest. "Daniel?" she asks, suspiciously. As if she half-expected me.

She lets me in, warily. Her nipples press at a long red Cold Chisel T-shirt that stretches down to bare, slender legs, what look like purple welts on her thighs. "Excuse this dreadful mess." She clasps her shoulders and blames "the boys"; a maze of laundry on the floor but no sign of boys, just the skunk smell of weed. Isabel's lecture when she spotted me out on the brick patio staring off into the canyon, sucking on a doobie. But I'm not sharing Sharen Wells's weed.

In a kitchen I barely recognize, Sharen offers me tea. I remind myself this woman lit a fire that could have burned a thousand acres and the town, eviscerated property, and no one called the police.

"Does Earley know?" I ask. "About the fire?"

Her eyes are strangely alluring, a blue glinting green that reminds me of coral, of Isabel's opal. Staring back so boldly.

"Seems he went down to Lakes Entrance with Elsie." She says it as though they're all great friends.

A sink of piled plates and angled saucepans towers precipitously. Shouldn't she be remorseful? Where did the bruises come from?

"I'm sorry about the furniture," she says. Her hands shake slightly as she plugs in a kettle. How old is she, forty? Australian years, all the sun and squinting. "I just kind of lost it with your father."

I'm nodding, looking around to see what's left, the floorboards bare, stripped of linoleum. The kitchen where my grandmother stood with the sun beaming in on her delicate English face, pouring her Earl Grey tea and placing homemade sultana scones on a silver tray, baking her special rice pudding.

Sharen Wells places the kettle on a cork mat. "The Landlord and Tenant Act requires twenty-four hours' notice for a visit from the landlord," she says, so ballsy. I have to remember I'm a lawyer.

"I'm not your landlord." I try not to look at her eyes. "And what you've done is a felony."

She pours hot water into pale green cups, my grandmother's gold-lipped china. "I know," she says too easily. "But I've been having trouble with your father."

"We've had trouble with him too," I say, take a sip and scald my tongue—serves me right for being disloyal. "But we don't set things on fire."

She looks down at herself, the cotton clinging to her narrow body. "It was self-defense," she says. "He appears on a horse at the window at all hours," she says, "and I rarely wear clothes in the house."

But according to my mother, he hasn't been on a horse in years. "I believe he can barely walk," I say, and still he has power over women like this.

"He'd crawl if he had to, Earley," she says. "He's at the door at midnight and when I don't answer he pulls out my marijuana by the roots."

"Why don't you just let him in?" I imagine her in tight-fitting jeans, smoking a joint on the front steps, watching out across the fields. I feel myself vaguely drawn to her

Australian-ness, her unvarnished-ness. But the welts on her thighs give me pause.

"Because he won't leave Elsie and now he wants me out of here," she says, hugs her steaming cup between her breasts. "He reckons he wants to move back in. Wants to die in his mother's house. Well, I want to die in his mother's house too."

I feel the onset of jetlag, as if my legs might cave, or is it this woman? My father's most recent endowment. "My mother owns this now," I say. I don't tell her how the whole five hundred acres, houses and all, are now in my mother's name, since my father was sentenced to life with Elsie. *Now I've got two bitches in my soup,* he once told me on the phone. I look over at this woman and wonder if there aren't three. But somehow I feel for her, her need to talk, her crudeness.

Scanning the squalor of plates and piles of paper, I can't believe anyone would want to live or die here. Maybe that's why she divested him of furniture. No sign of a pending Christmas here either. I walk into the bare living room, the Munnings print has gone. I loved that faded painting, the horses being led back from the gallops with blankets over their loins.

He sure can pick 'em, that's what my mother says.

The last time I visited, my father was *buying the farm back,* as my mother coined it, on his deathbed in the Dandenong Hospital, pale in one of those paper gowns with pneumonia and congestive heart failure, a shriveling man in a narrow metal cot. But he was still working the nurses, wheezing, flirting, as if there was something left to live for. His wrinkled farmer's eyes attending the bright young nurses in their robin's-egg blue. Offering them trips down here to "The Estate," telling them he'd take them out riding, as if he'd soon be back on a horse. Half dead and still handsome, still believing he was in with a chance.

"I've had him up to here," says Sharen, the roach in her nail-bitten fingers cutting across her throat. She looks at me as if gauging loyalties, her blue-green eyes more defiant than tearful, but is she more angered or excited by his unexpected visits, the skulking? Or angry that he skulks no more?

"Anyway, I'll take him to the tribunal if I have to," she adds. "How dare he try to evict me after all I've been through?"

"You won't take him anywhere," I say. I don't move to comfort her, feel no need to share the obvious—my father's always been a hands-on husband, women pressed against the fridge, my unsuspecting girlfriends bailed up on the hall-stand, that Lipman woman emerging from the haystack with my father behind her in the middle of the night while my mother slept alone up in the big house, the lantern standing dim above the roses. She probably already knows, the way she's apparently befriended my mother.

Sharen lights a Marlboro, a sudden twitch in her shoulders.

Maybe it would be good for him to stand before a tribunal for something before he dies. I lean on the ledge and try to summon my lawyerly training—any landlord and tenant claim could only be against my mother, since she now owns all this, but Sharen Wells has no cause against my mother, except perhaps some cloven empathy. Still, this woman with her cleavage and teacup wants to lay some stake out on this grease-stained floor. A black oil patch where it looks as if someone has dismantled an engine, takeout food containers adorning the boards. The rocker-recliner my mother mentioned. It could be an artist's studio, better in some ways without the furniture from Coventry.

"Are your horses still here?" I ask. The pair of plump Anglo-Arabs I've heard about from my mother, her voice loud on the headset in my office on the forty-first floor, telling me how one of those "useless creatures" foaled unexpectedly and Earley went ballistic, ordered them off the property. How they keep reappearing, mare and foal and other stray ponies, munching on the precious pasture saved for the cattle my father still thinks are his.

Sharen has a hand on the mantel, a certain swivel in her hips, reminding me how she pays her rent and horses' board "regular." And I've heard how she visits the big house, speaks loud enough so my mother can hear, charms her in front of the old AGA stove. She brings treats for the dog and drinks tea and partakes of my mother's stale Arnott's Teddy Bear biscuits, laughing. She helps with the jigsaw puzzles, placing tricky pieces in the blue miasma of sky. Sharen Wells is not stupid. She will not be *railroaded.*

"What's going on with Ruthie?" I ask. Perhaps this is the reason I'm in this house at ten o'clock when I should be with my tight-lipped mother.

Sharen looks up at the stains in the ceiling as if deciding what to tell. "If only he'd been there to see it," she says, still talking of the fire. "I mean I lit it for him and I reckoned at least they'd call him out of Elsie's bed, but only after did I find out he was gone. Serve me right for blazing a joint and drinking a Tooheys at once." She lights a second cigarette as if reminded. "The next morning I took her a bunch of jonquils. What Ruthie puts up with here, poor old thing, out there in the night when she shouldn't have seen all that."

I assume she means the night of the fire.

"I don't reckon she even had shoes on. I had to do something for her. Ruthie's my only real friend around here so I got her flowers, you know, from near Genoni's gate, the bit where it's green from the septic, along the fence of the caravan park."

"I just want to know about her health," I say. "You know how she won't see doctors." The time on the phone when she made me repeat: *No more hospitals.* Made me promise, even though I wasn't here.

"I don't blame her," says Sharen. "You know I'm a psych nurse over at Dalkeith in Koo Wee Rup so it's good to have me here."

I'm looking at her as if that's a plus.

"Anyway," she says. "I would have gone through the paddocks because it's direct but those three black horses snort me down like I'm some toy, and it's not bloody funny the way they are. One always lifts its head and they all stampede, so I have to go round by the road. They still came over the front paddock hill with their necks all up like big black swans. As if they smell me." She sips her tea, pleased to have an audience. "It's always further than you'd think, the walk from the Station Road corner." Her strange need to give me the details, the way she's almost poised when she gets going. "Cars whip through there like sharks on wheels. Jimmy Saddler in his trailer piled with plumbing stuff. He usually slows down to take a squizz but he didn't even wave." I imagine this woman on the gravel with her flowers, the shapes of those horses along the fence, taunting her, the clouding dust from Jimmy Saddler's Ute.

"I got no house or car, just blisters on my feet and flies on my eyes and those limp flowers." Is she really trying to woo me with quaintness? "Sometimes I get the bipolar, the merry-go-round in my head." She talks as though I might understand. "Ruthie's nice to me when no one's around, the time she saw that cut on my arm and she knew somehow it wasn't an accident."

I feel a bit woozy, sitting on one of the wooden fruit boxes surrounding the enormous grease stain on the floor.

"The jonquils in December were a sort of Christmas miracle anyway. A septic miracle." She laughs at her joke and I sip from my grandmother's teacup. A *Women's Weekly* on the floor, an empty Tooradin Pizza box, her laundry basket draped with socks, the wall bereft of pictures. An ache behind my eyes.

"Because I felt awful for what I done with the car. Ruthie there to see it." She pauses in a kind of reverie and I can't tell what's for effect.

I imagine her passing the row of old stumps that snapped clean off in some freak storm, as if the devil blew down on this place only and felled half the trees. Some would have seen it as Biblical but my mother just called it a face getting stripped of its features.

"Them Pond Paddock ponies coming to sniff at me over the fence, that skewbald pony Patch and that spotted creature that came all the way from Singapore."

Spotted creature? A description my mother might choose, borrowed. Sharen wants me to know she's part of life here.

"Ruthie's roses searching out at me like starving children. I plucked a healthy red one and pricked my finger. Serve me right. Took a jasmine from by the tank."

Apparently, my mother didn't answer the door. "So I went up the hall, I'd never been into the inner sanctum. Found your mother laid out on the little bathroom tiles like a rag, her head caught over the rung of the wooden chair." She felt my mother's breath against her fingers, pried her neck from the chair legs. "How long had she been there?" I ask, but how would Sharen know? The medical pendant around my mother's neck, the one she's supposed to press to call for an ambulance. The one she refuses to use.

"She was breathing," says Sharen, "but real soft. I rolled up a towel and cradled her head, not sure if I should just stay and hold her, you know, let her die in my arms. That's what she'd want, I reckon. But I did my Reiki on her. I'm not a master yet but I've done my level two online."

I'm not sure whether to smile or cry. Sharen rubbing her hands together and tracing some sign in the air, cupping a palm on my mother's brow, or her chest. My mother prone, like a small palsied bird, her pale breasts visible through the frayed cotton nightie, while this woman with chipped indigo nails plays healer. My mother who isn't keen on being touched.

Sharen's gaze is off me now, her eyes are tight. "The dog licked Ruthie's face," she remembers, and I wonder how much of this is for effect, if her unmade-up eyes are greener in daylight. "I told her you love her lots, and I said I was sorry, just in case."

I imagine the oblong of sunshine from the narrow bathroom skylight funneling down onto my mother's face. Sharen humming, her hands curved about my mother's ears.

"Anyway, so we fixed her, me and Pip." She blows her cigarette smoke softly over toward me.

THE BURNT-OUT CAR appears in the dark as the carcass of a gutted beast, chunks of charred wood underfoot in the grass, the rocking horse somewhere among them. And Sharen Wells now standing in the window, watching. Samaritan, healer, psycho, snake. I'm not sure, too exhausted to take her on properly. Isabel warned me: "Don't get too involved—get in, get out." Still, I imagine my buckled-up father before the Tenancy Tribunal, fending off assertions. An old man accused of shuffling around his own mother's furniture, brandishing his cheeky smile, some fumbled but fervent pursuit of flesh. Then yanking out her marijuana as vengeance, using eviction as currency. It's not his reputation I care about; that's been lost and gone. It's an elderly man on the dock of some petty assembly, collapsing, carted away without a chance to limp down the end of this short, dark hallway and climb alone between the sheets of his mother's four-poster bed.

"You'll kill him," I told Sharen before I left the cottage, but she just stared out past me, into the bay-windowed night, as if the pleasure would be all hers. She's staring out at me now.

"Then I'll go to the police," I said and she smiled as though she wouldn't mind. Or maybe she knows that I won't.

The night is clear, the garden light turned on up at the big house on the distant hill for my benefit. Evidence of my mother. Then, at the edge of the night I see her by the windmill gate, a frail shape in the dark. In her pale blue nightgown, like a sheet in the breeze above the grass. A skeletal woman, waiting, hugging herself in the dry night air. And I feel the sadness that doesn't invade me deep like this in California.

I walk over to her. She's wearing her jeans under her nightie, moored to the earth by my father's oversized boots, her shiny button eyes. "Accomplish anything?" she asks. Her nightie blowing against her ribcage. She's almost phosphorescent, as if she's Eleanor of Aquitaine, betrayed but undaunted. Her face gleams as if lost territory must be retaken. But her body seems shaky.

I wrap her in my jacket and place an arm about her shoulders, an unlikely liberty. I find myself wishing for Isabel; maybe she'd think all this was charming and strange, and maybe I would too, but without her here I feel the old unrest. Walking my mother through the silence.

"Don't worry," she says. "That spindly little English stuff, you could barely use it anyway." She exhales dismissively and together we trudge through the night, back up to the main house. The tiniest sliver of moon.

"The Munnings is gone," I say.

My mother squints up at me. She loved that painting too, the fine shapes of well-bred horses rendered in such perfect detail, walking back hot from the gallops. A print, but it was signed. She always had her sights on it. "Your father's a sloven and a slut," she says, then gazes ahead.

"Would he have insured it?" I ask. "Any of it?"

"He can barely keep a car registered," she says. "But don't panic." She gazes out over the spread that extends flat and black as bitumen before us. "You'll end up with all this." Shrouding me back in an old unholy alliance. Me, the lucky one. Schooled as a boy not to care for my father, my mother's disenchantment laid as a bounty at my feet. How she advised me quietly that my father's side of the family may have been good-looking but they weren't particularly bright, that my father's parents, *truth be told*, were actually first cousins. "That's why they had to leave England."

My father, the only surviving son of the runaways, charming, square-jawed. At nine, I could beat him at Scrabble, or would have if I'd bothered to play him, too busy doing crosswords with my mother, measuring up to her vocabulary, while my father was out chasing skirt. A mother too tough for my father to compete with: on a horse, at cricket, at cards.

With her three sisters, she played on the first women's polo team, against the men. She rode jumping horses in

England at the Royal Windsor Show, studied agricultural science at Melbourne University, played tennis as if she were Margaret Court, and came second in the Australia-wide bridge pairs with Fidelia the cook. My father who'd begged her to marry him until she gave in. "He wouldn't leave me alone," she once told me. "So eventually I said yes to shut him up." I was both prodigal son and surrogate husband. There was no competing here.

The windmill creaks above us where the three gates meet, again the hoot of that unseen owl, and the weight of this old conspiracy, my arm around the matriarch—part-parent, part-child, her confidant. All I'd tried to escape conspiring against me already, on my first night here. I glance back at her and feel the weight of jetlag and misgivings.

"We'll get Old Nev to clean up the mess," my mother says, forgetting that Neville's as old as the empire, can barely cut wood to keep her in logs for the stove, that he could no more clean up that blackened wreck than run for mayor.

I think of Sharen at the fire station telling her woes to the boys over smokes and a beer. "We should call the police," I say, but my mother laughs. The laugh she uses when she hasn't heard, in case what's said is supposed to be funny. In lieu of a response she motions at the dark billowy shapes of the heavy horses in the distance, grazing quietly in the next field, as if all is forgotten.

"We should just change the locks on the cottage," my mother says, and I realize she's heard all along, reminding me she doesn't approve of involving outsiders; she'd have preferred we fought the fire ourselves.

"We'll also need to keep your father out of there," she says. "Once he gets wind of this he'll want to move back in with his harlot." Poor Elsie. My mother seems to be gaining momentum, no longer a wavering stick in white cotton, but plotting as we did in old times. She might even have her hearing aid in. "Next thing you know he'll be dead and we'll be left with *her.*" She talks as if she isn't six years older than him. She holds course for the lantern in her garden on the distant hill, where the dog is shut inside the enclosed part of the veranda, barking.

We head along the old tractor path and she hitches up her nightie. "Remember at Carbrook we had those Dutch people?" She talks as if I was alive then, on the farm where she grew up. "They used our chairs as firewood. Too lazy to go out and chop their own." It's why I was taught to hate the Dutch. I realize I haven't mentioned Isabel, let alone that her father was born in Holland, or that her mother is Venezuelan. That they were never married, or that her grandfather was a general in the army in Caracas. A black-and-white photo of a handsome man in cap and uniform with a crop-eared Doberman at his side.

On the hill by the chicken coop she pulls free from my arm and climbs the stile unassisted. We both know if she fell she'd shatter a hip. Balancing in the night breeze she looks back down at me. "When I was a kid," she says, "we used to ride our ponies bareback and help spot bushfires from up on Two Bays Road." She shields her eyes as if we're in broad daylight. "The firemen gave us canvas knapsacks of water and we'd spray the remains." She goes to step over the wire but stops. "I'm a good firefighter," she says.

I suddenly feel a strong desire to defend the dignity of this old woman, who stands up in the dark like something immortal.

"You're the reason I stay alive," she says, then boldly steps down to the ground.

She walks on ahead through the wood chips by the chopping stump, leaving me this side of the fence, split in pieces of my own—the part that yearns to be here with her, to stay like this forever.

He don't see me, just old ghost Ruthie floating through the dark, she hears me make my currawong sound, but she don't look up, she got no need, she knows it's Reggie Don sits up this windmill looking down on them. That son come all this way and now he's flighty and indignant, but Ruthie, she's the real one here, she knows what's true on horses and this whole farm, even Sharen burning beds 'n' chairs for nothing.

Make my owl hoot and the son look up but he don't have his night eyes back coz he been gone too long. Want to tell him how Sharen's my mum and she's unlucky sometimes, 'specially when there's men.

Peel my eyes on these two walking, the son with his arm round Ruthie now, he must want things. Why she saying about this all being his, after what she told me? Climb down from here and follow. The way she looks at him from up on the stile, all playful and proud like she might be ready to fly. I hope she don't forget 'bout me now he's here.

Don't worry about Reggie, I want to stay and scare 'em.

I'll hunk down on the veranda and see them through the window, breathe in the wood-stack smell where Pip lifts his leg and watches me. That dog doesn't trust me, in there beside her as she plops into her big arm chair. He jump up beside her like always and do his dog stare out at me as if he about to growl. Ruthie hairbrush him so he arch his back and keep a secret. She eyes me too, out over her jigsaw table past her socks and undies on the clotheshorse like this window is the telly and it's just me that's on the screen. I'm the Reggie Dumbalk Show.

If this son wasn't here I'd go in and watch myself. We don't really laugh at TV jokes, me and Ruthie. Just a smile that sneaks into the wrinkle of her cheek and she pretend she deaf but she don't miss so much. Unless she got one of her old memories going. You better remember what you promise me, old girl.

Some nights when she call out "Reggie" so I climb down from in her roof where I sleep sometime and ease in through her dream, how they gallop through her head and wire fences coming, mud flies up in her face but she rides on racing. The only one still left on top and all those other horses running with her with no riders and she's afraid there's no way home. I just say it's okay, Ruthie, you just dreaming. I clear the mud from her old eyes.

Flick my ciggie onto this veranda, watch it smoke. Yeah, it's me, old girl, up in this window screen. Him there in his fancy dacks, standing over at the desk, his hair with gray already ash and dialing numbers on your phone. Trying to get through for something but I can't hear him coz of the wind in the trees and those big birds from out the inlet landing. The way they squawk and streak the bark with shit. They kill trees.

I seen that son once when I was small and up on Walker's shoulders when we came down here for a one-time visit. Looked about this place from there on Walker same way I look now, from up in the roof and in the trees. Or right here window-level.

Walker told me how he done the fencing and cattle and mucking out on this place when he was young and with my grandma Gracious. He never went to school like I never did hardly. They couldn't keep me in the room, and then they said I had difficulties, like my mother. But I got eyes in the back of my head like Ruthie. Walker said she kill a snake as quick as look. Jump down off the horse and jerk a stirrup with her off the saddle.

She come up to us that day and she was pretty friendly, considering. She knew what Earley did to my dad Walker. Then the son walk over all superior on a big dun horse he called Dunedin, as if he want Walker to know he owned the place already. Now he's back and so am I. He got a hand in his pocket itching and his face gone red with talking Sharen and he keeps dialing over.

Push my ear against this window and listen. "Isabel, hey it's me, can you hear me?" He got a pretty-name girlfriend.

He listens to the phone and looks around sly as if Ruthie can't hear. "Yep, already." Then he looks at Ruthie, recollects hisself as if he sees a sadness coming. "My father has this woman in a house out the back," he says, "a tenant. She's bipolar or something. She burned all his furniture."

That's my mother you talk about, Danny boy, careful.

"Lucky the whole fucking place didn't go up," he says. He's looking up at the pictures hanging. Some of himself when he was young on horses.

"Well, it wouldn't have been ideal," he says. Who talks like that? He pretends it's funny but he's not easy with it, I can tell. All I know is Ruthie dreams of these trees burning down and cracking on this big house roof like great big matches, photos of her riding on the beach and out hunting poor bloody foxes, and all the walls and bookshelves melting down, the fridge with the nut loaf I eat and her old rings and bracelets in their little leather boxes. She saw me take her

jewry once but she understood, she don't go to balls and par-
ties no more, she just watch me take her value things, climb
thru the manhole and keep them safe up in the roof.

She turn again and see me silent through this window
glass like I'm the real son while the other one laughs all ner-
vous in the corner. Leans against the desk and whispers to his
girl, then he stops as tho' he seen me too but I don't move. Just
feel my own smile creep along the flywire.

MY MOTHER STANDS up from her chair like a twig in her nightgown, looking out the window, her mottled sunspotted hands push about her lips. Then she turns to me. "Do you have everything you need?" she asks, rubbing at a blotchy terra-cotta cheek, her small bird face and small bird eyes. I point to the receiver, let her know I'm talking, but she doesn't care about phones, walks right by me to the kitchen. I watch her hover over the ancient microwave, pressing buttons, waiting for her wheat bags to heat.

"I'll call you when I get up there," says Isabel and then we're silent for too long.

"Have a fun trip," I say. "Sorry about how I drove to the airport."

"Maybe I should come out and drive you around," says Isabel. I watch my mother, wheat bags in hand, wafting past me into the dark hallway, a sarcastic good-night wave over her shoulder as she heads up the hall, drifting to the left and nudging the old church pew. She told me it feels as if she's spinning when she lies down in bed, calls her condition *left-side neglect* when it's probably strokes and vertigo. Isabel no longer on the phone, just the dog perched among the sitting room pillows, watching something out the window.

I wheel my suitcase up the hall, catch a glimpse of Aunt Emma Charlotte's portrait streaked with possum piss. It gives her a thin damp smile. My mother didn't ask me who was on the phone, as though my life beyond here is not worthy of mention.

Through her closed bedroom door I can hear her radio blaring—3AW talk and oldies, the throaty roll of

Burl Ives from her rickety bedside table. I no longer sleep in the shearer's quarters, with its tongue-and-groove ceiling festooned with dusty horse-show ribbons, but in here. *The Senator's Room.* The light unveils the familiar ornate molded roses on the fourteen-foot cobwebbed ceiling, a fresh rent where chunks of plaster have fallen, a dark hole up into the ancient slate roof. The room is named in honor of a series once filmed here, still decked out as the master suite of the television senator's house: the blue floral wallpaper, the only wide bed in the place. My parents' two single beds were once parallel parked in here, separate and unequal, in a house where men have found it hard and women have struggled on their own.

I heft my bag up onto the re-covered chaise and wonder which came first, my mother's unwillingness to share her bed because she realized what she'd married, or that she didn't share herself and he went elsewhere? First to sleep in the campervan and then with Elsie, out in his dead mother's cottage on the lip of the bush?

It's hard to imagine my conception here, thirty-five years this last November, my mother looking up into the cobwebs, a vague disgust in her eyes, or maybe just wondering what all the fuss was about. The irony of parents still strangely in love, even now, a love so fraught with disappointment it manifests as acrimony. A pattern I pray I'll not repeat. Not with Isabel. I hope I'm not her compromise. I should call her back and say good night.

On the mantel a sepia photo shows my mother swinging wide at a polo ball, her body clinging like a monkey's to the side of a horse at a flat-strap gallop. Beside it leans a picture of my father in New Guinea, standing on the beach with the others. I try not to look at him there. My childhood clock on a small, varnished table beside the bed, its hands set dead parallel at 9:15; branches scratch the corrugated veranda roof, up to the ceiling where possums gnaw the electrical cables. A vague smell of burning, as if the whole house is quietly smoldering.

Out in the dark I hear horses; one begins to canter, followed by the thunder of elderly geldings galloping up to the old pine plantation, pummeling the sandy earth. I climb into the Senator's bed, the same cream-colored sheets washed and wound through the wringer, the vague smell of mothballs but also of wheat. Against my leg is a wheat bag, heated and carefully placed by my mother, even though the summer night is warm.

I try to sleep but lie awake, remembering the look in Sharen Wells's eyes, the kind of stricken ferocity that has never quite left my mother's. I hold the warm wheat bag against me and listen to the burr of my mother's talkback radio, the groans of the cypresses; I imagine slipping into bed beside Isabel, her luxurious linens and silken skin, both feminine and boyish, her strength and fragility, and a childhood of her own. But I don't dream of her.

"Reggie . . . son?" calling out in the night like an idiot when he's probably up some tree or camped out in the bush. Just hope he's not prowling the town giving folks the willies, like they say his father used to. Just pray that bastard Walker doesn't find us this time coz I got nowhere to go and that Mitsubishi was a heap anyway. Even when it worked. I saw Daniel and Ruthie looking at it, that sad look in his fancy man's eyes. Didn't know what to make of me, did he? I kind of like that. The way he's taller than Earley and half the age.

"Reggieeeee." I shouldn't be out here in the bracken in these new Uggs. Got 'em fresh off the steps from yoga class in Cranbourne, walked in barefoot then left early. Took my pick of the slip-ons at the door, didn't I? Forgive me Jesus, you know I can't help it. But you never did nothing for me, did you? Just gave me a son who scares me sometimes, and a husband who scares me worse.

* * *

MONDAY

I wake sweating in the night, light-headed, stare up at the molded leaves and roses in the ceiling, the hole in the plaster where there was once an attic. A dream where it was crammed with rows of wooden coat hangers, old leather handbags hanging from hooks that turned into small curing pigs. Is someone staring in the window? Sit up but there's nothing, just the image of my mother's head over the rung of that bathroom chair, looping through my mind. Playing with death like she's found a new friend. Half-dried rose on the end of the bed. How the hell did that get there?

I feel as if I've been backed over, waiting here for the first sign of morning. Isabel driving up the coast, or maybe she's taking the Ventura Freeway, the Valley after the rain. We could have been holed up in the canyon for Christmas Eve, Isabel making clove oranges, or painting ornaments with gold leaf while I bought turkey and vegetables ready-made from Bristol Farms, boysenberry pie from Greenblatt's. We'd pretend I made it from scratch, tell stories of this place, romanticize what we could make of it some day—an organic farm, an origami farm, country restaurant, retreat house, eco-friendly subdivision.

When I next wake it's morning, a hint of yellow sky slants through cypresses. But even in daylight it's dark in this house. My mother letting Pip out onto the veranda, the sound of him trotting along to pee on the woodpile.

She knocks on my door. "Are you having Christmas without me?" As if I'm pleasuring myself or something.

"Christmas is Thursday," I tell her.

"Oh." She lets Pip in and I hear her trundle back to bed. Wonder what Isabel will be telling Mona, how I drove like a mad thing or didn't say good-bye on the phone. A car coming up the drive has me up and looking out the window. A Camry station wagon with a train of dust behind it. My father. He parks it under the hedge and clambers out with agonizing difficulty, his face like a twisted sandwich, the station wagon sagging so close to the ground. Shocking to see how one leg is now visibly shorter, his bad hip receding. A time he could run fast as my mother, but that was thirty years ago before he fell from old Billabong and broke his hip the first time. Now she calls him "Hoppity-go-kick." Ordered off his own land for just wanting to be with a woman he could touch. If there'd only been one.

WHEN I GET to the kitchen my father doesn't see me. Straining to reach for muesli and wheat germ from the tallboy,

his eyes on the kitchen TV. *Good Morning Australia* still with
that compère girl, Moira. He seems besotted with her elegant
face on the screen. His face is rutted as a quarry, holes in his
green windcheater, and an abundant shock of almost white
hair. How much he loves it when a woman smiles.

As I grab a glass from the sideboard he turns. "I'd have
put on clean trousers if I'd known," he says, a square-jawed
smile of his own. He places the cereals down on the table
and limps over to hug me. I try not to stiffen, let his head
rest awkwardly in my chest like he's the boy. His spine bony
in my fingers, sinking into itself, his hair slightly greasy. He
smells of musty hay.

"Your mother wouldn't tell me when you were appearing," he says.

"I thought you were away," I say, retreating.

Heading to the fridge he catches sight of Sharen's letter
on the table, searches back at me to gauge what I know. I try
to soften my glare.

"I thought me and Sharen had an understanding," he
says, folds the letter and stuffs it up among envelopes in the
mantel, above the old wood stove.

"Did you hear what she did to her car?"

He throws his chin up as if it's kind of amusing. "Silly
girl," he says. "Thought I'd knock up some breakfast for
Ruthie," he says as if leaving the bed of one woman to set up
breakfast for another is normal. He plucks a jar of kumquat
jam from the fridge. "Then I'll head out to assess the damage."

I don't tell him to keep an eye out for the glinting remains
of his mother's armoire. Let the scorched trumpet-leg chairs

be a bonus. The burnt remnants of the Munnings. I wash my face at the kitchen tap, to cleanse myself of these people with the fresh icy water. Cupping my hands I drink water piped straight from the roof to the tank, the roof veined with moss, the water absorbing fungus and lead as it flows over the lichen and slate. An American thought, the obsession with hygiene. I fill a glass to take to my mother; wrigglers squirm in it like microscopic eels. I imagine them converting inside me, mosquitoes blossoming in the bloodstream. My mother must be full of them, and yet the water tastes pure as dew.

While my father sections a pink grapefruit, slathers it with sugar, I pull Sharen's letter from the mantel. "Let's talk about this," I say, but he's staring out past the television, through the pocks of the fly-screened window. Some shirtless kid lopes along the bottom of the Boy's Paddock, right along the fence line with a whip or a stick and those three black horses following him, not chasing, but spaced out evenly as if he has them trained, their trots extending as if it's some parade.

"What the fuck is that?" I ask.

"Sharen has a boy."

THE BOY DISAPPEARS as if in a dream and I'm left standing up, eating Weet-Bix drowned in milk, topped with Manuka honey, watching out the smutched window, through the cobwebbed flies. Now there's just a single Murray pine scratching up at the sky, the heat of the day already on the verge of shimmering, the fences stretching away to the bush. What kind of boy?

A fierce light punctuated by the distant hump of Sharen's car, a purple scar rimmed with black and the dot of my father gimping down toward the windmill. I watch him shuffle, a short, stooped creature, on the way to inspect what he's wrought.

"Are you ready?" My mother in the kitchen doorway startles me. Somehow up and dressed, her nightgown tucked into her jeans and still she looks thin as a picket, leaning precariously on the counter as if she's just tipsy, a Fair Isle cardigan over the top of everything. "Let's go down the town." Her hair sticks up one side like a seawall. "What have you done with my list?"

There's no evidence of a list, just Sharen's letter she takes from the table. "That was addressed to me," she says, stuffs it in her bag.

She attempts to hold down a crest in her hair, but she still can't seem to raise her left arm properly—her hand suspends oddly as though balancing a platter. The dog stands by her, ready to go, as the arm descends limply. "The *New Idea* will be at the *newsagence.*"

A slight slur—she means newsagency, doesn't she? Or is it "newsagent's" here? I suddenly can't remember. A prune-colored mark on her forehead where she must have hit the chair when she fell. I find myself eyeing the shape of her face. It doesn't sag.

"We need to get the mail, don't we Pip?" She speaks as if only the dog would understand.

I put down my sogging cereal. "Can we talk about your fall in the bathroom . . . remember?"

She moves farther into the kitchen as if on tracks, secures herself on the lip of the sideboard, and pulls the dog leash from its hook. She's wearing her hearing aid—it signifies business. She selects a faded sports cap from the pile of them on the ledge beside the egg cartons, reaches for her blue dilly bag, and steadies herself again. She fossicks in the drawer. "Then we'd better get going before I have another one."

Gently, I place my cereal bowl in the sink. "Wouldn't it be better if we went in later on?"

Jauntily, she straightens the bag poised over her shoulder and glares out from under the sports cap, its World Equestrian Games logo from Stockholm, from our last big trip overseas. "Have you found the list?" In Sweden she hoarded food from the breakfast buffet, stashing lunch and sometimes dinner in the folds of her coats and pockets, refusing to pay for tickets on the underground, burrowing beneath the turnstiles as if she was twelve, her coat loaded with croissants and muffins, sachets of butters and small jars of marmalade, plastic knives. Apprehended by a subway guard, she advised him in English to get a real job, ran so fast he couldn't keep up in his military boots. She was only sixty-five then, back when there were Christmases she still played cricket in the garden, the fastest bowler in the family, hitting "sixes" out toward the carpet-weed that now marks the dried-up pond. She had that kind of body—she didn't have me until she was forty-six, back when women didn't do that. She told me she never wanted a child until she had me, that she was too busy with horses outdoors. That I was quite the surprise.

The key for the post office box in her fingers, she counts the coins from her old vinyl change purse. She prefers change to the bright Australian notes she stows in their thousands in her leather hatbox in the linen closet. Satisfied with her funds, she hooks out her arm to be escorted. "Come on," she says. "It might be our last."

I feel the weight about the edges of my own face as I take her scrawny arm and follow her out past the meat-safe, her movement slightly stilted over the capeweed lawn. The ponies in the Pond Paddock lift their heads, alert at the sight of her. Her little skewbald Patch walks up to the gate.

"I'm a bit stringhalty," she says, announcing it to the animals. "Hocks have gone a bit spasmodic."

We pass the maidenhair fern and the septic tank where the grass stays green all summer. She veers me away from the Prius, her face contorting as if appalled by such extravagance. "They already reckon you're from out of space," she says, and I'm unsure if she meant to say it that way, but *out of space* is exactly how I feel, the world closing in on me and wafting away at once.

She spies the Camry. "Where's your father?" she asks, as if he's my fault.

"He's gone to sort things out," I say it as if that's always been his strong suit.

"Let's take his car then." His car that's actually hers.

At the dusty back of the Camry, she hands over the dog leash and stands free, attempting an exercise, a calisthenic effort to swing her arms, but her left one just wilts, her sleeve like a long empty sock. "The extent of my damage," she says.

I resist a desire to help her as she makes an effort to walk straight, determinedly picking her way along the side of the car. Her Levi's worn like a teenage boy's, her footfalls uncertain. I imagine her crawling around in her room to get dressed, feeling her way down the hall to the kitchen, and then standing erect at the threshold.

At the passenger door, she halts abruptly. Against the cypress trunk rests a stick, rough but tapered. It's been whittled. "Look who made me a walking stick," she says, wandering over to examine it.

"Who?" I ask, but get no answer. It looks as if it's a garden stake, the sort she'd use to right a sapling. I hope her mind's not been affected; I don't dare ask her the day of the week as I barely remember it myself. A day lost in the air, the line drawn down through the Pacific, jagged and arbitrary. Landing three days shy of a midsummer Christmas.

I open the back door for Pip to jump in but he's sniffing over at the tree, then yelping up into it with a pitch so high it's barely audible. His front legs scuffle up the trunk as if he wants to climb.

"What you got up there, Pip?" I ask. The tree I hid up in as a kid, on a platform I made where two branches fork and I couldn't be seen. The twin Jack Russells, Digby and Tudge, used to obsess over possums up into those branches, before the night they went out hunting and met up with a pack of wild dogs.

"Leave him alone, Pip." My mother's tone is fierce and the dog looks back at her, prick-eared, confused. Called off. She leans on the stake as if it's a crook, her expression severe as though her facial nerves have been restored. Then she slants into an effort to walk to the car. "Get in," she orders and the dog canters to her, cautious, obedient, jumps in the back.

"I thought you liked him hunting," I say.

"Not what's up that tree," she says. She folds herself down into the car and pretends to look comfortable. I look at her from the driver's side, the stick a primitive javelin beside her.

"What is it?" I ask.

She drops the car key on the driver's seat. "We got a visitor," she says.

Travel bits and soft clothes, camomile or cashier, whatever they call it, smooth as lamb but make no sense in this heat. I prefer the feel of sun and keep my dirt shoes. I reckon I can feel where water flows underneath. Artesian, Walker calls it, reckons I could be a diviner if I wanted. But he reckons too many things and I'm glad to be away from all the rustling, the things he makes me do. Dig deep and pull a shiny white headphones machine says Beats Music. Probably cost a hundred, and who got a hundred here to spare but Ruthie hidden in her linen cupboard safe? I reckon she knows I take my share. It's not so much coz I can live a week on thirty, I get my snacks from fridges. She even leaves me some food in the boot room.

Nice gold pen tho', different, heavy with a point shape like a violin and unscrews. Look. And dribbles. Parks a little blue turd on his pants and lucky they dark. Wipe my fingers on my face and see what else. A hard thing down the bottom. Wrapped in a shirt, I pull it up slow, a silver frame photo of a girl. His rich city one, smooth skin and blackcolor hair, earrings like a movie star, Spanish maybe, probably famous. A model girl. The one he had on the phone maybe, who make him laugh and then look sad. Wonder if Ruthie seen this.

Do a freeze for footsteps, head up to the ceiling hole. Can't be Earley, saw him gone. When I asked Sharen if she's called him Earley coz he comes too soon she said he's too old to come at all, but she didn't think it was funny. Footsteps in the hall. It's that ol' egg lady Margaret Boatwell. She never come in this far.

Need to be quick and hitch up this big white cupboard door and shim my way through these spiderwebs to my plaster hole, to get back safe. But I got even better this time. Put on my big new headphones and press play for music. Listen to some weird guitar and jerk myself to Danny's girl.

"DON'T STOP." MY mother's cutthroat whisper beside me as we pass Sharen out on Langdon's Road. My mother raises the carved head of her curious stick as best she can and tips the brim of her cap, then stares out ahead. "She'll be the death of us," she says as Sharen disappears in the rearview mirror, misted in dust. I feel as though I've been here for days. My mother beside me, resurrected, pursing and parting her lips, resilient inside her own bleak thoughts, staring out over her land, over the Station Road Paddock that's virtually empty, none of those brown Devons that used to be boarded, just a few Herefords now, and those black horses seem to make their own arrangements.

My mother examines the grooves in her dappled walking cane, pale against her marbled hands.

"Just a stick," she says, calm as you like, dissolves back into her silence, save for the nervous tap-drip sound from her lips. I glance over at her ferrety face, the gleam of tenacity in her deep-set eyes, and feel myself being swallowed, by her and by the heat of the day, the angry glare of the sun as it skewers the windshield, the dead insects and flies in the cobwebs that shroud the wipers. In Los Angeles they wash their cars all summer as if the water supply is endless, not stolen from the north. But here the sky feels as though there might never be rain, until it floods. It used to still be green in December, but not in a year like this. The light so harsh, eats everything up. My tiny carcinomas that get frozen off with liquid nitrogen by the flirty dermatologist on Bedford Drive. The spots that appear on my right arm and temple from this no-ozone heat, all the years I drove on this side of the road with my elbow out the open window.

Thinking of Isabel, I swerve in the gravel, turning right onto Station Road.

"Keep your shirt on," my mother says. I look over, heartened by how she seems mean and marvelous as ever, regardless. The disloyalty lodges in the pit of my stomach for leaving her here.

We pass the Albertinis' farm, the house low and painted pale olive now, veiled in natives: acacias, banksias, a melaleuca. "That nice gray thoroughbred of theirs was bitten by a tiger snake. Dead as a stove in the grass," my mother says.

I've forgotten how death and hardship are passed off here like so many handkerchiefs, laughed away with a weary acceptance. It makes my Los Angeles life seem self-obsessed, but here we have our particular breed of narcissism, just earthier, parochial in its own way.

Off to the right, my grandmother's cottage peels into view. Its faded green-striped blinds look more ripped than I remember. In daylight it seems so innocent, save for the blackened sedan crouched in the field. One of those horses reaches to sniff the charred bonnet, its head extended straight from its neck while the other two are off grazing, picking at the tussocky grass.

"I love those big horses," my mother says.

I pull onto the verge, roll to a halt among the rumpled trunks of long-dead wattles. "They seem to have the run of the place," I say. The rise of the land folding into the edge of the scrub, pocked with the white star flowers of the wedding bush. My chance to actually talk to my mother. But the dog's up in the back, prick-eared and whining, and my mother stiffens, leans forward.

It's Earley emerging from behind a windbreak, holding onto his deerstalker's cap. He's examining the carnage in the field, what's left of England blackened and strewn.

My mother drapes a hunting scarf over her cap, trying to poke the ends in the neckline of her Fair Isle, as if primping. My father moves to the other side and kneels in the grass. "He's pretty agile for a cripple," she says, readying herself to get out and supervise from here.

Unaware of us, my father shoos the horses away then looks up at the sky. He shouts something out but his oaths are swallowed in the wind. She holds her stick between her hands and regards the lopsided figure now scuffing through the dry paspalum in his gumboots toward us.

"You don't seem to have married anyone," my mother says as if it's such an accomplishment. "What are you, forty?"

"Thirty-five," I say. "But I've met someone."

My mother doesn't seem to hear. "Let's go," she says, "before we have to cope with him."

Gazing down at the windblown grass, my father approaches the fence line and I consider getting out to greet him, to avoid watching him deal with the fence. "You know his parents were cousins," she says. "Hence all the problems." As if she hasn't told me a hundred times. But the words feel sad now. "Hung around like a spent penny," she says, tensing as he inches down low through the barbed-wire fence, snags his windcheater. He tries again, raises his dilapidated face and attempts a worn-down smile, as if to say life is much more than any of us bargained for. I get out and pull up a wire. The roughness of his farmer's fingers clutching mine as I lift him up. A silent moment's contact that might mean something.

"Thanks, son," he says when he's up, but he's limping over to the car to deal with my mother. "Bloody unbelievable," he says but my mother doesn't answer, playing with the dog leash.

"Does she have her hearing aid in?" my father asks me. Provoking. The hearing aid now covered by the scarf, as if it's a national secret. A deafness especially designed for the timbre of my father's voice. He turns to me, motioning to the car out yonder and shaking his head as if familiar with loss. "What a bloody shame."

"So you've sorted it out with Sharen?" My mother forms the words clearly and loudly, no slur at all, as if making allowances for *his* hearing, the fact of him out in the wind.

"I dropped off another Order to Vacate." My father's tone is obedient, talking now as if he's an employee. "Gave her two weeks." Words half-directed to me in case they need repeating.

"She's not going anywhere," my mother tells him. "She delivers some illiterate letter. Burns your supposed antiquities. Shining us on, that's what she's doing."

My father pushes a swath of gray hair from his face but the wind blows it back. His scabbed hands cup the top of the wound-down window. "We'll have to get her vehicle out before a horse gets hurt," he says. The anger in the clench of my father's jaw, his teeth worn down, hers rotting, her pouted lips. Me as some kind of conduit. Like little old children they play our parts.

"She burned my rocking horse," I say.

For a moment they both look at me, unsure if I'd care. Then my mother shakes her head. Tries to turn around. "She's coming. I can feel it," she says.

I glance in the side mirror. A figure striding along the road in our direction. Sharen at a hundred paces. My father fighting with the back door, struggles to get inside. "What do you think you're doing?" my mother asks him and the dog's growl is low, but I'm helping him in, going around to start the car.

Bloody Earley. Just like him to tell me to take the road to meet him out here and there he is peering round at me through the dirty wiper-shape back of Ruthie's car. So much for going to the cottage and sorting things out. It's so friggin' hot it makes me wish I'd shoved that bath towel over Ruthie's nose and snuffed her. They'd notice me then. On this burning bitumen pulling these stupid Genoni sandals off. Can't even tell if what I'm doing's for real or just for effect. No one left to watch, and if my eyes weren't so sore I'd cry but they feel raw as my feet and my eyeballs are burning. No zinc on my nose and no cars to run me over.

"What you doing, Naika?"

Reggie's a shadow, calling me little duck or little dog or whatever it means in his made-up language. His bare feet beside mine and his jeans are frayed big time now, cut off high to make them short. His legs tanned and his hands and they hang loose as usual. I shade my eyes and look up at him—stripes smudged on his cheeks like ink. "What you done to your face?"

He doesn't offer me a hand. "Think I found myself a girlfriend."

"What do you mean?"

"In the big house," *he says.*

I know to be careful round him. If I say one wrong thing I won't see him for days. "Isn't she a bit on the old side?"

"Maybe," *he says. His hair is bleached from the sun and from living out. He's even woolier looking. The shape of Walker right there in his cheekbones, getting clearer.*

"I been back in your house early," *he says.* "I refurnished."

Oh Jesus. Give him a room and he makes it a tree house, invites the possums. "Where you sleeping?" *I ask.*

He stands with one knee bent, his foot pressed against his skinny upper thigh like he thinks he's some old-time aborigine. "Been up the trees." *He points off into the bush.* "And I got a new roof place for naps. I been fixing it too."

I'd try to stand and be like a mother but he'd still be taller and what's the point? "Where you going now?"

"I got some money," *he says.* "Going to town."

"Where you get it?" *I look up at him suspicious and scrunch my eyes.*

"Not nothing bad or nothing," *he says.* "I just take some payment for what happened to Walker and Gracious."

I know it's half in his head because his bloody father and granny were sent away a hundred years ago. "Got some for your mother?"

"Go get your own," *he says.*

I pull Earley's crumpled eviction notice from the pocket of my jeans, hand it over. "They've gone and made it official. Fuck the lot of them."

He frowns and makes mouth shapes as if he's reading but I'm not sure he can. "You should change the names around," *he says.* "So it's them that's got to leave the house."

He gives me a pen as if that's easy then he takes a passport from his shorts and points to the emu and the kangaroo. "Look what I found? I just need to fix the photo."

"Whose is it?"

"Who do you reckon? He has an American and Australian," *he says.* "He's not going anywhere. Anyway, I left him the American one so he can go back where he came from if he wants." He shows me the picture of Daniel with his hair slicked back from his face and wearing glasses. His eyes stare out all serious as a judge.

"I could put my name on this one and get a photo of me stuck in. Easy peasy," he says.

I taught him easy peasy when he was small and it makes me want to smile.

"You better put that back," I say.

"Don't worry, Mum, I just borrowed it for the day."

And I got nothing but Vicki Genoni's stolen sandals dangling in my hand and they don't even fit right. Reggie looking at me as if I'm tragic then he kneels. "You gotta learn to look after yourself," he says. I know he's right. He's the one does fine with nothing.

"You know what I heard Ruthie say about you?" He looks at me hard like he's my teacher. "If Sharen can't make a home, she'll break one."

"I still got a home," I say, point to the cottage in the distance.

"Yeah, and how's that going?" he says and spits on the road.

I feel myself sagging, being lectured by my own son. I look up at him. "Why you so mean to me, Reggie?"

"Coz you're the mother you have when you don't have a mother." He kisses my head and leaves me, walks off as if he's already forgotten.

IN THE REARVIEW mirror there's no Sharen in the distance, just the dog eyeing my father in the backseat. I switch on the wiper washer but the rubbers just scrape the glass, smearing insects. "Well done," says my mother.

When I ask Isabel to marry me will I even tell these two? No: *Have you met anyone?* My mother wouldn't leave here if she could, she'd stay to feed the dog, keep an eye on the animals. Does she even remember what I do in LA? Twenty-something hours since I landed at Tullamarine and I barely remember myself. The alternate universe of the forty-first floor at Pickering Lardner. On a windy day, the view runs all the way to the bridges of Long Beach and the hills of Palos Verdes. Piles of documents rowed up on my desk like Stonehenge—Val Verde Unified School District, Tehachapi Valley Health Care District, Victor Valley, Pasadena, Centinela, the agency financings that run together in my head. Work I'd never stomach back here is bearable elsewhere, especially when a green card came with it.

What would it be to have parents who wanted something more for me than to just come back here to pick up where it was all left off, saving them from each other? From themselves?

"Did you tell Dad how Sharen found you on the bathroom floor?" I ask to shake things up.

"I just felt a bit woozy, that's all," she says, the bag and dog leash clasped in her lap, her fingers kneading gently like her lip. "Took a bit of a toss." She stares out at the mangrove-choked river and returns to her thoughts.

We pass the spacious playground at the primary school, speckled with children already out for recess, cheeks plastered white with sunscreen, scarlet slouch hats for shade beneath the eucalyptus.

"We'll take you in to see Dr. Orry this afternoon," I say.

"Over my dead body," she says, then laughs at the irony.

Friday nights I was allowed to come down here from school and play tennis with the Tooradin juniors, Bobby Genoni, and the Tomkins. The tennis courts rippled with weeds and now there's a glinting machinery shed. Then small mansard-roofed houses crouched on each side of an orange brick edifice that rises up from behind a white ironwork fence. Old man Genoni's house.

"Monstrosity," my mother says, the word she always uses when we pass all of these buildings on what was once part of the farm. The town creeping out in our direction, over the bracken-covered rise we called Fox Hill, just a fibro shack with a family who worked on the place. They were sent away when the Genonis bought, back when my father called Italians "New Australians."

"What's this?" he asks from behind, leaning forward to pull at my mother's new stick from beside the seat.

"Sharen's son made it," I say, just guessing.

"His name's Reggie," she says as if I should know. She scratches at her psoriasis, tiny flakes falling as snow on her shoulders.

"They'll be gone soon enough," my father says.

My mother turns to me, her face freckled dark as a basket weaver's, the side of her neck gathered like a lizard's. She could be a peasant from anywhere, but she's the daughter of a dead postmaster general. "Your father's sorting things out," she says and then there's silence as we round the bend.

The inlet always surprises me, the fact of this town right on the coast, the farm so near the water. Pelicans and fishing boats, the gray sand foreshore, a far cry from the white sand of the Ninety Mile Beach or the Great Ocean Road, a further cry from the winding highway up the California coast. Here it's tidal; armies of miniature crabs pock the mud.

I picture Isabel on the cliffs at Big Sur, watching out to sea. I picture her sitting outside on the sidewalk at that restaurant on Larchmont with its blue and yellow Provençal tables, speaking French to the waiter, or trying to, her hair swept back by sunglasses. As I arrived I watched her as she braided her hair into two long plaits and tied it up behind her, then she pulled her glasses down over her eyes and smiled. An African bangle easy on her arm and the small tattoo of the virgin.

My mother examines the coins in her purse as though they might be her last. It's Isabel who comes from nothing, who's re-created herself, encourages me to do the same.

"Park there," my mother says, pointing to the sandy hillock by the pale green fibro hall where she always insists she walk in from, where the Tooradin Historical Society hosts its annual chair contest. My father, society president, deputizes Margaret Boatwell to beg my mother annually to donate a chair from the big house, but my mother annually doesn't. Earley wins anyway, with the tablet-armed chair of his grandmother's, a dark cherry-wood with one arm widened for writing, as though turning into a flattened upturned hand, where he believes his own great-grandfather once worked on sermons back in Barnard Castle in County Durham. A chair now charred out in a field.

I pull the Camry onto the rise beneath the draping evergreens and for a moment we sit with the view. The town divided by the South Gippsland Highway, more a road than a highway by American standards, but branded *impassable* by my mother nonetheless. Semitrailers hurtle through on their way to Inverloch or other Gippsland towns, Korumburra, Leongatha, Sale. The narrow bridge over Slocombe's Inlet with sluice gates below, and the rock pool, where local boys still swim in the salty water. Grumpy Unthank walks his bulldog, maybe not the same dog but similar. The wall of the foreshore and a narrow gray beach akin to some coastal town in an oven-baked England, the sand leading out to the channel, the mangrove islands toward Bass Strait. Tourist buses burn through full tilt but sometimes stop for fish 'n' chips from Cova Cottage or a ploughman's wheel from the bakery.

My mother tries to turn to the backseat. "Sorry about Hilma's furniture," she says as if he's just appeared, then she gets from the car abruptly, her movement jerky, pursing her lips in the shade of her cap as she manages the leash and her blue dilly bag. "C'mon, Pip," she says and the dog jumps down, prick-eared and ready to be led. Despite the heat, my mother pulls on the cream nylon parka I bought for ten dollars in Manila twenty years ago. Over her jumper. She says her bones never thaw from the chill of the night.

My father is still in the back, left like a shopping bag.

This is their ritual. She'll walk in from here and he'll drive on ahead and sit at his table at The Pelican, hold court, wait for unsuspecting tourists returning from a weekend of fairy penguins waddling up through the dusk in their black-and-white thousands. A windswept beach down near the Nobbies, sixty miles farther on. Since Elsie, my father's been relegated to this side of the road, the tired side. The row of bright, multicolored shops on the far side of the highway is my mother's side.

And I am shepherding my mother who wanders off ahead with a grim, unsteady determination, her new crook and her dog, trying to keep her stroke-canted limbs in measure. She shields herself from the back of Genoni's agricultural machinery yard, a red Massey Ferguson tractor, a John Deere combine, tractors with cabs much taller than ours on the farm. A lot that was once full of weeds and unsold slashers is now awash with gleaming mulchers and balers for silage, mowers for hay. My mother admires the feat of farm production but she isn't keen on trade, or those who work in it, or Italians. I think of the crumbling walls and plumbing those Genonis have traveled to this end of the world to avoid, to this town where my family has old money, such as it is, stashed deep in hatboxes in the house with its own crumbling plaster and echoing pipes.

My father passes by in the Camry, hunched low against the driver's-side door. He gives a halfhearted wave, as we venture the rest of the way on foot, as is the custom. The only difference is I'm here now.

The roar of a truck on the highway, the inlet at low tide and the warm salt wind off the briny water, the mire. The dog's head up in the wind as it lifts its leg and irrigates a shine on the raised black letters of a new bronze plaque near the bridge: *Tooradin. Aboriginal for bunyip. A mithical animal of the dreamtime. Donated by Royal Genoni.*

My mother scoffs, endlessly buoyed by the misspelling, hauls the dog onward, forges the pointed end of her crook in the dirt. My father parking outside The Pelican, getting himself inside to settle in his usual chair among the Ken Doane plastic tablecloths. From the street, I see him smile up at a straggle-haired waitress who pours him tea, his deerstalker's cap held down in his lap, still in his favorite green sweater with its minor stains and holes. And still lord of the manor in there. I observe him through the sun-glinted window as my mother waits a few doors up at Tooradin Collectibles, pretending to examine the curios.

But I can't take my eyes off my father. The way relatives seem different when they don't know you're watching, more themselves but strangers somehow. He appears even more shrunken, struggling to settle his hips in the chair, to turn and greet an elderly couple eating scones at another table. He grins up at the waitress as if she might get snared inside the creases of his smile.

"Heard a rumor you were back." Mikey Duggan, stout and aproned in the plastic fly-strip doorway.

"So it seems," I say, not meaning to sound snooty. I

summon a wink of collusion, pass by him through the veil of plastic, head over and kneel by my father. "Dad, I spoke to Sharen. I think she's a bit unstable. Why do you have these people on the farm?"

He stiffens, his beefy hands about his mug, staring into it. The old couple seems riveted in our direction. Mikey is listening, his waitress too, so I whisper to my father again. "I guess Mum ended up out there fighting the fire."

My father's attention draws down to the hat in his lap, the mug being choked in his fingers. He clearly didn't know this. "We should go to the police," I say. I dredge up allegations from long-ago studies of torts and crimes, malicious mischief, arson, growing dope, if that's still illegal here, countered by my father accused of harassment, unwarranted entry, all of it aggravated. Sweat in my shirt and under my collar; getting embroiled brings blood to my muscles.

"I'm sorry about all this," my father says looking at me in the eye, his lids sagging and red with disappointment, his slightly dank coffee breath. "We might need your help this time," he says, and I'm nodding, touching his shoulder as I rise.

"First we need to get Mum to the doctor for tests."

He's nodding, as if with me here that might be possible.

As I leave, I allow a half-apologetic smile for the waitress.

Outside in the sun, I breathe in the sea air and run to catch up. My mother's well ahead, waiting at the new pedestrian crossing, impatient to get to her side of the highway. To the Tooradin bakery, the post office, Cova Cottage, and the newsagency, to secure her crossword magazine. As I glance back, my father, hunched in the café doorway, starts limping this way.

"Blast you," says my mother. "What did you say to him now?" Then, unannounced, she launches out to cross the highway, her jagged step and no light in her favor, just the dog as it eagerly pulls her across, her crook half in the air. A truck whines to a stop. At the shriek of its air brakes, I wave in apology to the driver. Oblivious, my mother's fishing in her jacket for the post office key on the pink nylon string, the material my grandmother crocheted into bath mats. She swats me away as I attempt to help her onto the curb.

"I told him you were out fighting Sharen's fire on your own," I say, and she stops as if unsure and I wonder if she's already forgotten. Then she notices Earley again, knotting along the other side, beneath the flowering gums, and she hands me the mail key. "And where the hell was he?" she asks as she loops the dog to the bench. "I don't want him over this side of the highway."

In an effort to avoid a scene, I head to unlock Box 90. A bundle of Christmas cards, some addressed to "RB & EW Rawson," as if my parents are still happily married, a few just to her, from those who've taken a moral stand. Again I've forgotten it's almost Christmas. There are no windows dressed; it's the middle of summer. Last Christmas in Manhattan when I met up with Isabel, it was snowing. Those elaborate New York traditions—Bloomingdale's and Lord & Taylor, the tree dressed up at Rockefeller Center. I bought her a cashmere scarf for seven hundred dollars because it was Loro Piana, whoever that is, when I only met her the night before. She said it was a red flag, but lovely nonetheless.

Here, the only thing Italian is old Royal Genoni gliding by on the footpath in a fancy four-wheel motor chair, the Lincoln-jawed face of a patronage statue.

"I hear you had a fire," he says, his accent more subtle than his satisfaction. "Not to worry, Bobby Genoni took her in. Poor thing had nowhere to go." As he passes my mother she smiles at him falsely, holds her dilly bag close as if fearing it might get snatched. She calls him a dreadful old fossil as we step inside the store, the jingling bell on the door the only obvious nod to the season, along with a big red stocking taped to the wall. My mother ransacks her change purse for coins to buy the *Herald-Sun* and *New Idea*, preferring not to break a note. She stamps a great fistful of coins on the counter, silver embossed with emus and echidnas, and waits for someone to count.

The locals monitor us from behind the shelves—the Savigo girl whose parents used to run the railway station when there was still a train. I remember how she was sweet back then, all glasses and spotty face. Now she's a sad-looking woman. I'd say hi but the way she stares is disconcerting, makes me want to say: *Yes, I'm the one who moved away.* Then she averts her eyes as she always did and, for some reason, I have a desire to apologize for leaving her here.

My mother nudges me, ready to go, but outside Earley is sitting awkwardly on the bench, petting the reluctant Pip. "It's Tagalong Shenandoah," my mother says, the name of some pony from her childhood or a private joke she still shares with my father who raises his head with an uncomfortable grin.

"Sorry about the other night, Ruthie," he says, his hat back in his boxy hands, and then he turns to me. "Can I have another word with your son?"

My mother's eyes draw down to the pavement, waiting, giving me the choice, and I feel tossed up between them, knowing my father can't really catch, my mother who might drop me for sport. "Of course you can," I say.

My mother folds her *New Idea* into her bag and I can feel her pull, her silent disapproval. Accusing me with her eyes as she points to the magazine cover: a Hereford bull with a bridle and saddle, a woman on board midair over a jump. My mother pretends to seem tickled, a jumping bull. "I rode the farm bulls when I was a kid," she says, "but we never thought to jump them."

As if running interference, sweet Margaret Boatwell parks her truck and gets out with her shopping bags and her face like a twisted sandwich, all brow and chin, keen to say hello to me but not daring. She can see we're in the midst of things. Old Cloudy Gray, on his way to the pub, is trying to listen in. Some woman watches out of the newsagent's window.

My mother walks on with her dog and her purse and her stick.

"It's strange she still loves you," I say to my father, but he shakes his head—he can't fathom how love could manifest as so much fury. We watch her recede in silence, wafting along in the hot sea air. The stick as her rudder, she heads away over the highway, a flimsy, meandering figure daring the trucks.

A couple of city people pull over in their new Range Rover, eclipsing her. They get out in their moleskins and polo shirts. Hobby farmers and their fifteen acres, moving down here to breed alpacas or Welsh mountain ponies, getting their tractors stuck in the winter mud. My father acknowledges them with a hopeful smile, touches the brim of his cattleman's hat, but they don't know him from a can of paint. Ruthie in the distance, already on the footbridge over the channel. She stands there, staring down into the swill rushing through the sluice gates as if daring herself, then she shields her face and looks out across the foreshore, to the rickety jetty where the few local boats are moored, over the mud and mangroves toward Westernport Bay.

I STAND BESIDE my mother on the bridge, both of us staring down into the mouth of the inlet. The walking stick is floating by the sluice gates.

"I don't need it," she says.

"But didn't Sharen's boy make it for you?"

"Oh," she says, remembering. "Can you get it back?"

"No."

I slide into the passenger seat, onto the ratty sheepskin beside my father as he keeps tabs on my mother who's climbing in the back with the dog. He starts the car but it's already running; the ignition screeches. "Want me to drive?"

my mother asks. She's not been behind the wheel since she had dental work done without anesthesia, then, on the way home, drove right through the florist's front window in Mornington. After that my father got the car.

He bumps it forward and my mother starts to make that tap-drip sound and the dog seems unsettled, shifting about on the seat, whining out at the trees as they pass. "What's going on, Mister Pip?" I ask. My mother strokes the dog's ears.

"The gifts your father brings into our lives," she says. "Marvelous." But my father says nothing, turns left at the school and drives through the new subdivision, accelerates up a newly paved street doing his sick-of-bloody-everyone driving, past a cluster of ugly brick houses. The land we sold to the Genonis too early and they made all the development money.

"Here we go," says my mother as he swerves off the end and we bump up the track, the back way to the cottage, as if it's old times, dust roiling out behind us, a smoke train, the dog poking its face out the window, eyes shut in the wind. And I wish I was on that Pacific Coast Highway with the cliffs jutting out like huge rocky sails and the rain sweeping in off the water. The weekend we drove up to San Francisco to see art at the Legion of Honor. *The Cult of Beauty—The Victorian Avant-Garde.* A museum and a movement I pretended I'd heard of and it was amazing—galleries of Whistler and Stanhope, and Isabel holding my hand.

Near Big Sur, Isabel spied a tree in the distance, a giant ancient cypress full of color. As we walked down the path toward it, we realized it was ornamented with bright vintage dresses, blues and pinks and yellows, hanging from branches and rippling in the wind. They were pinned with prayers and dreams, hundreds of them, written on old-fashioned cardboard luggage tags. She wrote and pinned some of her own and I envied her, attaching a prayer to a tree and believing it might be answered. "You never know," she said. As though it might be that simple.

We trundle over the cattle grid, across the hummocky paddock. Bracken and shiggy scrape the underbelly of the car, the tires jolt in the ruts. "Jesus, Earley," my mother says. "Must we?" But he ignores her this time, parks by the fence that's supposed to keep animals out of Sharen's nonexistent garden. A scrawny roan calf scuttles out into the field through the garden gate.

"Wait here." My father's out quicker than you'd think, a slam of the door behind him and we watch him limp across the sandy lawn, banging on Sharen's brown door, then letting himself right in.

I move to get out as well.

"I wouldn't if I were you," my mother says wearily, but the house door's left open and I can't resist.

In the pokey kitchen, the stack of filthy plates and pizza boxes remains. From the sitting room, the smell of sage and paint, eucalyptus. Sharen crouched on one of the small wooden crates, my father stands beside her, staring at the wall above the fireplace. The plaster painted black as onyx, white letters on it where the Munnings hung. *SHAREN LIVES HERE.* Branches inside, eucalyptus, bridal bush, three old tires piled up as a seat.

"All I need's a decent piece of quiet to take care of myself and Reggie."

"You said you'd get that little bastard out of here." My father grits his jaw and hisses in a way that reminds me of childhood. But Sharen ignores him, watches me as though I'm her witness.

The words seem to pierce the dullness of the room. "Who wrote that?" I ask.

"Bloody kid's everywhere," my father says.

Sharen cups her cleavage as if she's doing Reiki on herself. "I'm so sorry, Daniel," she says. "Coming home to all this."

I try to summon the landlord and tenant's laws here. The Landlord and Tenant Act. But all I remember is the "rule of rentals is that renters rule." Sharen looking at me with those parrot-green eyes. I decide to check the rest of the house, head out through the frosted French doors past the place where my grandmother's desk and prize-winning chair sat until recently. The front door is open, the late morning sun lancing through. Outside, the rocker recliner is splayed in parts on the path as if there's been some incident. Beyond it my mother has the dog off its leash, and it's running a bunny down into a burrow under the green corrugated shed. A second poddy calf skitters from sight.

The other room is empty. Another discarded *Women's Weekly*, this one with a cover titled "The End of Dame Edna," a tangled mess of sheets and laundry. Hearing boards creak down the hall, I move toward them, wary, but I want to see this kid close up. Apples of dark green manure, neat and piled on the floor. I turn from the murky light of the hall into the bright-lit bedroom. No bed, just a small white pony, stock still, regarding me standoffishly, its forelock long between its eyes. Its head extends to check the air and its eyes reflect darkly. "Bloody hell," I say, then hear a noise from outside.

As the pony cocks its head, one eye goes pale, opaque in the light and out the window, my mother peers in, shading her face through the bird dirt. The flinty sound of her laugh makes the pony restless, shifting its feet and turning, its reflection in the wardrobe mirror, twinned with the white of its eyes and its dusty angular rump.

Retreating into the hall, past the loamy manure, I glimpse Sharen and my father through the sitting room door. Awkward, together, looking around to see what's going on.

"Should there be a horse in the bedroom?" I ask. I know if that pony explodes and comes rushing out, my father's one good fall away from a wheelchair, but I just leave them to it. She's not allowed to keep a horse in the field so she put it in the second bedroom.

My mother stands by the gate, staring at the distant road the way a captain might watch out to sea, and I feel a kind of debilitation unfelt since I was young. What Doctor Orry called "the ready tiredness," but I suspect it was a bewildered depression. My mother right here as if nothing has changed, ready to be driven home, putting the dog back in.

One of the three big horses approaches and sniffs the car. "He's a character, this black horse," she says. Has she forgotten the pony in the house, or is she no longer fazed by strangeness? I open the door for her, playing the consort, sidekick, as she thinks it should be. "What's his name?" I ask.

"This one? Trombone," she says. "Out of that great big Lady Lime." She points to the other two in the distance. "Satchmo and Goolagong," she says. "Remember the twin foals?" The pair that stands on either side of the burnt Mitsubishi eating grass. My mother calls out to them and they raise their heads like sentinels. She scoots into the passenger seat and I remember when they were a pair of darkening foals, one named after an aboriginal tennis player and the other a jazz musician; how political correctness bypassed us here.

As I get in, I glimpse the pony's face through the bedroom window, turned about with its head now facing out, the window as its stable door. Another of Sharen's stowaways. The black one nuzzles the windshield and Pip barks, but the looming horse ignores him, looks in at us until I beep the horn. I wonder how my mother bred such supercilious horses.

"They're all sired by that big-boned New Zealand horse that stood up at Caldemeade," she says. In her element now. Horses and son. "You remember him, Sonambulo?" Parts of her memory are sharp as scissors and her hearing has somehow improved. "Trombone. Satchmo. Sleepwalker. All of them black as creosote," she says, "but out of that same creamy mare. That mean old Lady Lime. The size of a shed." My mother the size of that stick left in the pool by the sluice gates. "But they took their father's color. Black as your boot, all three of them. Thick as thieves. That's how we used to be."

I drive off and feel the weight of the time change, the lack of sleep. We've left my father behind. "What are we now?"

"Arm's length." She bathes in the late morning sun refracting through the windscreen. The sign on the gate says *STRICTLY PRIVATE* but the gate's wide open so you can only see the warning as you leave.

"I have a girlfriend," I say. "She's part Venezuelan." Starting in a way my mother might understand, with bloodlines. "We're talking about getting married next year."

"Oh," she says. She feigns neither judgment nor interest as we turn through the gate and bump back down the track onto Wedding Bush Road. These places that recur in my dreams as I sleep cupped with Isabel, holding onto her as if she's a raft.

"I guess we've left the lovebirds to it," my mother says.

I look back at the house in the dust unfurling behind us. And that's the end of the Isabel discussion.

"Where the Munnings hung," I say, "something's been painted on the wall."

I keep my eyes on the gravel but sense hers growing narrower.

"He's out of Sharen," she says, "by that bloke who was born here in the bush. Remember him? Walker. Old Gracious's son. Walker Dumbalk." She grimaces. "Small world." She turns to me and her face almost softens, then doesn't. "Reggie thinks this place is part his," she says, "because his father was born here."

She watches back out toward the Albertinis' place. "Might as well be, I suppose, if your sights are set on Venezuela."

She starts humming one of her tuneless tunes, the one she always used to when she clipped the horses. "Danny Boy," her favorite.

"Her name is Isabel," I say.

SHE DROPS HER shopping bag on the kitchen table. The *Sun* and the mail, the *New Idea*, all of the reasons we went into town seem unimportant to her now. She's feeling fragile, I can see it in the glaze of her eyes as she hangs the dog leash on its hook then disappears up the dark hall, touching the wall for balance.

"Do you need me?" I ask her, but all I get is her half-hearted wave. As though letting me know she's familiar with neglect. And I'm left in the doorway wondering if I'd not been here would I have ever heard of her fall. The way life only seems real if witnessed firsthand. If at the moment of her death, I'll sit bolt upright in my bed in the canyon with a streaking thought of her.

Alone, my focus is drawn to the phone on the desk, to the life where I'm not. I dial the "0"s and "1"s, the familiar string of numbers. "*Your international call cannot be completed as dialed.*" A polite Australian accent.

The dog watches me as I try again. Do they even have cell phone service at Esalen? It makes me suddenly anxious. Only days ago, we stood together at the law firm's painful Christmas party, taking the faux fur–collared coat off her shoulders at the door of the California Club. Her slender Versace knit dress I bought for her birthday, spending more than I ought. But it was worth it—she looked lovely. The narrow slope from her ribs to her hips, her buttery skin. The woman the partners tried not to notice in front of their wives. The dress my secret penance for being drunk at the summer associates' dinner in August, right before Isabel said she was moving out to LA. I told her about Farideh, the Persian girl from Duke, how under the table our legs pressed against each other's. I told myself that's all I'd done but then we'd danced too close. "You're a man," said Isabel, "I like it that you're so honest." But I didn't tell her how I wanted to take Farideh back to my office in the middle of the night, lay her on my desk and push a chair against the doorknob; how I wanted that when I was so in love with Isabel.

The telephone ring sounds far away. I imagine the crystal bowl tone of her iPhone's ring, rummaging in the pockets of her bag. If we'd flown out here together and we'd witnessed my mother and the dog hunting that possum along the picture rail, she'd have been so polite, suggesting a side trip—Bali, Lizard Island, or at least the W in Sydney. She'd have read up on restaurants, Bilson's and Aria, the Bather's Pavilion, ways to explore the reef. Would I have stayed here in this dark sitting room where that brumby foal once slept on the couch? Would Isabel have understood? I've seen her grandmother's tureens of sacred cowrie shells, oracles and talismans. Her grandmother who taught her that the White God doesn't talk or dance or even come to visit. The White God hates the feel of flesh and the sound of laughter in the night. The White God would reject her. And how she shouldn't be with me.

The line goes dead and I'm redialing, wishing there was wireless here, that my mobile might work.

"Daniel. Hey, *lindo*." The slight burnish of her accent on my name.

I look up the hall to be sure my mother's not prowling. "*Mon amour*, can you hear me?"

"Yes, I'm here." My accent feels broad and croaky, unprepared, my words swallowed up in an echo of wind on her speakerphone. "You're driving." Near San Simeon maybe, or the beach where the famous seals dot the sand. "Are you nearly there?" I ask. "It must be getting dark."

Her easy, guilty laugh. "We're on the PCH near Topanga. We just left." I can hear Mona laughing. "*L-O-S-T*," she says, her *Latins-Only Standard Time*. I imagine the sun glinting silver off the water and the shadows of the cliffs.

"Don't worry," she says. "Mona's driving."

"Her car?"

"She doesn't have one," she says and there's laughter. She's driving my Jeep.

"It's lucky I love you," I say. "Why didn't you just take the 101?"

An echo breaks onto the line and it's harder to hear. "We wanted to see the sunset from that big rock, near where the sand slides down the hill." The day we tobogganed down on cardboard sleds and sat on the giant rock with a view of the ocean, the towers of the naval station at Point Mugu.

"And we wanted to see the surfers." Repeating Mona, and I feel a twinge of envy, the two of them together spotting guys changing out of wetsuits right on the side of the road. The colored sails of the late kitesurfers at Zuma. The beaches with Spanish names: El Matador, El Pescador. "You should stop for the night at Pismo."

"We'll be fine," she says but I can feel her smile trail off in the wind, and I can feel her colluding with Mona, a playful roll of eyes.

"I told my mother about us," I say, but she's having trouble hearing so I shout it.

"Well, I should hope so," she says as if that's no big deal. I look up through the dimness, along the sitting room picture rail, a photo of me jumping High Colorado at Melbourne Royal, but the horse has been speckled with dots.

"You're so strange, *lindo*," she says. "Are you okay?"

I want to tell her about the boy and how I miss her but the line starts shrieking as though it's a fax so I lay the receiver down, stand up on the couch, and reach. Me in jodhpurs and short elastic-side boots, but the horse's bay rump is painted as if it's an Appaloosa. The other photos, my mother with a stirrup cup with the Findon Harriers, the line of framed Lipizzaners with their different airs above the ground, are untouched. The phone is beeping.

WHEN I OPEN my eyes it's already late, slants of last light shelve through the motes of dust, through the sharp speckled light, and then I see what's woken me. A half-naked boy slithers silently up from the top of the wardrobe, up into the hole in the roof.

"Reggie," I say, sitting up in the bed. "Get down here and talk to me." But there is no movement. "Did you go through my things?" Still nothing and I wonder if I imagined him, somewhere between dreaming and awake, it doesn't seem possible to get through that hole from the wardrobe, it's too precarious. "I just want to talk," I say. "Why are you up in the roof?" As I pull on my jeans, I remember the ladder leaned up against the trellis outside.

The flashlight I grabbed from the top of the fridge smacks on the doorjamb, the ladder not that tall as I lock the legs wide, but I'm climbing, suddenly wary of putting my head up through this hole. Black as a well, the ragged edges barely wide enough for shoulders. The whine of the dog and my mother is up with her fierce night eyes. "What the hell are you doing?" she asks, coming over to steady the legs but her hold just makes them shakier.

"Just checking," I say as I poke my head up through, cobwebs wrapping about my hair, the acrid smell of rat dirt. I open my eyes to others that shine back at me. I spray them with light. Possums, mother and baby, staring from torn-up papers, debris. Rafters exposed with fine shafts of light from the last of the sun through a crevice.

"See anything good?" she asks.

The possum skulks behind a fallen beam and I glance down. "Sharen's boy, I saw him. I think I did, I just wanna make sure I'm not going bonkers."

I see smudges in the dust on top of the wardrobe, but a possum wouldn't just be standing there. Pushing my head back up into the darkness, I try to shed the light on what's behind the chimney, illuminate something—a blue blanket with pink checks and I make out a row of baby swallows, their heads from nests tucked under the eaves, but no sign of that boy.

"We need to fix this hole," I call down, but my mother's lost interest; she's stepping back toward the bed.

"How would the possums get out?" she asks. "They'd starve. Stink the place up."

As I pull my torch arm through, his face appears from behind the chimney, then his half-naked body shining with sweat in frayed denim shorts, and I'm staring as if I'm the one intruding. "This is yours," he says. "I borrowed it." He holds up the photo of Isabel and I shine the flashlight on her face, her almost-smile. The boy smiles too as if he's sorry for the inconvenience. His dry surf-knotted hair bleached pale by the sun.

"Give me that," I say reaching to him as he kneels to hand it over. As I try to take her from him, the ladder swoons sideways then jerks from beneath me, ripping out under my feet like I'm a man being hanged.

A DIZZYING PAIN stabs at my eye as I try to sit up; trees rush by in the dark. The dog observes me from between the front seats and my hand aches, blood on my shirt. Two fingers strapped tight with electrician's tape, and what is it? Thinly peeled bark underneath it, the smell of eucalyptus. A crease in my palm oozes red. I remember the wardrobe mirror coming at me, my hand stretched out. Touch my forehead where the skin feels raw, my eyebrow swollen. I'm about to throw up.

Rising again, I want to make out who's driving but it's as though the car is roving on its own. The night seems furry outside and the car lurches above the gravel. Pound Road, this stretch between hedges where the Anderson boy ploughed his motorbike through those hawthorn hedges and wrapped himself up in the fence.

Hoisting myself up, I make out my mother's gray hair through the headrest. The pain strikes back in my eye. "Turn on the headlights," I say.

She leans into the steering wheel as if it holds her up. "They're on," she says but it looks as though it's only the parkers.

"Where are we going?" My voice is hoarse, from far away.

"Emergency," she says. "You broke the wardrobe mirror. You were out like a wino, your hand was bleeding." She winds her window down and the night blows in at her hair. "It looked like an axe wound."

"How did I get to the car?"

She doesn't answer, her concentration is out in the shifting darkness and I remember the face of the boy in the roof and those blood-grained eyes. He helped her. Maybe she likes him because he helps, because he's the only one here.

The pain pierces through my head. "You shouldn't be driving," I tell her but she leans farther forward, her shoulders clenched high by her ears, her small hands clawed on the wheel, straining to stay on the gravel, smelling her way through the blackness. I watch the farms pour by through the bug-smeared window.

I come to, squinting through a white, fluorescent light, laid out on my back in a hospital bed. A dark-skinned doctor looms above me, examining my hand. It aches as though a nail has been run through it. "We'll need to stitch this," he says, his accent clipped, Anglo-Indian or Sri Lankan, but he's talking to somebody else.

"Hello there, Mister Daniel," says a nurse as if she knows me, her hair stringy, gray-blond. She places her clipboard on the table and bends low to winch up the bed. She looks like a friend of my father's.

"Where am I?"

"Berwick Medical Center," she says.

The room is a pale lime green and trimmed in pink, plastic-smelling, a deep window with a view out into a bright-lit parking lot. I don't remember Berwick having a hospital. A line of silvery poplars shines in the night, lit like popsicles. I feel nauseous.

"You have a concussion," says the doctor in his pristine coat, "plus a good cut and some abrasions. You must have taken quite a spill." He peers down through gold-rimmed Gandhi glasses.

"Went for a burton," says the nurse as if she needs to translate.

"Who wrapped bark under the tape?" asks the doctor.

I blanch as the nurse uncurls a small bloodstained strip of bark. The depth of the cut, a gorge between my thumb and first finger. The mirror broke my fall, shattered, the glass must have sliced me. I imagine my mother fetching gauze and tape and that boy running out for a ribbon of bark off the blue gum.

"They do that with bark where I come from," says the doctor, "in Punjabi villages. They say bark clots the blood."

"Did we run off the road?" I ask but the nurse looks at me confused as she pinches a needle in my palm and I clench my eyes at the pain. "Where's my mother?" I ask as the feeling of the anesthesia pushes through my hand and I don't hear an answer just the shunting sound of a train in the night, the cold comfort of iron clattering on tracks. Isabel's face in that silver-framed photo, down in Battery Park the weekend we met in New York and she leaned against the boardwalk fence, the way she hugged her shoulders, the sky bright against the sea behind her, then she did a little ballet. She'd be quizzing this doctor about brain swelling, bleeding, demanding an ambulance to a city hospital. I should insist on an MRI.

The numb sense of the needle sewing, webbing the skin between my thumb and forefinger. The train-throttle sound and I'm staring away from the numbness, out through the window. My mother is down there in the parking lot, flimsy as a thread. The thought of her holding the car on the road as if it were an airplane landing, and the boy's spittled leaves and the bark now on the tray.

"Just one more," says the doctor and I look down at the miniature knots being tied, the catgut and tweezers, the neat little stitches. A tremor weaves inside me as the doctor wheels back on the stool and then stands. He walks around to the window and looks down as if intrigued. The dark and silent parking lot, the little woman with the dog by the car.

"Is that your mother?" he asks.

"She doesn't like hospitals."

My mother rights herself with a hand on the car door and the doctor removes his glasses, rests an end of the frame on his coffee-stained teeth. "Will she be driving you home?"

With that my mother looks up and regards us.

"She drove ambulances during the war," I say.

SITTING ALONE IN this stark hospital room I'd call Isabel, if my hand wasn't wrapped like a mummy's, and if I had my phone. Why can't I remember her number? I want to listen to her strange stories, not deal with my own. How her New Yorker father had factories in Caracas and Cartagena making fine leather gloves and belts, a wife in Manhattan who knew nothing of his secret daughter in the Bronx. When she was eleven and he took her on a picnic to Central Park she knew she shouldn't but she told him how the *Babalawo* came to her mother's flat with two big cages, one full of doves and the other had a rooster, and how everyone huddled in the grandmother's room with the altar where the *Babalawo* sang and shook his shells and called in his spirits, his jangling beads and crazy eyes. Coaxed by her father, she said it cost a thousand dollars for a night with the *Babalawo,* she told him that and stared down at the tartan picnic blanket, told how the doves were taken from the cage, one by one, rubbed all over her body, how scary it was as the *Babalawo* took out his knife and slaughtered the rooster, squirted blood from its neck right into her mouth so it ran down her throat and over her skin. When her father asked why, she could tell he was angry. She said she was being prepared in her grandmother's ways for womanhood. She remembered her feet sticking out from the end of a sheet and how they were sticky, bathed in blood and bird guts, and how her father took her home from the picnic and from her bedroom she heard shouting, folded her ears and buried herself in her pillow. Then the door slammed and she knew it was the last time she'd hear her father's voice. That it would be the last of the glove factory money.

* * *

TUESDAY

◆———◆———◆

The taxi squeals slowly to a stop by the concrete dome of the underground tank. I glance at the meter. Sixty-three dollars for fifteen miles.

"Nice old place," says the Indonesian driver, sweating from under his burgundy head wrap. "You never would guess this was out here."

Over the seat, I hand him seventy dollars in the bright-colored cash, feeling ridiculous for getting in the back of the car out of habit, when we're nowhere near a city, but glad my wallet is in my pocket, the way my mother just drove out of the hospital. An overnight stay for just over three hundred Australian dollars, when I'm uninsured here.

Stiffly, I wave at the driver then limp past the dying lilacs to where the dinner gong hangs on its wire like an owl. Sore in one leg like my father—two days here and I'm lame as he is, my hand freshly bandaged and a plaster on my forehead, plus a white paper bag with a jar of seven Vicodin.

When I asked what would happen if I took them all at once, the nurse said I'd probably just vomit.

Standing in the kitchen doorway, I have the sense of a second arrival. I peer through to the dark living room; the television's on but silent, no possum being hunted. An ache in my ribs at the sight of the boy kneeling at my mother's feet, his jeans hanging low as a rapper's; my mother obscured by the back of her recliner, but I can see she's in a dress. He's bathing her feet in a wooden bowl of mud. Leaves and a branch from the flowering gum.

"What's this then?" I ask. The boy stares up with a covetousness that gives me a chill. My mother turns and shrugs as if there's little she can do. "Reggie's softening up my toenails," she says. "You can cut them later if you like."

"They're hard as hooves," he says, massaging her toes, kneading her brown buckled feet. Weird with him in here still shirtless, his young hands on her colorless arches, the purple tributaries that crisscross her ankle. Painting mud up the backs of her calves and on the ridges of her varicose vein. My mother who never wears dresses.

"Sit down, Danny-Do, and watch the tennis," says my mother. She doesn't inquire about my hand.

"Why's he even in the house?" I need to sit down but keep the advantage of height; my mother's gaze returning to the muted rhythm of tennis, her other blue-veined foot taps the carpet lightly. The boy looks up, a smile in the edges of brown-blistered lips. His knotty hair and big dark eyes. "I just came to live on the farm for a bit," he says. "Isn't that right, Ruth?"

Ruth?

Her mouth softens as she hears it, the way he handles her foot, pulling her toes so she smiles as it tickles. I feel the dog against my leg. The dog that usually clings to my mother like a sidecar.

"Sometime I come in," says the boy. "To help. Coz no one's here. And now you come and fall off that ladder." My mother seems to nudge him with her muddy foot, a warning. Everyone here conspires in pairs.

"Without you here," I say to him, "there'd have been no ladder." I feel churlish when I should just grab him and turf him out. Instead, I move farther into the room, my good hand poised on the back of the couch for purchase. "Shouldn't you be with your own mother?"

The boy works on the bridge of her foot, the mud darker than the shining wet skin on his wiry suntanned arms. "Can't live with Sharen all the time. She's crazy." Then he levels up at me. "Anyway, this is my place too," he says. "My dad was born here."

I feel my breath get shallow. A memory of round-faced Gracious who worked up here in the house, her sweet, ashy smell, as if she'd been bathed in smoke. A photo somewhere with her holding me as a baby, bundled in her wrinkled arms.

"Before you lot was even here, my Uncle Worry used to work with sheep, when there was still sheep, and Walker ran cattle. Some of them cattle was his." When the Genonis demanded they leave and Earley, keeper of peace, drove poor Gracie and that son of hers, Walker, up north somewhere near Gundagai in the back of the old Ford Ute. I remember them leaving. I must have been eight or nine.

I can see Walker in the boy's face, in the rustic strength of it. I rest a knee on the arm of the couch, pretend to be comfortable.

"I told you he was Walker's son," my mother says.

"Walker Dumbalk," says the boy. I don't tell him how his father gave me nightmares as a child, that I'd see him marauding in the paddocks. My mother called him Darcy Dugan after some famous prison escapee, but sometimes she called him Walkie Talkie because he barely said a thing. Mean dark eyes and bushy brows. He used to slaughter the meat, skinning sheep that hung in the meat-safe, but I never knew he owned cattle.

"Where's he now?" I ask.

"Down at Yarram," says the boy. "Where I left him." But he looks away, shifty.

"Why did you come up here?"

"To get away from him," he says. "Find my mother."

"Reggie wants to be where his family comes from," says my own mother, as if correcting, baiting me. She once told me I wasn't raised on a farm; a farm raised me. "There is a belonging," she'd said, but I wasn't sure if she meant a belonging to the land or to her.

It's not just the dull ache in my bandaged hand and being laced with Vicodin. This Reggie troubles me; something restive in his bloodshot eyes, his lashes long and laced with dust. His hands are too friendly, plumping my mother's skin in the mud and brown water.

"You like me, don't you?" he says, and with that my mother turns too; she gives me an almost inviting smile.

"When I come back he'd better be gone," I say.

"*You're* not coming back," she says, and I know she means for the long haul.

As I stand to leave, the ache between my stitched-up fingers jabs into my arm. "Perhaps you should attend to your own mother," I tell the little roof rat.

"Remember, I'm the one healed you," he says. His eyes are keen, not dull and angry as his father's, but fractious somehow, dutiful. For all I know he's a godsend.

OUT ON THE veranda I bathe in the late-morning heat, let the day blind me. They call this sun a "hot white bell." A hot white bell that takes its toll. Sucks the life force from you and leaves the seeds of melanoma. The dumb eyes of the cattle as they lift their heads and chew their cuds, regard me.

From behind the high wall of the bluestone barbecue, my father appears unexpectedly at the fence line, kneels to roll under the post and rail. He lies flat in the grass and then turns himself over beneath the bottom wire, arms stiff by his side as if he's in some imaginary straightjacket.

"What happened to you?" he asks.

"Fell," I say, unsure if I have it in me to tell him the details or walk over to help him get up, but there's a slope and he seems breathless, struggling to stand. Cast in the grass, the way a sheep gets cast in a field, or the way the disabled girl crawls in the grass in the famous Wyeth painting.

My father who won't get his hips replaced, afraid his heart might not survive the anesthesia.

I extend the fingers of my good hand down to the roughness of his palm. His skin hard as bark from all the years of axe handles and shovels, rasping horse's feet, and I'm suddenly aware of my own. Once coarse as a farm boy's because that's what they were, they're softer and pale but already burnt and ingrained with gray sand, returning to their old selves. Away from Isabel's creams and lotions. If she could see me here, standing out in this grass in my socks, bandaged and sore, wrapped in the red plaid cut-off shirt I wore when I was seventeen, my father on the ground.

I hoist him up; this little weathered man who I almost wish could just stay in that bleak house in "Bitter Snug" with Elsie, beyond the reach of my mother's revenge. Part of me wants to hold him and whisper, *Thank you for looking after the place*, despite everything, *I'm sorry I've been gone*. My father who rises up light as a marionette and I can almost hear his hips, just bone against bone, crying out for cartilage. Glassy-eyed but smiling still, he stands, hopeful for a moment with me.

I brush the grass stalks and prickles from the back of his pullover. "Mum drove me to hospital," I say. "Last night."

I notice a mark on my father's neck. Skin cancer or hickey? He lifts his shirt collar up to hide it. "Over to Berwick?" he asks. "The new hospital? There's a nurse called Jenny. Did you see her? They're terrific, the girls there."

"I wasn't there for the nurses."

My father nods, kicks at a sandy divot in the lawn, a

place where a rabbit has dug and then perched. "Of course not," he says.

He forgets there's no audience for that talk with me. "So what have you been up to?" I ask, try not to fixate on his collar or his too many layers of clothes in the heat.

"Oh," he says, cocking his head to conceal, "sorting things out with Sharen."

Unsure what that might involve, I try to imagine what Sharen could do that my father wouldn't endure—what would she have to incinerate? The houses, the stables, the horses? "Did you get that pony out of the cottage?" I ask him.

"Nearly knocked me down in the hall," he says and tips his head back with a tight-creased smile, the way he, like my mother, passes off adversity, leaving me with a thin coil of guilt. "I said it could live in the paddock."

"Will she pay for it?" I ask.

"She's a bit pressed right now," he says with that old apology in his red-rimmed eyes. He's re-ensconced her.

"Her offspring means business." I point to the roof with my bandaged hand. "Did you know he nests up in the eaves?" Again, a bite of pain between my fingers, the thought of the bark and pulling at the stitches. "That's how I ended up with this."

My father collects himself, an extra brush to the seeds on the arm of his sweater. Taking it in. "He's just a kid," he says. "Fourteen, but skinny."

"He's giving mum a mud bath."

The droop in my father's lower lids deepens as if preparing for a great weight of water.

My eyes draw away from Daniel leaving me, the disappointment all over him. I look past the roof into the bright yellow mouth of the sun. The same space between chimneys where I see the old man sometimes, a shape that appears in the memories that run about inside my eyes. If I blink it'll be gone; a trick of the heat but it haunts me, driving old Gracious and Walker up over the border in that blue Falcon Ute, away from here. Seven hours straight it took me, with the two of them in the back just to make me feel bad. They wouldn't sit in the front, neither of them, they wouldn't look at me. Walker glowering at the back of my neck. I was afraid of his fist through the window. All of their things stuffed in three old yellow suitcases and a few hessian sacks beside them.

Before we left I'd tried to explain how it wasn't my fault, and how it was a favor I was doing for them, taking them, but Walker just spat in the dirt near my boot. I tried to tell them it was Royal Genoni throwing them off, not me. I didn't even own that piece of land anymore. But they refused to understand, and they didn't believe I could do nothing about it, other than drive them away. They both knew what was true—nobody wanted Walker on the place, least of all Ruthie.

Near Holbrook, I ran into a dust storm and in the rear-view mirror their faces went a dull kind of orange. Gracie's white dress got covered but still the stubborn buggers wouldn't sit up in the cab. Eventually, Walker banged on the roof and pointed directions to some fallen-down shack way back off the road in a patch of ghost gum country. It was on the way to Junee.

When I drove in through the dust to deliver them, Gracie's ancient brother was there waiting, as if he knew. Wiry gray hair and a black birthmark in the middle of his brow, so still the flies looked stuck to his eyes. Uncle Worry, they called him. He was born down here before my time, but I'd heard of him through Gracious. Gracious who raised me but wouldn't even look at me now and this old brother of hers who didn't move to shake my hand, his eyes boring through me. Walker walked right past him, took their bags into the house, and the uncle watched as I left him with his sister by his side and his face kept coming back in my head as I drove through the night all the way home, hardly daring to stop for petrol.

When I got back down here I was so exhausted, it was like I woke from a sleep, and there he was up on this roof, in my mind, over and over I saw him up there. Uncle Worry. When I look now he's gone. Close my eyes for second and he's not there but it doesn't mean I'm not worn out by what I think I see.

I head inside and see what the hell's going on with Reggie. Sometimes when I look at him I see the uncle in his eyes.

Coming in through this back door is dangerous these days. Ruthie and her rules. Even if it was the front door when I was a kid, when we drove in through the avenue of gums and down the Pond Paddock hill, back when Gracie looked after me and took me for walks around the pond. Back before Walker was born and Sharen didn't exist, and that cottage wasn't yet there.

In the Senator's Room the fallen ladder and the hole in the ceiling. I'm not allowed in here and still I'm the one gets blamed for not getting it fixed.

"Wasn't there for the nurses." Snooty little blighter. Coming back here and stirring things up. It was better without him; everything goes worse when he's around. I forget, last time he came he had me sign those papers so I lost the land. Just because I wanted to sleep with Elsie. That's all I wanted, a body to lie with. Ruthie never even gave me that. Only an occasional cuddle under sufferance, if I was lucky.

I loiter in the hall by the pew as if I'm a burglar in my own house. Sounds come from the living room like distant gunshot but it's just the television turned up too loud. The tennis at Kooyong or wherever it is nowadays, that new place with the dome and the roof that opens up like an overhead cupboard.

From the doorway I spy her in her usual chair, the blue court on the screen divided by lines. Is it Phillippoussis, the Greek kid with the serve? Or hasn't he played for years?

"Where's Reggie?" I shout above the sound, but does she hear? She's wearing a dress and the dog licks her ankles, a bowl of dark muck at her feet. Like Yarra pudding. I go over to it and take it away. "I want to talk to Reggie," I shout again and she motions her chin at the half-open window.

"Better late than not at all," she says and the crowd on the television roars.

THE HORSES PICK on the last remnants of green as rabbits disappear into burrows. I stand among them down by the pump shed in the Boy's Paddock hollow. A richness of chewing and crickets in the silence. Leaning down I pull up a dockweed with my good hand. I could lie down in this grass how I did as a kid and pretend to be invisible, let my retinas burn, but a vehicle rattles up the drive, changing gears near the stables.

Almost relieved at the chance of outsiders, I listen to the sound wend up to the house.

Heading back up the hill, I climb the stile cautiously, step down near the compost heap, and watch out past the end of the shearer's quarters. A truck pulling up by the old magnolia, clouded in dust. The dog barks from the garden steps. A four-wheel drive with a high diesel stack. A new silver Land Cruiser with an elaborate tray. Bobby Genoni with a woman beside him, sitting too close. And Jesus, it's Sharen; they've seen me.

Trying not to limp, I move across the unmown grass, coop my dressed hand in my opposite armpit. All of a sudden my fingers ache hard. The tray of the truck decked out with ledges of tools, shovels and pipes, a pump with a bright green tank. Bobby gets down with a brown cigarillo, his face red and blustery, smiling. Sharen slides out from the same side. Her gingham sleeves rolled up, her hair clasped back, her eye shadow blue to cage her emerald eyes.

Bobby's neck bulges from his collar, his hair thinning over a crimson Australian scalp, and I force a tight, distant smile. "Hey, Bobby G.," I say.

I'm shaking his hand, reaching slackly with my left. "Sharen said you were in town so I came by to confirm, wish you all Merry Chrissie." He butts out the cigar on the gravel even though it's barely been smoked, twists it in with his heel. "You look as if you've been in the wars, Dan."

I shade my face in the sun. "Took a bit of a toss," I say, sounding awkwardly like my mother.

"We're on our way to Cranbourne," says Bobby. "Anything you need?"

The slap of the flywire slamming, my father shuffles along the path behind me. "Maybe you should keep a lookout for antiques," I say as we watch him emerge from beneath the shade of the ficus out into the sun.

"Thanks for letting Sharen stay in the cottage, Earley," says Bobby. His hands jingle coins in his pocket.

My father stands atop the bluestone step beside the flagging roses and gapes at Sharen. The longing in his eyes reminds me how he once told me: *All I want is a woman who'll hold me.* If we could only learn to hold ourselves.

"I heard she was moving in with you, Bobby." I pick a deadhead from the nearest bush and feel the dull persistence in my stitched-up hand.

My father inches down beside me. "I told her she could stay on," he says apologetically, humiliated. A mixture of shrunken and fawning. Despair in the red of his eyes.

Sharen acknowledges him with a cautious smile, but she's standing by Bobby, her peacock eyes now strained on me, giving me a glimpse of what these men find attractive. Is it the audacity? Or that her jeans sit low for a woman her age, her midriff tan, the silver stud in her belly button?

"Dad, you know that house isn't really yours," I tell him, holding Sharen's gaze. Her cheekbones are high, freckled by sun, and the air tastes raw. A new red mark stains the side of her neck. Our silence broken by the clang of the dinner gong, echoing through the afternoon.

"Lunch," my mother shrieks through the trees from behind us.

My father brightens, as if we might all be invited, but I don't move. "We need to do something about Reggie," I say to Sharen.

"He never hurt anyone," she says, defensive, but I hold up my bandaged hand as evidence.

Two fingers press against her thin dry lips. "He never did that," she says.

"He's not Walker's son for nothing," I say. "Just get him off the place. Take him with you."

Bobby looks confused, squints at Sharen for details.

My father snuffs at Bobby who doesn't know who's fathered whom. "She's a wheelbarrow full of surprises, our Sharen," my father says, tries for a diffusing laugh, but his words incite a new glare from Sharen. She retreats to the truck and climbs up into the passenger side. "Fuck yous'all," she says, slamming the door. Bobby looks on, a sudden spectator.

"She'll keep you on your toes, Bobby," my father says, his smile weak, lopsided, a display of silver-capped molars. As he turns to me I wonder if it's more than the usual water welling in his runny eyes.

"Someone saw Walker down at the caravan park," says Bobby.

That strikes each of us silent. Except for Sharen who stares out the truck window, down into the dust.

ANGLING THE QUEEN Anne chair under the doorknob and wedging the windows shut, I collapse on the bed. The evening heat leaks in as I listen, think of that boy climbing all over things, blowing dirt in our faces while we sleep. This house where nothing locks, silent now but for the crickets and the snort of a horse from out near the pond, the echo of dogs from the greyhound kennel on Finks Road. The gruesome thought of Walker.

Out the window, the dull black shadows of the cypress trunks and distant lights from the refinery at Lysachts. And the photo of Isabel, left on my pillow with the glass cracked, brings on the need to hear her, but it's the middle of the night back there. We could have had Christmas with her mother. That little walkup off Westchester Avenue in the Bronx. How her grandmother Rosario understands English but refuses to speak it. I remember her kneeling in the candlelight, petals on the white lace cloth, and the cross with Jesus festooned with beads and a bowl of grapes and bright plastic flowers. The odd thing was the urn of feathers. Isabel said it was nothing; her grandmother had once been a priestess of Palo Mayombe, some old voodoo thing. She had small mirrors and a cauldron of water. *When I was a kid she cast out demons*, Isabel said, *consulted the dead through patterns in tea leaves and slices of fruit.* Only later did Isabel let on her grandmother was probably casting me out, didn't want any more white men infiltrating. I looked too much like Isabel's father.

Don't panic, Isabel assured me. *I don't believe in the color of gods.* But she still has her superstitions—throwing a bucket of water into the wind for the New Year, her own altar with pictures of Amma the hugging guru, and her grandmother's stories passed down: the Chupacabra that sucked the blood of calves and goats and children, leaving nothing but their carcasses with puncture wounds.

She told me how her grandfather was once a well-ranked general and they gave him the moniker "The Chupacabra of Caracas." He had a son, Isabel's uncle, who dressed up as a girl and wore bright makeup, and one day got brave enough to parade himself in front of his father. The general beat him so badly the son ran away and her grandmother never saw him again—a teenage *travesty* on the streets or "disappeared" by her grandfather to clear the family name.

Me staying out of sight, the snort from the paddock and I sense it out there in the dark. Not just the three black horses down by the pump shed, but someone out there, me crouched low as a lizard, and I know the shape of him, feed in his hand and a halter. Walker come rustling, one hand outstretched like a tongue in the night and horses will go missing. Walker come for Reggie too and my breath gone cold. The big one sniffs at a carrot and Walker try to catch him with the rope, one then another, to load them on the secret truck and drive them down for sale. Bairnsdale or the knackery at Poowong. I know those ropes. Horses there in the night and gone in the morning. I know the sound of Walker's whisper.

"I know you're out there," he says to me, voice low and pretending he's nice. Wants to drag me back to Yarram but I gotta hide myself from that life, threats to send me off to Rhon Rhon, a prison down there that he went to, but it doesn't exist anymore.

"Come help me, Reggie." His whisper through the dark but he won't catch that gelding, not without me. "We just gotta get them to the place off the highway near the egg farm. Truck's coming. I need you, son." About to put the halter round the big mare's neck but she backs away. "Look at these buggers," says Walker. "Dodge the three of them together and we'll have a truck of our own." The way he always talks about us "doing business." You and me, Reggie. Walker and son. And the mare eats out of his hand again.

I reach for a stone and throw it low and then the dog comes out of nowhere so the mare she spins on him and gallops off, all of them turn from his carrots and rope and go.

"*You little bastards,*" *he calls to me and to the dog. "I'll catch you too, don't fuckin' worry.*"

But I lie here in grass and dirt with my own breath coz I'm not his prisoner boy no more, don't do his rustling, not here not nowhere. Riding horses bareback through the night to wait on roadsides or in the room in Yarram when I pretend to sleep and he tells me I'm his precious little bastard and how we make a business work together but it's just because he's drunk and knows the animals trust me.

His torchlight sweeps near me so I get up and run with the dog and the horses, but me, I'm low and silent. He won't catch me this time.

A PANADEINE MUTES the ache in my hand but the gallop of horses and the distant greyhounds howling in their cages make me restless, sparking an old desire to steal up to the city. Get drunk on rum and Coke and circle the curbs around Grey Street and Barkly waiting to spot a St. Kilda girl who might suit me. Thoughts like that make me want to take the Prius to Tullamarine, catch the Qantas flight in the morning—be in LA the same morning and rent a car there and drive up the coast. Esalen by midafternoon.

Almost asleep when I hear pushing at the chair that holds the door, a knocking. My mother whispers my name.

I wrench the chair free from the latch and see her standing there disoriented, folded into her nightgown. "Pip's disappeared," she says.

I get up and look down the dark hallway. "He's probably on the veranda," I say. "In his bed."

My mother wipes her eyes, gummed-up and watery. "When I woke I got lost in my room," she says. "I was crawling about on the floor."

I turn on the hall light, fearing the boy might be slouched in the fanback chair, or in the pew, waiting. "I'll find him," I say. "You go back to bed."

As I walk down to the living room, I take my grandmother's knotted mulberry cane from among the shooting sticks and umbrellas that sprout from the hallstand. Then I see the cane that Reggie made for her, last spotted at the sluice gates, returned, but I am less surprised by such mysteries now. The boy must have followed us down the town.

Through the curtains into the shadows of the dark

enclosed veranda, I make out Pip's small canvas bed, an empty burrow of blankets. The doors are shut. The dog is gone.

Barefoot with the cane, I slip into the night, call Pip's name in the powder-lit garden. The cypress trees creak like ships. The sounds so distinct and the quietness is scary, the sense of that boy. I hear the word *pernicious* in my head. In LA risks are everywhere but somehow I feel safer there. Here there are no witnesses, just the mute regard of the trees, and the dull acceptance of the animals. This place I so often conjure when I close my eyes and dream.

I head past the compost pit and stand on the stile. The air is black as iron as if the night is dead, the shadows of the ibis roosting in the trees like folded tents. An old Welsh pony raises its dished face from grazing, a pony I remember. Vonita. I climb down and put my arm around her thick bay neck and scan the shadowy distance. No sign of the dog, just the moon that hems a great raft of clouds with an edge of light, the bare bones of distant hills. The pony's smell is familiar, musty and salty, and the night is warm and high, suddenly lit up by the barefaced moon.

My soles brush through the dry paspalum. I should be in boots; my feet were once tough before these years in loafers and wingtips, lawyer shoes. I'd be out in the night as a boy, fear and freedom running through me indistinguishably, the chance of snakes in the grass. For all I know, I'm being tracked by the boy across the cool gray sand to the rabbit warren. I head on down near the Lagoon Paddock gate, the breath tight in my chest, eyes on my footfalls, and the cane in front of me.

I swing up onto the corner gate with barely a sound from the chain link, and land easily on the other side. I could probably still swing up onto a horse, but my body is achy from the ladder, and the hand I've forgotten to favor begins to throb. The incinerated car lies ahead, a low monument. Moving through the night toward the three black horses. That dog when it goes hunting and forgets its name. My underarms sweaty as I cross through the ti tree and over near Sharen's fence, as though it's where I was headed all along.

I don't knock, just push the front door open and stand in the entry hall, stare into the living room. No Reggie, just Sharen on a blanket and cushions on the empty boards, a pale sheet pulled up around her. The painted wall above her. She rises up abruptly, a quick sound in her throat as she hugs her arms to her knees in the shadows.

"What you want?"

I feel the carved grip of the cane in my hand. A bruise on her cheek seems to shine in the moonlight. "Pip's disappeared."

She looks cautious; her green river eyes and a hand on her heart as if for protection. "Do you want help?" She looks almost innocent in the dark, the sheet off one bare shoulder, but I'm not sure what I want. Her surf-bleached hair about her face, a small tattoo on her upper arm, she clasps herself to cover her bruises. "Ruthie must be worried," she says and I study her. Pretty once, and in a weathered leathery way still. I can see Reggie in the shape of her mouth and eyes. There's no doubting he's hers.

She stands, struggling to stay covered, tucking the sheet under her armpits; she reaches down for a pair of red denim shorts and pulls them on, facing the window. "Give me a sec," she says, but as she grabs her gingham shirt, the sheet falls and I see the narrow curve of her back, a glimpse of a breast, her attempt at modesty. Makes me want to move closer. She'd smell musty as old hay, musky, so different from Isabel, lucerne to freesias and rose.

"What happened to Bobby?" I ask.

"He was afraid his wife would find out," she says, buttoning her blouse. She looks down at my bare feet, the thistle burrs on my pant legs. "You gone native?"

Searching her eyes for something, a part of me that wants her just to stay undressed, to kneel and be near her, and I wonder how different I am from my father, from men like Bobby Genoni. I feel different from myself, back here, out here, as though I'm near the end of something.

Clasping the walking stick, I stay in the doorway, the soles of my feet on the boards; my plastered hand begins its ache. "What am I doing here?" I ask.

Picking up a worn-out Blundstone boot, Sharen stops and turns, pushes her hair from her eyes. "No accidents."

I look about the emptied room, the words on the stippled wall. The pile of clothes and blanket, so far from how it had been. No inlaid table or grandmother's chairs; she's left herself with no bed. I think of Isabel's Frette sheets from the outlets at Morongo, a quilted satin comforter. "I need to get back," I say, look out into the faintness.

"Wait," says Sharen and I can hear her slipping on her other boot.

I step into the color-blind eye of the night. The constellations spangle light across the gray grass, past the windmill and all the way back to the big house. "Pip," I call as if I'm calling myself. I try to remember my real life, what I do. Securities laws, the "blue sky" surveys, treatment of debt under the laws of every state and Puerto Rico, Guam, the Virgin Islands. A row of Zegna suits, a high-rise office with a view, a 401(k) and benefits; all of it incongruous under the breadth of this sky. The sound of Sharen shutting the garden gate, following. She shouts the dog's name so loudly the three black horses raise their heads. The simultaneous pricking of ears and they're trotting to us, spanking through the grass. Sharen's white pony now follows them, a new disciple, as they break into a canter.

"They scare me, those big ones," says Sharen.

I reach behind me to assure her, feel the bareness of her arm. "Stay close," I say as the three of them come to a halt just feet away, puffing, heads rising up in alert. The baldy-faced mare steps forward, extends her neck to sniff me, the air too warm to mist her breath. "Hello, girl," I say, gently reach out my good hand and rub her velvet nose. She nuzzles my neck and I let her, her nostrils on my throat, whorls on her forehead. Then Sharen's pony pushes in and there's squealing and they scatter then stop in their tracks. The bigger gelding stands aloof in the dark, suspicious, its mane growing thick and almost straight up. "That's the one that spooks me," she says and as she says the words, the horse snorts, wheels on its haunches, and all of them take off, thundering across the moon-dappled meadow. Together we watch the shadows galloping, and from nowhere the dog appears, haring after the horses through the grass with the moon on its back. The dog that never chases stock.

"Little bugger," says Sharen, calls the dog off as if it's hers, but the dog races on like a greyhound let out of a cage. The night is the only one listening.

I LEAD THE dog home through the dark with my belt looped through his collar. My mother delights in dogs that are deaf to instruction and then come back all proud and smiley.

At the windmill, the dog's still panting. He only stopped chasing when those horses turned in their tracks to strike at him, then he took refuge under a boxthorn and came straight to me. As I let him drink at the horse trough, I hear the same strange hoot of the owl. High on the edge of the tank is a shadow. "You up there?" I ask.

A laugh is laced with something akin to mocking. Ten feet up, a knee to his chest with his skinny arms wrapped around it. A silhouette of twisted hair.

"Why do you like to be up so high?"

"Safer," he says. No shirt even at night and the moonlight on his open face, one dusty foot dangles down the lichen-covered bricks of the tank. "Gotta keep an eye out." His glistening eyes stare out toward the distant window lit on the hill, my mother waiting. "You know she shouldn't be up there alone." He lets both legs hang and spits into the tank, hums the way my mother does as if it's how he soothes himself, and the fins of the windmill creak. "Walker's around," he says.

"What's he likely to do?"

"Wants to take me back."

The dog begins whining as I lead him home through the warm slices of night, the groan of a truck without lights rumbling along Genoni's Road.

* * *

WEDNESDAY

◆———◆———◆

"C'morn, C'morn."
I wake to the call from down in the Boy's Paddock flats and it has me rising up from the bed to draw the senator's curtains that never quite close. This life proceeds without me. A bright stroke of daylight and a view of my father summoning the herd of old ponies that live near the house, his call echoing up as I walk outside in my boxers to pee. Last night feels somehow distant, the pain dissolving from my hand as I stand on the edge of the veranda like I did as a kid, making patterns in the lawn.

My father hobbles through the distant capeweed in his gumboots, still hollering at the geriatric ponies that ignore him. Then one raises its head and begins to trot stiffly, followed by another, and the elderly geldings thread past, their movements pottering, not pummeling the earth as they used to or as those black horses did last night. They're far away on the Lagoon Paddock rise, lined up as kings, as the brood of rickety ponies disappears over the hill to the yards by the sheds, my father left far in their wake. It makes me think of running brumbies up past Briagalong, my father stopping at a waterhole with his horse's neck stretched down to drink. Taking fright at a branch that cracked, it leapt out into the middle of the water. We laughed at my father then realized the horse couldn't swim, panicked and sinking, its eyes rolled high in its head. In the turmoil of dragging the panic-struck horse to land, we forgot my father couldn't swim either, floundering on his own in his oilskin coat. We had to help haul him out too, saved by the wax in his Driza-Bone overcoat. He'd broken his hip for the first time.

The phone rings and it has me rushing inside, through the mean glare of the morning. I hear my mother's "hairlo . . . hairlo" as I open the rattling sitting room door, "Whoever it is can't hear," my mother says, handing over the receiver as if it's a grenade.

"This is Daniel," I say.

A faint echo. "Oh my God, was that your mother?"

"Thank God it's you."

My mother glares, waiting to see who it is, refusing to leave. I'm nodding but not speaking, strung between them.

"We stayed at Pismo," she says. "Now I'm up near Big Sur and it's raining like crazy. There's no reception at Esalen so I drove up the highway to call. I'm near where we saw those dresses hanging on the tree."

"Are they still there?" I ask. Maybe now's the time to pin a prayer for me, my mother tidying the desk as if searching for something by the phone. "Breakfast's ready," she whispers urgently and I nod.

"Are you okay?" she asks, a crackle on the line. "Hello." I must have missed her answer.

"Yes," I say. "For some reason my mother's loitering." I don't mention my fall, the ladder, my hand, the gleam in that black horse's eye, the boy on the rim of the tank.

"Tell her to leave us alone," says Isabel laughing.

My mother's examining the calendar on the wall, crossing out yesterday with a Sharpie. "Mum, please," I say.

"Oh my God, you sound so Australian," says Isabel. My mother looks daggers at me then smiles.

"I feel it," I say as my mother returns to the kitchen. "I just wish you were here." But I'm not sure if it's the phone that sounds hollow or me. "You seem so far away."

"Don't be melancholy. Listen, I found this poem for you," she says. "A Rumi one."

I forgot she was there for a workshop called *Rumi and Ecstatic Dance,* how she started reading Rumi in Spanish and then others I hadn't heard of, Mirabai, Rilke, and the Lebanese one. "Listen to this," she says and there's rustling. "It's perfect . . . *This being human is a guest house.*" She's speaking slowly but it sounds as though she's in a tunnel. "*Every morning a new arrival. Welcome and entertain them all, even if they are a crowd of sorrows.*"

"That's beautiful," I say.

"*Even if they are a crowd of sorrows who violently sweep your house empty of furniture.*" She pauses for effect. "*Still, treat each guest honorably. She may be clearing you out for some new delight.*" Then silence.

My mother slams a kitchen cabinet.

"See, it's no coincidence, the furniture, that woman. Maybe you're just supposed to be kind."

The phone cord on the end of its leash, I move to the kitchen door. My mother's halved a grapefruit for us, cutting sections, the small enameled knife with the curved blade. She's not eating without me.

"I miss you, Señor Daniel," says Isabel.

"I miss you too, my belle," I say. "Thanks for the poem." My tone sounds reedy, thin. I sit on the arm of the chair under the dim standard lamp and try to get back inside myself. Think of her birthday at the Immaculate Heart in Montecito, up near Santa Barbara. We made love in a small monastic room with paper-thin walls while the nuns in their habits observed the great silence, and then we looked out the window.

"What would I do?" she asks.

I pick up a tiny photo of my mother in jodhpurs leaning against the hood of a car. Her diary on the desk, her cursive letters. *Daniel Arrives.* December 21. She's crossed off that day and now two of them since. Today is still blank.

"What do you mean?"

"If I was there?"

At the monastery, in the great hollow quiet, a sketch of Mary smiling from the wall, holding the baby, and I never wanted a child until then.

"Keep me out of trouble," I say. "Or at least sane." I look out through the curtains, the leadlight windows. My father coming back up the drive with the hitch in his step. "Save me from these people."

"Even if they are a crowd of sorrows . . ."

My father stands on the crest of the drive, his full head of hair blowing across his face, pushing it back almost boyishly, surveying the farm as if it's all still his. Then he turns to the house but it looks as if his legs are buckling. He's staring up at the sky.

MY FATHER SEEMS shaken but he won't say why, leaning against a garden fork that's been planted in the lawn. He watches up at the slope of the roof, the slate tiles and the archipelagos of lichen. The heat already shimmers off the chimneys. "Sometimes I think I see old Uncle Worry," he says.

I look at his pink-rimmed eyes, their whites scorched with rivers of brown. "He must be dead twenty years."

"That's what concerns me," he says then casts it off as a joke, gives himself a shake. "I'm moving pretty freely this morning," he says. "Got the horses up."

The dinner gong sounds angrily. "Daniel, will you ever come and eat your muesli?" my mother bleats down the path.

"Could I come in with you?" my father asks. "I need to sit."

"We can give it a shot," I say and he allows a shallow laugh.

I put my arm through his. He seems to barely come up to my shoulder. My mother at the door with her hand on the gong, at the ready. "What are you two plotting?"

"Can Dad come in for breakfast?"

My mother's lips clamp. "He's not supposed to be in here." She holds the door open, addressing me.

"He needs to sit down."

"He can make his own coffee," she says and walks back inside.

As I usher him through, my father's eyes brighten. "Things are looking up!" he says.

"Jumped up corporal," she says to him and then she starts at me. "My own poor mother warned me on that picnic blanket at the Melbourne Hunt. 'He has a wandering eye,' she told me. She didn't mention hands."

As my father sits down with his coffee, she leaves: the old rattle slam of the door. "She's worse when you're around," he tells me, his knotty fingers around the mug, as if she's my fault.

OUT THE SITTING room window, through the gauze of the fly screen, my mother's in the Pond Paddock framed between two cypress trunks. With the boy. They look akin to something from a plein air painting. Her helper hefting a small pine tree up on his shoulder. My job. The old woman following in her gingham shirt. The word "chutzpah" rises from me, the boy's narrow hands cradling the tree, like they cradled her callused toes. I watch them cross where the tennis court was, past the single rotted post where the net once stretched to the other post that has since disappeared. Where I'd play against her in the cool of evenings as the ibis landed in clumps in the high branches, nestling and squawking, tainting the bark with their guano. The fine red gravel tennis surface barely recognizable now; *en tout cas*, she always called it, all-weather, submerged by weeds and dust. Her strokes were clean and solid, shouting at my scratchy backhand: *Lift your game, for God's sake.* Smiling as she sliced something by me or lobbed right over my head. I barely beat her before I turned sixteen. There was no outplaying her through cunning.

Now she herds the bare-chested boy to the gate, a rusty tree saw over her shoulders, the dog inspecting the rabbit warrens. Maybe the stroke has realigned her somehow, made her stronger, that boy as a project or replacement, or some strange mascot. But she's not unlike the boy herself, both of them wiry, a similar height, both of them slatted by the shadows of the row of trunks. The paddock that had once been a forest of conifers before droughts and Christmases took their toll—just a few huge pines left in the distance, towering and yawing, aching to die. The pity of cutting the last young pine but at least she's broken her moratorium on Christmas since the year she turfed my father out. She's boycotted each Christmas since. *What's the point?* she told me. *All of you gone. It might as well be wartime.*

She hangs the handsaw on the fence and instructs the boy. Her short gray hair seems almost blond in a streak of sunlight. They stand where the jonquils bloom in the spring, spawned by the first decent sunshine. She's taking the tree from him. I rest my coffee mug on the sill, an instinct to tear out to help but she widens her stance and hefts the pine, the boy observing her from behind as she moves up the slope of the lawn. Then the boy stares up at the house, sees me. I'm not sure why I'm nodding.

My father still in the kitchen, drying breakfast dishes, mesmerized by a strange-looking Asian woman on SBS reading the news with a stilted British accent. *Preparations for this evening's Carols by Candlelight, Melbourne's Christmas Eve ritual at the Sidney Myer Music Bowl.* The silhouette of my mother out on the veranda, pulling the living room fly-screen free. Taking the direct route.

"We still have doors," my father says, cocky now he's in the house.

"She's bringing in a tree."

I help her slide up the hard-wedged frame. The smell of pine needles breaking as she hoists the young tree inside, buried in it. The trunk grows tall as it emerges into the room.

"Watch out for my Wysocki," she yells in to me, obscured by branches as the tree passes over her jigsaw table, the puzzle of children playing in snow. Pieces missing, as usual. If the puzzle had horses she'd frame it when done.

"I would have helped you," I say.

She begins to clamber in through the window and I reach to give her a hand but she shoots me a look. For whom is she showing off? My father? That's the part that somehow breaks my heart.

Inside, she averts her eyes, removing detritus from her shirt, and then checks that her hearing aid is still covered by her hair.

"Thought we'd stopped cutting down trees," my father says.

My mother ignores him and I think of all those Christmases she's been here in this big house alone, Earley off with Elsie in some restaurant, now me with Isabel and her homemade tree. Next year she says she wants an *aluminum* tree with a small rotating tree stand, color wheels, and retro lights mixed with her homemade ornaments. She says she likes the tinny smell of spray-on silver. I called her a huffer.

My mother sits herself down on her jigsaw stool, pretending she doesn't need a breather. "I'll get the butcher's grass," I say, the boxes of ancient decorations in the linen closet.

I step up on the wooden trunk full of bone china, reach for the cardboard case, the green plastic grass to wrap around the base. Everything still there, the basket of creased wrapping paper. She recycles strange things, socks as dusters, her hands inside them like puppets. Regifting was always normal here. When my grandmother's memory was gone we'd rewrap the gifts she'd just given, present them back to her the same Christmas day, laying bets on whether she'd notice. If she did we'd stifle the laughter, my grandmother smiling politely. If she didn't realize, the room filled up with a hushed sense of victory. It didn't seem cruel to me then, just sport.

I think of the sterling silver bedside clock I brought with me for my mother this time, the same present left for Isabel, double-gifting for mother and girlfriend, I know. But I'd run out of shopping days and there they were—a pair of silver clocks.

On top of the carton of dusty decorations, I balance the butcher's grass and a small frosted Santa with gray kangaroos in the sleigh. An old sleeping bag is laid out along the top shelf with a pillow. The pillow smells musty and sweet, creased with sweat. Does Reggie sleep in here too?

Back in the sitting room my mother perches, poised with a lit cigarette, as I set the Christmas paraphernalia on the couch. She hasn't smoked since the doctor gave orders. "Why are you doing that?"

"I always smoke at Christmas," she says, holding the cigarette up as a prize, supporting an elbow, not furtively as she used to, but boldly. A box of Craven As in her lap. The brand with *craven* in the name.

"Weren't those discontinued?"

"They keep if they're in a hard pack." She nods down at the cigarette box and looks up as my father appears, maneuvering the familiar container of bricks he always uses as a makeshift tree holder. He grapples the barrel across the room, doesn't look at either of us as he kneels, taking out bricks, his square hands working as they always have, his upper body still strong, but now all I really see is the strain in his face, the creasing of his eyes.

I unravel the green plastic grass. "Did you cut this tree on your own?" I ask my mother.

She coughs then breathes out a flute of smoke as if all the hard labor has been accomplished. "Just decorate it," she says.

As I used to, I kneel and wrap the butcher's grass around the rusted tin, once a feeder for horses, then used as a receptacle to drain the chemical toilet from my father's old Airstream caravan, emptied down under the hedge. It appeared at my twenty-first birthday, full of rum punch on a table in the boot room. My father assured me it had been swilled out, but I was doubtful, advised my friends not to touch the punch.

As I release the tree it stands askew, so my father slides around on the floor, lodges a length of wood from the fireplace to right it. "Well done, Earley," my mother says.

I fish the translucent Christmas star out of the carton, careful not to break the glass pinecones or the shiny clip-on birds with holly in their beaks, and my father raises himself up by his arms so briskly that I realize he has the upper body power of a paraplegic, compensating for his legs. He shifts an armchair over, secures it while I climb up on the cloth of the arm, and affix the five-pointed star by its loop to the top of the tree.

My mother takes a deep drag on her annual cigarette. "Gates, can you go and buy some cooked chooks and ready-made salads from that place near Brunt's in Cranbourne?" Their play is over; she's called him Gates. Memories of gates he left open and horses out on the road.

My father looks suddenly forlorn, his knobby fingers fumbling with a ribbon on an angel. "How many are you having over?" he asks.

"Not sure," she says. "Perhaps I'll ask your friend Sharen. She loves to get inside this house."

"She's probably having it with the Genonis," my father says as if he thinks that's funny.

"And where will *you* be?" asks my mother.

My father turns to me for support.

"You'll be with Elsie," I say. "Won't you?"

"We go to the Chinese up in Hampton Park," he says bravely. "With her sister."

My mother butts the half-done cigarette on the sole of her shoe. "We can have a Chinese Christmas here," she says, gesturing widely with her good arm. She slides the stubbed-out remains of her cigarette back in its box.

I sit on this narrow cot in this damp cabin and glance at the small silver clock he gave me. I've set it to Australian time and I keep trying to imagine him there on that farm I've seen in photos, where it's already tomorrow. Already Christmas in that bleak house. Hot and dry while out this window the rain sweeps in from the Pacific and wipes the view away. I hoped I'd be relieved to be free of his moods but the yearning feels like hunger pangs when everything is supposed to feel so enlightened up here, but I'm getting unstrung. The Turkish eyes of Oresh, the yogi dervish who's going to teach us to whirl. I'm afraid if he knocks I might not say no, just to spite myself. Those Turkish boys understand me. "Like the birds of the sea, men come from the ocean—the ocean of the soul." Rumi knew about transcendent men, spiritual and curious, but I don't want some doe-eyed, elastic yoga boy. I need my craggy Australian, the one who's attached to the earth. If only I hadn't let him go slip away into that farm world. The world he didn't invite me into when I've shown him where I'm from. The Bronx, mi abuela, a glimpse inside her priestess room, her Madonna del Pianto, Lady of Tears, the statue of Jesus with dollars pegged to his hands and dogs at his feet. I knew it would be awkward, but still I took him—I wanted him to know.

Now I try to create a traveling altar, light a candle beside my photo of Amma, incense smoking from the wooden bowl and the white lily I picked floats in the water glass. The heater pants in the corner like a sick puppy as the rain comes down in black sheets. Tomorrow we'll be dancing with sitar and drums, chanting our way through Christmas, and for some reason I'm dreading it. I drove five miles north up the highway in search of phone reception but his voice sounded so odd and conflicted, and he didn't catch the significance of the poem. He didn't even seem able to absorb it; all preoccupied as if he's been possessed by that place. Then on the drive back, in the spray of headlights I noticed that tree by the road where the colored vintage dresses were hung with the prayers pinned to them, where Daniel stopped the car and we walked down. But the branches of the tree were now strung with Christmas lights and wedding gowns writhing white in the dark, blowing out toward the cliffs; some had ripped free. I watched what looked like a veil fly up into the rain and then a giant deer crossed the road in front of me, stood in the middle of the blacktop in the dark and stared. Right into me, as if it was a warning.

I want to head back out with my flashlight and find a land line but the office is closed and what would I say? "I thought you wanted to marry me?" That same alien ring tone and probably the message. "This is Tooradin Estate, the home of Ruthie Rawson." His mother's accent so strong at first I thought it was a joke. And who would put the name of their house on a telephone message. White people, my grandmother would say, but Daniel's never felt that white, not American white. The way they fall in love but won't take you home to meet their mothers. Still, here I am alone, whispering: "Don't lose yourself." Repeating. As if a prayer might bridge the distance. "Please don't lose yourself." But I'm not sure who it's for: me or him.

* * *

CHRISTMAS DAY
(THURSDAY)

I sit at the head of the table, the spread of the cold collation before me, and tear a last piece of the succulent white meat free. The red-nosed snowman, candelabras, a gutted chicken. I watch my father carve the second bird, the sun arching in through the window behind us; he's a stooped silhouette framed by the old velvet curtains, faded from orange to dust. In a long-sleeve shirt with a grim, unfestive woolen tie. My mother and Sharen in the kitchen as if they're friends, when it suits, or maybe enemies, colluding to edge Earley round the bend.

The light from the twin window motes in on an empty tablemat, an extra setting. "In honor of Granny Rawson," my mother announced with a smile that edged along her lip. Places set for the dead. But she never treated Earley's mother with anything but ridicule, counted her as too fine-spun for here, or worse, discounted her as not so bright.

"Should have stayed where she'd been born," she said once, "among the dainties." Next she allowed as how it was actually a setting for Elsie. "Just in case." The maudlin Elsie who refuses to set foot in here for any occasion, not while my mother's alive. And my mother who's even done place-names, her ballpoint scrawl on cut-up greeting cards. But not one for Elsie. Just an unexpected *Sharen* smudged on shiny yellow. The dusty plastic orchids drooping from the Royal Doulton vase. Everything as it once was, save for that creased yellow card and Sharen's laugh amid the clatter in the kitchen.

Heat sifts through the propped-open door to the end of the veranda, a door rarely used. A hundred degrees on Christmas day. I can barely remember what that means in Celsius. Burl Ives singing "Jingle Bells" from the record player in the living room, my mother and Sharen tending the Christmas pudding like sisters. The echoes of the dishes being extracted, the steamer on the back of the AGA stove. I think of the coins she'll have buried inside the pudding mix, old shillings and pennies when I savored the taste as a boy. Traces of copper and silver cooking into the richness, brandy and breadcrumbs, grated nutmeg, raisins and almonds. The excitement of biting down onto an unyielding sixpence.

I stare down the table past my father. A table generous enough for twelve, without its leaves, but just the four of us now, spread out with feet between us, the empty setting alone at the end, opposite me. Earley sips from one of Granny Rawson's sherry glasses, his thoughts behind his eyes, drinking his Christmas Frangelico and waiting for the women to return. He peers across the table as if unsure what to say, gazing into the rustling fireplace.

"Are you expecting Father Christmas?" A joke my father doesn't deem worthy of a response, and I wonder if he's chosen to spend the day here to be with me, Elsie launched on her own to meet some sister-in-law. Poor Elsie. Or, more likely, he's come for Sharen. Lured and now disappointed as Ruthie toys with her out in the kitchen, monopolizing her on purpose.

In the thickening heat and the silence between us, I eat without waiting, my attention drawn to the array of portraits watching down from the walls, my shovel-jawed grandfather, "all bottled trout and polo," as my mother once called him, and Great Aunt Emma Charlotte, black-veiled and now possum-stained, the maiden great aunt from some horror film. The table set with the "occasional" silver retrieved from deep in the sideboard, the green-framed hunting scenes from Stubbs. Parents who met out hunting with the Findon Harriers, my father appearing at every crossing, hounding her. That's what she called it. As if she was the fox.

"We're coming," she shouts and then a gale of laughter and I imagine the pudding being delivered to the floor and frantically scooped up. But Earley isn't amused. He won't start without them. Now he's gazing up at the oil of his own shiny-eyed father.

"He warned me she'd be no day in the country." He says it half under his breath, as if talking to the portrait.

The dog barks and Reggie appears like a shock in the

veranda doorway. Dark and shirtless as usual, his hair wet and plastered down. Standing in a pair of loose-fitting pants and black shoes, his feet in them are more like branches forced into flowerpots.

"What are you doing here?" I ask.

"Ruthie," he replies, but he seems more cautious than usual. His skin looks shiny as if he's been oiled, not ashy as it has been. Maybe he hosed himself down in the garden, or stole some body lotion. "Invited me," he says and then, gingerly, he takes the seat at the far end, as if knowing it's his. The artificial flowers and the snowman, the Christmas candles lit between us. I don't reach forward to move them, to examine his face as he leans to take an empty plate, his fingers folding around the Wedgwood. Rounded nails not bitten like mine or ingrained with dirt like my father's. He's made an effort to clean himself up and it has me both sad and more fearful somehow, wanting to go to the kitchen and shake the truth out of my mother. "No sitting at this table without a shirt," my father says suddenly, the lines ruckle up from the sides of his eyes, but the boy takes eggs and pulls at the chicken with his fingers. My father slaps his hand so fast the boy retreats, stunned. The speed of my father's move-ment is as quick as when he'd swipe me as a kid. A stickler for shirtsleeves at table, my father obsessed with unlikely manners, cutting toast in quarters, napkins in rings.

"I don't have a shirt," says Reggie.

My father turns to me but I'm shaking my head. "Really?" I say. This boy who's already rummaged through my things will not be swanning about in my clothes.

Ruthie comes in, doesn't react to who's sitting at the far end. "Everything okay, boys?" she asks. I feel myself glower in disbelief—it's Reggie who's standing, clearly relieved.

"I need a shirt, Ruthie," he says.

She studies him, wipes her hands on her cockatoo apron. "Hang on," she says, and disappears into the hall.

The boy seems heartened by her, and I observe him leaning forward, using his fork to scoop the macaroni salad. He pierces some beetroot, ignoring the silver servers, and then hauls the last leg off a chicken. Probably starving, poor kid, but I doubt it, the wisps of my compassion curried with uncertainty, the sight of Reggie chewing as if there's nothing here but food, then glancing up at the image of Aunt Emma Charlotte. He points at her with his fist around his fork. "That one spooks me," he says. "Ev'ry time."

How many times would that have been? This room so familiar to him; this room only used for special occasions. It's more than just stashes and blankets stowed up in the ceiling, the bedroll in the linen closet. He knows the place by heart.

"The forks are for eating, not pointing," my father says, still huffy, and I wish my father would talk about something other than etiquette. So English and irritating. Nonetheless, Reggie has locked his elbows, looking down at the mess on his plate.

Sharen is heading from the kitchen out into the hall. "I'm taking a leak," she announces and I wonder if that entails scouring the cabinets for pills and medicine, trying my mother's goanna oil and tiger balm, hunting for lipstick.

Good luck with that. I imagine Isabel confronted with this. Would she be amused or sympathetic? In sympathy with whom? I remind myself I'm not the underdog here.

Reggie leans forward to eye the store-bought ambrosia, soft marshmallow infused with cherries and fruit. Please God don't put your fingers in it; then Reggie glimpses his reflection in the great-mirrored sideboard, his skin against the shelves and tarnished silver. The ache in my hand as I pour myself another Pimm's from the jug my father's prepared with dry ginger, mint, slices of orange. I feel the dog under the table, resting its head on my foot.

My mother returns with a bright blue-and-gold-striped shirt. Mine. Left here years ago. She balls it up and tosses it down the far end, her aim still strong; her dexterity seems to be returning. She knows how throwing things inside annoys Earley, unless he's the one having a tantrum and then the rules turn upside down, ancient lamps can hit the floor. Then she returns to the kitchen, leaves the boy pulling the shirt over his narrow shoulders, the colors brought to life against his chest. He leaves the buttons undone. "That okay for you, Mr. Earley?" he asks.

My father's disdain looks somehow hopeless.

"Don't call him that," I say and the boy averts his eyes, looks back out the door he came in, then he reaches for a red and silver bonbon.

"It's a Christmas cracker," I tell him for fear he might think it a napkin. I know it sounds patronizing, as I remember the ornate ones my grandmother always gave us, with tiny wooden hand-carved toys, miniature Aston Martins

and Mini Minors, hard-boiled lollies that tore cuts in the
roof of my mouth.

I watch the slender arm and narrow wrist of the boy,
the shining cylinder wrapped with twists to contain its
trinkets. "Someone has to pull the other end," says Ruthie,
reappearing. She walks down to Reggie's place at the table,
doesn't make sure her thumb is well extended; the way she
used to be sure she'd win. She wants Reggie to. "Now," she
says and crepe and cardboard burst open.

The boy leaps back in fright, the glossy bonbon still
in his hand, Ruthie retrieving an orange plastic dinosaur
that bounces on the table. She hands it over. "This is yours,"
she says. He picks out a card rolled inside a plastic ring and
reads haltingly: "'Your ship will be coming in. If you can
stay a . . . board.'" He smiles and unfolds a multicolored
paper crown, puts it on his slicked-back head of twisted hair.

"King Reggie," says my mother and he beams a nervous smile, but Sharen comes through from her visit to the
bathroom, wiping her hands in her hair. The bruise on her
cheek's been covered in makeup.

"It's time," says Ruthie, motioning Sharen back into
the kitchen and to my amazement Sharen takes her order
in stride.

"For what?" I ask, but in a moment she's back, emerging with oven mitts, the steaming pudding on a plate she
sets down before me. She pulls out a cigarette lighter from
her pocket and next thing I know, the pudding's whooshing up in flames, right near my face, brandy burning blue
and orange.

"Merry Chrissie," Sharen whispers to me. "We're glad you're here."

It draws me back, the liquid green of her eyes, and I feel I'm sliding both into them and yet retreating. She picks up a bone-handled knife and as she slices, the innards steam and the blade scratches against the buried coins. An essence of the boy reflected in the shape of her brow, the way I see myself in the blue of my mother's gray eyes. I glance over at her but she's bewitched by the pudding, so I glance at the boy in the paper crown, spooning the remains of the ambrosia from her good crystal bowl.

My father refuses to look at the pudding or Sharen or anyone, studying his glass of Frangelico, as if doing all he can to stay in his seat. A time he'd have thrown the drink at the fireplace, but he's already on probation in here. He stares at Ruthie with a sudden vigilance. "That place was set for my mother," he says.

"Your mother's no longer with us," says Ruthie.

It makes him stare up at the portraits, his red face darkening as if almost in tears. Sharen pays him no mind, awards me a lavish slice, the euphoric brandy smell of Christmases with my grandmother here, when I was young and wore that same striped shirt, buttoned to the top to be formal, tucked into my burgundy flares. And I feel a prickling guilt, growing up with this odd hard privilege, and this boy who has nothing and just wants more. Impulsively, I find myself reaching down near the dog, feeling for the gift for my mother stowed on the floor. I rip the card free.

"I got this for you," I say to Reggie.

Everyone stares, especially the boy, as I stand and present the blue-wrapped parcel and Reggie searches my mother for guidance, but she clutches a hand to her chin and is silent. Sharen puts down the knife.

Cagily, in a kind of slow motion, Reggie unwraps the gift. Greasy fingers on the Tiffany blue and the brown leather case, and inside it, the small polished silver clock revealed uncertainly, as some unwarranted accomplishment.

"For helping Mum with the tree," I say.

The boy's eyes get larger, suspicious. He strains to hear if the clock is already ticking.

Against my wrist, I feel the brush of Sharen's hand.

THE DOG BARKS then silence but for the din of crickets, the occasional flapping of wings cast up by the night. My fingers throb, my hand re-bandaged too tight. Steadily, I unwind the gauze, feel the roughness of the stitches, scabbed slightly. Then a vague thrumming, like rain but far away on another roof. I look for my watch. Two in the morning. Still that sound. Not my mother's radio, no static; it's from the small bathroom down the far end of the hall, the shower's running. The image of my mother splayed out with her neck caught in that chair. I spring from the bed, wrap myself in a towel, wind the bandage back about my hand.

Without knocking I open the bathroom door, a shroud of steam through the light—a cattle-hide vest strewn on the floor, giant work boots, jeans with a leather knife sheath thrown at the chair. No sign of my mother, just a too-large silhouette in the white shower curtain, the top of a wet, balding head above the rod. "What the fuck . . . ?" I shout over the sound of the water as a wide weathered hand appears round the edge of the curtain, another hand wiping water from a gaunt windburned face, freckled and undaunted. A high receding brow but still easy to recognize. Walker Dumbalk.

"What the fuck you doing?" I ask, my voice cracked with fright.

"Sharen locked me out," his voice is raspy and deep, his stare unblinking. Leaden rings below his eyes.

"It's bloody two a.m.!" Tucking my towel as if it might protect me from the dark wells of his eyes. "I'm out looking for Reggie," he says. Steam rising off him like hot damp smoke. His unshaven jaw even meaner than I remember, flecked with gray. "I know the little bastard hides up here."

He disappears back behind the curtain as though this is his house too, for all the years his mother put in cleaning here and cooking, not spending time with him. Washing himself with my mother's cloth, her soap in his underarms, the acrid smell of his steaming clothes, as I stand here on the tiles. His work boots on her towel, a thick leather belt with a silver longhorn buckle drapes off his jeans like a python.

He opens the curtain again, his face creased up as if inconvenienced. "I'll be out in a minute," he says. An accusation in his tone that has me close the door behind me and stand like a child in the hall. The memory of him out in the paddocks making trouble, while his mother served us food. Coming back to haunt us. All that happens as my mother sleeps.

The dog chews a small slab of meat on the living room floor. I kneel and hold him, pray he's just been silenced, not poisoned. A squeal of taps from the bathroom, the scrape of curtain rings then a hollow quiet. The dog skulks off with the piece of red flesh in his mouth. I wonder if this is the ritual, if Walker's been up in here before, and what would have happened if I searched his dirty pockets?

Edging my way to the phone, I view the list of numbers in the dull light on the wall. *CRANBOURNE POLICE: 59910600.* I pick up the receiver, just to let them know, but the bathroom door skreighs open, the shadow of Walker's head in the hall. "Wouldn't if I was you." He says it casually but I think of the wood-handled pocket knife in the sheath on his jeans and know better than to dial, than to tangle with the likes of him when my hand is already in gauze.

I wait, uncertain, as Walker gets dressed behind the bathroom door, unsure if I should search for my grandfather's rifle in the linen closet, sleep with it. I enter the small room with its high rows of shelves, folded towels and blankets, napkins, the same for thirty years, leather suitcases and wooden boxes of cutlery. I kneel and reach behind my mother's safe for the canvas gun bag, but there are only rolls of old Christmas paper, fading maps of the original farm. Whispering the dog's name for it to follow, I creep back up the hall, hinge the bedroom chair tight against the doorknob. Back in bed, I cradle the dog and listen for creaks, this house with its myriad doors and windows, lost skeleton keys, ancient rusted locks. I look into the dog's open eyes and think of the bruise on Sharen's caked cheek, wait for the footsteps in the side hall, the scratch of the flywire out onto the bluestone, and the sound of his boots stepping off the veranda into the dew.

* * *

BOXING DAY
(FRIDAY)

The vulgar glare of Boxing Day morning has me driving the Prius to town. No sign of Walker when I woke, just his dirty boot prints in the hall, the licked up blood from the meat on the sitting room floor, but meat from where? The image of Sharen's bruised face, Reggie ogling the silver Christmas clock. "Love that timpani blue," said Sharen, quietly prizing the gift from the hands of her son but he didn't let go, his eyes fixed on the delicate leather-cased silver. The things they know that we don't. Only once did Reggie glance at me, unsure whether to smile, unclear if it was a trick or some new alliance. I wasn't sure myself. All I know is there's no alliance with Walker.

The car runs eerily silent on the bitumen, past the caravan park where Bobby Genoni first saw Walker. The "new-car" scent better than the Camry's engine oil and wet dog smell. The fence lines sliding by like the years already have, the landscape greened by the aviator glasses I bought at LAX. I never imagined I'd yearn for Los Angeles, the strange realms of it just down the canyon—driving Sunset Boulevard, Santa Monica, Melrose, the distractions. Isabel. To take me away, I push in the Krishna Das CD she gave me for Christmas—repetitive mantras with sitar and percussion. A relief from the radio versions of "Silver Bells": Bing Crosby's to Wilson Pickett's to Olivia Newton-John's. A local girl who made good.

Strange my mother didn't want to come with me, said she needed to "hold the fort" even though I didn't mention what happened in the night. Wonder if Reggie watched his father from a tree?

At the South Gippie Highway, holiday traffic peels past, en route to Cowes or Wilson's Prom. Everything abbreviated, holidays to hols, Gippsland to Gippie, Promontory to Prom. Falcon wagons mounted with surfboards, pulling boats, or trailers with sand bikes, jet skis. Pale people hungering for the beach, drinking in sun with zinc on their noses. City people. I come from a family not beckoned by water, from this local, unappealing coastline, not the cream sand beaches of Portsea or Flinders, or the cliff tops near Cape Schank the locals call the Gaza Strip, where the rich Jewish families from Melbourne build their weekend mansions.

I try not to keep searching the side roads for Walker, examine my hands on the steering wheel—my fingers dry and wrinkled, morphing into their true selves. Fried as a kid in this sun that beats down now through the slope of the windshield. I turn the CD off. Making the U-turn through to my mother's side of the highway, I park in the service road in front of the bakery. It's now called *Buns in the Oven*, a new sign I didn't notice the other day. My mother's instructed me to pick up a ploughman's wheel. Thick rolled pizza bread with onions, tomato, and cheese, served cold and mushy.

Isabel tells me I eat without appreciation, using food to stuff feelings; she says it's nothing to do with weight. She wants me to join her for therapy. "Couples," she calls it with a kind of relish. *Open up in a safe place, talk about what intimacy looks like for you.* Her tone so kind and encouraging it urgently makes me not want to go. Not keen to be trapped in some office with three Miró prints hung behind a cushiony couch, cornered, waiting to be torn apart by the sincerity of their concern, sharing some varnished version of the truth of all this.

Stepping out of the car, I see Cloudy Gray making his way from the butcher's to the pub with his paunch and braces, pushing loose strings of hair away from his face in the wind, plastering them back on his mottled red scalp. As I turn to head into the bakery, I spot Sharen and Bobby Genoni at an outside table at the Kettle Café. She sits cross-legged in faded, red denim shorts. As I make my approach, Bobby gets up with an awkward smile.

"I thought you two had put a lid on it," I say.

"We're working out what's next for Sharen," he says.

Bobby Genoni: career counselor.

I cast my eyes on Sharen but she avoids them, gazes off to the fish shop on the foreshore, the circling seagulls.

A hand covers her crow's feet from the sun, her bruise still covered with makeup below the line of her white sunglasses, her bare legs where the welts have faded into her tan, the fine blond hair on her thighs.

"She needs furniture," says Bobby sitting back down to his coffee.

On Sharen's middle finger, a cracked turquoise ring the color of her eyes.

"She needs more than that," I say. I watch her turn, a shadow creeping around the edges of her mouth. "She needs security."

"I'm getting her a weapon," says Bobby as though he's ahead of the game, ready to play the Italian. Put a gun in his pyro girlfriend's hands.

"Is that you want?" I ask her but her sunglasses reflect so I can't see her eyes. She carefully pastes Chapstick on her pink splitting lips, neither nods nor answers.

"Don't all Americans carry guns?" asks Bobby.

I suddenly realize how I feel safer back there, where my accent can somehow diffuse things, where strangers don't maraud about inside at night. "Walker took a shower up in the big house at two a.m.," I tell them. "I think I should report him to the Cranbourne police."

Sharen shades her glasses with her open palm. Her head does a small sad shake. "I've already talked to them," she says. "They call it 'a domestic.'"

"He doesn't live with *us*," I say.

"Yeah," says Bobby. "Maybe you can tell 'em someone you've known since you were a tyke just used your bathroom."

Sharen watches out over the mangroves. "I just need to keep him from Reggie," she says.

BACK AT THE house, my mother doesn't hear or see me leave her fresh ploughman's wheel on the kitchen table. She's on her knees in the dining room, crunching wads of tinfoil to stuff holes in the baseboard, trap the rats that leave tooth marks in the grapefruit, their dirt in the muesli pack.

Alone in the sitting room with the tree that needs to be taken down, I search for locksmiths in the yellow pages, call one in Hallam who's mobile and try to explain the seven outside doors and twenty windows but he tells me you can't replace those skeleton keys and he doesn't travel this far. Another says he can get to it next month for twenty-five hundred dollars. The third one, in Tooradin, is called Bound Safe and Smart and the owner seems to know this house. "Let's be real," he says. "If anyone wants to get in that place, they will. Regardless. But I can come out again if you like."

I'm not sure how oblivious my mother is of Walker, if she knows what happened to the rifle, but in her state of determined flimsiness I decide to leave her alone.

I slide the laundry door closed behind me, the smell of Joseph Lyddy saddle soap and the sweat of saddle cloths. Silence, save the flies already hitting at the window, trying to escape. Cool in this enormous brick room with bluestone slab floor, two sinks, a row of old machines, the ancient wringer. A bag of ropes and halters that looks as if it's been cut open with a knife. The New Guinea axe with the woven grass handle. No obvious sign of the gun bag with my grandfather's Winchester.

I reach past a cardboard box of wooden boot trees to slide the window open, let the flies out, but the frame won't budge. I hate the sound of them bombing the glass, struggling in the cobwebs. I'm staring at farm clothes soaking in the big cement tub. Earley's boiler suits. My mother who still takes in his washing. Probably does Reggie's too, if he ever changes clothes.

Touching the dusty suitcases shelved along the wall, I spot Granny Rawson's portable turntable, her wicker picnic basket, and a brown leather case I don't recognize. Dark frayed stitching and bronze reinforced corners, the kind Isabel buys at collectible shops and plies with orange oil, piles them up like a stack of giant books in the corner of the studio. I could smuggle this home for her, as an offering.

As I pull the case down, I think of packing up and heading off somewhere, the lavender farms in Western Tasmania. I place the suitcase on the ironing table, rub dust from the flaking gold initials. *E.W.R.* Ernest Wilkes Rawson. Earley's father. I called him "Bop."

Inside lies a silver flask and an old canvas wallet with a memorial war coin from 1914, and a clothing rations card with sections torn off. *Director of Rations, Sydney.* Everything but the gun he tried to teach me to shoot, back when there were wallabies and roos here and I missed them on purpose. Nothing more depressing than a wounded kangaroo.

Beneath is a sepia photo. A fine-featured man in military garb on a cavalry horse. Probably the one that dragged him by the stirrup over the ploughed fields of the Somme, before he was shipped back to England with multiple fractures and nursed by his young cousin Hilma. The one he hauled out here and married.

"Saved his life, that horse." My mother standing in the faint light startles me. Armed with a rusty Mortein insect sprayer, she sallies over and launches a great plume of poison at the window. I reel from the haze of toxins. The brand name—*mort,* French for "dead," and *ein,* German for "one." An army of blowflies fighting for their lives.

"Do you know where Bop's old trench gun is?" I ask.

"Haven't seen it for years," she says.

From the suitcase I pick out a small color shot of my grandmother. Hilma, petite and fair. My mother steadies herself on the washing machine and peers at it. "Didn't even need to change her last name," she says. The old story. I place the two photos together. The likeness is strange, my grandmother and grandfather could be brother and sister.

"Poor things," she says with a kind of weary relish. "They lost the other son. He was taller. Earley was all they had left."

I feel the Mortein settle on my eyelids, irritating. "Remind me why you married him?"

She tucks her insect sprayer under her arm. "Without him there wouldn't be you," she smiles but that's no answer. I look away from her coffee-stained teeth. A pair of faded board shorts draped on the wooden clotheshorse. I drag out my old mountain bike by the handlebars. "That's Reggie's," she says.

I look at her sharply.

"Well, he's been using it," she says, pulls out a stained envelope from the suitcase. Photos of the old brown Vauxhall. My father is young, standing in front of it on some mountain road. "That was our honeymoon," my mother says. "We went to Gelantipy!" I can feel her wan smile. "It wasn't exactly Paris." Up near where my father found that brumby foal. A town in the High Country where that big family ran brumbies and where those Snowy River films were shot. I shuffle through photos of horses and polo, my father the day Prince Philip played at Coldstream riding Minta or Bandy, the best day of my father's life. Then a picture of a bare-chested Walker out in the bush block, chopping down a tree. He must have been seventeen. Like Reggie but taller and thick-limbed, not wiry.

"Why wasn't he allowed up in the house?" I ask.

"Gracious wouldn't let him," she says. "She was afraid for you. Walker was ten years older, rough as pineapples even back then." She touches my hand and reaches for the doorjamb for balance, as if we're aboard a ship.

"Did you know he's back around here?"

My mother presses her lips as if to keep her face from falling. "I guessed," she says. "I saw Sharen's face."

Closing the suitcase, I hear photos sliding all over each other, the mixing of trips, honeymoon in the mountain shuffled with black-and-white snaps of old Gracious with me as a baby in her arms.

"He wants Reggie," I tell her.

A duffel bag falls and a thick horse bandage rolls out across the floor. "He can't have him," she says.

"It's the only way to get rid of Walker, unless we go to the police," I say.

"We can handle it," she says, taking her leave. I'm not sure if *we* means *us* or her and Reggie.

"We can't even find the Winchester," I say but she's already gone.

OUT ON THE pathway I straddle the red vinyl bike seat, ride down the dark gravel drive and into the crisp gray hints of light. The pedals whine beneath me as the rim of the sky turns puce ahead, a chill in the air and the face of the moon still high. Not the dull-featured one of a hazy Los Angeles sky or off the beach in Malibu, but wide-faced with wide-set eyes and a tight mouth.

The bike scrapes along Langdon's Road toward the lane where I used to ride away from her, the lane now regaled with a sign not yet buried in trees. *Genoni's Road.* An unmade track with no traffic that runs alongside the farm. Nothing to do with the town or any Genoni, just local bootlicking. I spit out an insect that lands in my teeth, and wend on, the back tire low so I have to work hard, wobbling a bit in the dust. I haven't been near a gym since I left LA, haven't even done my sit-ups. Exercise for its own sake feels self-indulgent here.

Looking back to the house, I see the blood-orange sunrise glistening on the windows of the shearer's quarters, reflecting, and I make out shapes under the rotary line. My mother and Reggie, motionless, watching. Some dull Australian version of Wyeth or Wood. But straining my eyes, I realize it's not Reggie at all. She's standing beside Earley's boiler suit, which she's now hung on the line, a slack ghost beside her.

An enormous lop-eared hare, almost the size of a wallaby, stands in the grass that divides the track. I anchor my foot in the sand and lean, watch the Old World rabbit bound away as I get off the bike and rest it in the ti tree scrub at the edge of the lane. I think of Isabel's book about animal totems—she'd say the hare is my guide. Yet it's as foreign as I am. English as my grandparents, breeding with its cousins, but I follow it anyway, in case I'm somehow supposed to; I climb the fence as the day comes in clearer, patterns weaving in the browns of the grasses. No sign of the hare but a figure appears in the distance. Ascending the rise, it emerges—just the crown of a dead tree with bare arm branches. The farm and the light playing jokes. The sense of being watched from somewhere.

Along the cattle path into the bush, I walk to the thicket of eucalyptus, high bracken, sword grass. The sheltered clearing with a stand of different trees, bark black and knotted, leaves fine and weepy as willows, maybe Murray pines. *Brennie's Brothel.* That's what I called it as a teenager, when I brought Brenda Ferguson here to lie with her in these lush fans of unlikely grass plastered long and flat and parted like hair where cattle sheltered. I lie myself down in the coolness of the dew, the late-morning light pleating down through the branches like a luminous skirt. Overhead, a sort of Casuarina, a she-oak, maybe, or a wild cherry. A sanctuary greened by a silent seep beneath me.

I close my eyes to the memories of Brenda, her short tennis skirt and the way it rose up when she served. Mrs. Ferguson in her gatekeeper headscarf who said it wasn't safe. She'd heard things about my father. "Like what?" I asked but Brenda wouldn't say as we stood on the cracked asphalt court, wooden rackets held in our hands, old-fashioned as the trees. For the first time I realized the wings of my father's reputation had spread further than the house.

A breeze swarms the leaves above me, then a rustle and humming. I sit up, spooked. Sharen on the cattle path, barefoot with rips in her jeans, the sun aglow behind her. It gives her a kind of radiance. She gazes into the clearing as if she knows I'm here, almost a smile but it's not in her eyes. Her hair twisted up. For a moment I think she hasn't seen me after all, but she's making her way in, over a fallen wattle trunk, knotting her shirt at her belly.

"Saw you riding up the lane," she says. She crouches, barely six feet from me, picks a stalk of grass and sucks the sweetness from it. "Followed your scent," she says. I wish I could have gone unseen, but I'm drawn to her knees pressing through the frays, her bare toes arch in the grass, toenails pink and chipped. I want to stand up, to give myself a chance, but I'm clasping my own knees tighter.

"I used to come here," I say, "when I was a kid."

She nods. "I bet you did." A rotting branch pokes up behind her like a big horned bird. She moves closer, squatting down, leaning. I strain inside for willingness to recall why this doesn't serve anyone, but she's combing my lips with her fingers, my arm reaching to her as if it's a limb on its own. I pull her fingers right to my mouth, and press them there, biting her fingertips. The taste of soil. Her nipples against me and I don't say no, I don't say anything. She smells of things low to the ground, of farm and house and childhood. I close my eyes to the salty sweat taste of her neck, pull her to me. A length of her hair falls down my cheek, gentle as water and I can't even feel the pain in my hand. "Maybe you need me more than you think," she says, my fingers diving down under the lip of her jeans, undoing myself and she's falling around me, down on her back and it all seems too easy, in through the moss to the warmth of the water, finding myself so smoothly inside her. Hoping Reggie doesn't see this, his mother's wetness on me, nudging her into grass and twigs, my mouth on her ear and her hair has the smell of apples as she arches up eager, so eager I groan as I flood her already, slumping too soon. My face falling down to the loose strands of her hair and the grass stems, and the feeling of tears that never quite come.

* * *

SATURDAY

◆━━━◇━━━◆

I wake to the far-off rattle of a phone, the smell of sex all over me. Last I remember, I lay down in this bed paralyzed in a sleep too deep for dreams. Up through the realms came an image of Isabel stepping out of a car on the drive, her Roman sandals touching the dirt as if it was a movie. But here at Tooradin. The dog leapt up on her cream linen skirt as I struggled to comprehend—Esalen to LAX to Tullamarine, now standing by my mother's dead roses, her hair tied back with her sunglasses high, that tuberose scent in the dry afternoon. Under these cypress trees. My focus sliding down her dress to the paw marks on her skirt, a lotus flower hennaed on her calf, to the dust that crept about her pale sandals. My own legs weak as folding chairs.

The phone again. What if it's her?

Up at the window, the eight o'clock heat through the glass like an accusation. The bike's on the lawn where I left it. Grass stains on my jeans as I pull them on and the memory of Sharen in the flattened clearing. No candles and music, just rutting against the earth. She had me finish so fast and hard and I'm still lost in the fog of it.

Heading out the side door and down the path, I pee on the flourishing lemon, the only tree that seems to thrive. The Camry wagon rolls up the drive and slowly edges alongside. My father winds down the dust-caked window. "Let's go for a drive."

I stand right near where I stood in my dream of Isabel. Thank God that wasn't real. My father propped up by the steering wheel, hugging it as if it might preserve his life. "I need to show you something," he says. Sharen not even rinsed from my mouth. I don't bother to fish for a seatbelt, just wind down the window and hope he doesn't smell her on me. My father jolts the old car forward as I rummage in the glove box for mints or gum but all I find is a pack of crushed Craven As and matches. My mother's secret stash. I light one up and it's so stale it almost makes me gag but my exhale provides a smoke screen.

We sit in a glum silence and I keep thinking of Sharen, how my neck craned to the sky as I slipped inside her and how it felt better than good.

My father hums "Moon River" for no apparent reason. The three horses by the stockyards, the same hot surrounding their big bodies settles about my face. I breathe out another haze of smoke, don't care where he's going, passing Myra Chaundy's pony stud and then on either side the asparagus fields spread into the distance, the soil pitch dark and peaty with a soft fur weaving above it, a dark green lace.

My father taking me away like he used to when I was a kid, to visit Gerida or Maeve or one of the others. Arriving unannounced for coffee and scones, as though it held a country kind of charm, their husbands not long buried or far away at work. Using me as a decoy.

"Where are you taking me?" I ask.

"Dalmore's closed up," he says, ignoring me. The peeling one-room school still sits among the trees, a set of broken goalposts. The place where I rode my pony to primary school and tied him up in the falling-down yard. A world that's been here all along. It's America that feels unreachable now as we wait at the South Gippsland Highway. I pray he sees the cattle trucks bearing down. They rock the car as they whoosh past like we're just particles of air.

The Tooradin Airport, once just a windsock in a field and out on the mudflats, the rusted hull of the old shipwreck. I explored it on my pony spooking in the wind. The mast still leans out on an angle, but back then there was the remnant of a flag, flapping like a small ripped hand. "We should charter one of those, fly over to King Island," my father says. Savagely, I butt the cigarette in the ashtray, wonder if I'll take it up again. In law school, I smoked Kretek cloves from Indonesia. "I came to visit my mother," I say. "She's dying."

The disappointment in his eyes reflects in the sun as we trundle along the highway in a new kind of silence. I imagine his heart going *phut* and me reaching for the wheel and the handbrake at once, careening through the fence on this bridge, landing down with the boats that lie on their sides in the mud of Cardinia Creek.

"One day Ruthie lay down in the dirt near the stables and curled up in a ball," he says.

I look over at his stubble, the stoop of his shoulders and his green woolen sweater in the heat. "What did you do?"

"The chores," he says. "Eventually Old Nev came past on the tractor and she got up."

My mother lying in the gravelly sand, waiting, while my father tosses biscuits of hay, mixes feeds for horses in the yards. How could cruelty seem so normal? And which of them is the crueler?

"So where's this girlfriend of yours?" he asks.

How does he know about her? Isabel, who heard her father leave one afternoon and hasn't seen him since, hasn't tried to track him down. Not because she doesn't want to but because he's not looking for her. "None of your business," I say. If I'd stayed in LA, I wouldn't be stuck in this dog-smell car.

"I mean, how's it going with her?" he asks.

"Splendid," I say flatly. As if I'd talk to him about it anyway. The ways she tries to polish me. The kundalini class in Hollywood, its teacher with Coke-bottle glasses talking about Jesus visiting India during his unaccounted years. The students' vacant faces in their culty white linens and headscarves. A hundred frog poses and still I'm stiff as a pylon, the dirt from here in the creases of my knees. And now I'm digging myself back in.

We gaze out at a stark café in the field, a manmade pond and picnic tables. "I'm sorry you didn't bring her with you," he says. "You might have had more fun."

I remember the dream. "You mean *you* might have," I say. "I wouldn't subject her to you."

He nods as if he understands but then his head shakes, refusing to let the meaning in.

"Let alone Walker Dumbalk skulking around," I add.

My father shakes his head in a kind of distant disbelief, as if that's not so unusual. "I was twelve when Bunny drowned," he says as if his brother's death is somehow relevant. "After that my father started to bring me here. He fancied one of the Greaves girls. They milked by hand then." He talks like infidelity is generational, dropping by the local divorcees and wives, leaving your own wife at home. My grandmother sitting alone in the Moorooduc house and laying it all at the bleeding feet of Jesus while her husband went out philandering. I come from a line of men for whom fucking around is a form of mourning, a way to forget the dead.

"Last year the buggers pulled the old homestead down before we could stop them," my father says. I know this time "we" means the Tooradin Historical Society, the local paladins of the past. All I remember is a weatherboard house under that empty stand of dying conifers. Falling down twenty years ago. Everything quietly falling down. But he remembers it as the place he came with his father who visited some blowzy young woman in a print dress and apron. Not prim and English like my grandmother, but a smiley Australian dairy farm girl.

"They do Devonshire teas now," my father says. "And they built a rotary dairy. Fifty cows milking at a time. It's quite an attraction."

We pull in. Only two other cars in the parking lot.

Adjacent to the café juts a shining silver shed, its oval roof slightly domed, a giant spoon. Is this what he wants to show me? A corrugated iron eyesore? A mob of angular Holstein and Friesian cows, patched black or brown and white, filing in from the thistle-dotted pasture.

I get out into the manure-scented air and think of Sharen bucking beneath me. He doesn't deserve to fuck a woman like that. Even she's too good for him. And I'm no better than any of them. The way I please others when I'm in America, pretend to be solid and worthy, when I have trouble caring much at all. Well, I'm back to basics here.

Heading over to the shed, I don't witness him hobbling over the gravel behind me; don't want to feel sorry for him. Up a wooden ramp, through a large swinging door, to a platform that overlooks a monstrous metal machine. A deafening sound of suck and pistons. Rubbery tendrils attaching to hundreds of teats simultaneously, cows hungrily pushed inside metal chutes so their buttocks are forming one great circle, a giant pulsating propeller of them.

A sign on the viewing platform says: *It comes from a cow not a carton.* Two Japanese women huddle at one end; each covers her nose with a handkerchief. My father's standing right beside me in his wide Akubra hat. "It's a big *deal* they've got here," he says. It has me confused how he's climbed up to this platform so quickly. "We could set up something like this," he adds. "You're the lawyer. We've got the land. You should come back so we can go into business. You could bring your girl."

I look at the udders, the cups on the teats and the milk swilling through. Think of Sharen's untethered breasts and how she fed one to me then the other, asked me to bite them.

"We could do a bed-and-breakfast riding school," he says.

I feel the collective pressure on all of those teats, a sudden post-coital confusion, and need to get air, walk to the door and stand atop some wood stairs for relief from the noise of my father's return to the fold ideas. I imagine the business, my father limping round the unwitting women, Reggie up in the trees, creeping them out.

My father shadows me still. "What do you think?"

Me pretending to care about groups of neurotic midweek ladies and their tragic unsound horses. "Didn't we already lose enough on your ventures?" That herd of Charolais he imported from France. Half the cows dead en route and the rest stuck out in the paddock, bloated on some toxin in the silage. *Eighty thousand dollars down the gurgler,* according to Ruthie. Then money from the joint account he "lent" to Erica Jeffers to set her up in a townhouse in Elsternwick, houses put in his girlfriends' names. Income from the farm drastically depleted so he might have some currency with women. Lucky Ruthie has a stash of her own.

"If you dwell on what went bad, you'll end up like your mother," he says.

The Japanese women look over, unimpressed by what they see and taken aback by the tone of my father's voice but he's oblivious, stares down into a steel pipe yard, a bed of fresh straw and a single Friesian cow with a full bag of milk. She bellows out toward the horizon where the dairy paddocks merge with the mangrove coast. My father in the shade of his hat, his skin marbled by the sun. *I'm more afraid I'll end up like you*, I want to tell him, to reach into the well of this man for more than a bucket of emptiness.

"You know the morning Ruthie took that turn in the little bathroom," I say, the image of her on those cold cracked tiles. "She told me she pressed her medical pendant."

My father's knotty hands grip the railing. He moistens his lips as if choosing words. "The alert people called but I couldn't get over there," he says. He sounds rueful but I'm not sure he's capable of real remorse. An old desire to strike him, just knock the bastard down.

"You know she'd had so many false alarms," he says, "rolling over in her sleep. And I was heading out with Elsie on our way to Wilson's Prom." He's captivated by the middle distance, the cars as they thread down the highway. The curtain of warm morning air between us feels viscous as water. I want to tear through it.

"I didn't want to ruin the trip," he says then looks away.

A dryness in my mouth, the word "unconscionable" fighting against the gate of my teeth. "Her head was stuck over the rung of a chair," I tell him.

A tractor motor reverberates. It has a front-end loader and a chain out the back, drags a dead calf through the grass. The cow is circling and wailing. My father closes his wrinkly lids. "Luckily she made it," he says.

The thought of Sharen there by happenstance minister-ing over my mother's canted body. "Did you even call her?"

My father pulls sunglasses from his pocket and puts them on, my face contorted in their bronze reflection. "You haven't been here," he says. "You don't know what it's like to keep the place going. Keep an eye on her. Getting calls in the middle of the night and going over to find her fast asleep."

I watch the calf being hauled by its throat, its neck extending unnaturally, mouth open. The cow pushes against the fence, agitated, bays out. Makes me wonder if I'm not capable of remorse either.

"We all do bad things," my father says. I feel him stare at me. The way he's turned this around, the sound of the cow. I need to get away from him, head back to the car.

"I never slept with one of my father's girlfriends," he says as I step through the swinging door.

Busted, I stay. Is that who we are? People who get to say things like that? The pain stabs my jiggered hand.

"I know what goes on," he tells me. "I got men on the farm. They know when a bike goes down the lane. Old Nev was grubbing thistles in the bush—he saw you. As if I wouldn't find out," my father says taking off his hat and pushing his fingers through his sweaty mop of iron-gray hair. I watch the small heaves in my father's chest, his lungs grasping bits of air, and remember how I once slept with a girl called April when I was too young and he tackled me like this. *You just wish it was you*, I told him then, but I don't say anything now.

The cow below us moans into the blazing day. The distant clinking of the dead calf being released from the chain and as the gears of the tractor grind, the cow below us bawls even louder, a fountain of her scours spurts fresh over the railing.

"I loved your mother," he says. "But she treated me like an unwanted dog."

A grave is being dug so the calf can be buried. The Japanese tourists scurry across the grass. They've smelled and heard and seen enough of things we see as normal.

"Does your girlfriend love you?" my father asks, but that almost seems by the way now. How I want to please others when I'm in America. The calf being pushed in the hole by the machine. Still, I find myself nodding.

"Then pull your bloody socks up," he says. "Or you *will* end up like me."

THE LIGHT ON the message machine blinks in the dull living room, the couch smells of dog. Three messages, two eerie hang-ups and then Isabel from the road to San Francisco. She sounds as if she's in a tunnel, an echo of laughter behind her. It's already afternoon here. I need to call her back, pray she doesn't answer. There's a click and whoosh, the unlikely event of reception.

"You sound like you're in a helicopter," I tell her, feel a pang at the sound of her innocent voice.

"We took off the ragtop," she yells.

"With the heater on blast," shouts someone else, then a squall of laughter.

"Who's we?" I ask, aware of the drag in my voice, my vowels flat and dying.

"Lauren," says Isabel. "She did that dress installation at Big Sur. Remember the tree?" When Isabel pinned a prayer and I didn't. "She's got a cabin. A place called Sea Ranch." Another *whoop* in the background and I imagine them on that Big Sur coast, cold wind off the ocean biting at their faces, the swoop around the curves. At least they're having fun.

"How was Esalen?" is the best I can do. The thought of some stranger driving my car. I suddenly hate those dresses.

"We whirled like dervishes," shouts Isabel. "It was amazing. I was almost the last one standing."

"She fucking was!" says her chorus. Another dyke in love, no doubt, leaving poor Mona for dead. I know I should feel more possessive; I've fucked up something precious.

"This Turkish guy Oresh led in a cone hat and white robe." Isabel all breezy. "You really missed something." Missed the dervish lusting after her in his floating kimono, the sound of twangy strings repeating as they spun their feet off the ground. It probably was amazing but I can't feel a thing. I bite my lip until it hurts.

Out the window, my mother's in the Pond Paddock with Sharen, picking up manure in the wheelbarrow. Sharen in a bikini top and cutoff shorts with the wide manure fork, the smell of her still loiters about my fingers. While Isabel was spinning I was low in the dirt with the local skank. She felt so strong and Australian, capable of anything, unafraid of pain. I can almost make out her bruises from here, her breasts as they struggle at the edges of her string-tied top.

"It was like we were standing still with the earth whirring around us," Isabel calls out from the other end. Some dark-eyed Sufi with eyebrows of death. I wonder if he screwed her, and why I'm only suspicious of her when I'm guilty. My eyes on a wet pink rut of my own, remembering how I lost myself in Sharen in a way I can't quite remember. In that same grass clearing where I felt up Brenda Furguson, felt the hungry moisture the first time.

"It was like flying," adds Isabel, while I'm in another hemisphere feeling the opposite. Wanting to dive my nose into the ground. If I were there we'd sneak out of the yurt and climb down to the beach, hide in the caves and I'd want to smoke weed. She's better off without me. Twirling to drums and sitar, she and the Turk the only ones left. They'd have made love among candles and cushions, sacred sex and mantras, tantra. But if he fucked her in his cone hat would she really tell me all this?

"Better come home soon," the enchanted lesbian shouts. They both laugh like kookaburras.

"Do I need to worry?" I ask, wishing I could just get on a plane and take my injured hand back to her in the canyon.

Out in the paddock, they're cleaning up around the old pine tree where my mother wants to be buried. Sharen's calf muscles jut from the top of sockless elastic-side boots; she bends down low as if she knows I'm watching. How she brings out the primitive in me, the animal I try to keep stored away. But what if that's who I am, if in America I'm just fronting? Poised and respectable, slightly rough around the edges in a way they find appealing.

"Well the Budokon teacher from Brazil was pretty cute," says Isabel, "What about you?"

"I'm here with me," I say. I don't ask what Budokon is. The dog comes in and jumps on the couch, leaving my mother out there with Sharen. I wonder if Sharen really slept with my father or just led him along for rent.

"What's wrong? You sound so weird."

I clear the thickening in my throat. "You sound high."

"Maybe you should be too," she says. "Why don't you come home?"

"My mother's going to die soon," I tell her. "There's people all over the place. I need to be here." I don't tell her I dreamed she arrived right out there on the drive like a warning. So clean and neat and tall. "You can come out if you want," I say, my mouth drifting from the receiver.

"You need me?" she asks. My mother walks with her carved stick toward the narrow woven-wire gate into the garden. "We could go somewhere nice," Isabel's voice straining. Sharen pushing the wheelbarrow through the sand to the giant pile under the draping shade of the trees. Her biceps taut, she tips the load. I listen to the wind howl in my ear as she stares up at the house, shading her eyes with her sunburnt forearm. I don't want to go anywhere nice.

* * *

SUNDAY

A dream where I'm out in the sand near the old dressage arena, digging the earth with a stick for the sound of a telephone ringing. My ear to the grit and it's loud so I keep gouging with my stick, hit upon an old Tarax bottle then bones of what could be a dog and the ringing gets louder but there are just bones and clouded glass. A man at the foot of the bed, dark river eyes that pierce inside me, but as I rise the figure melts through the rippled glass window, and it feels as if I'm awake, staring out into the crow-black dark. But I'm already standing.

At the window, what looks like a distant fire are just floodlights that flank the new roundabout way out on the highway. Then I hear words from somewhere behind me, floating down the hall: *Jehovah Raffa Elohim*. An American preacher's voice. Now I know I'm awake. My mother's radio in the other room picking up a different station. *All-sufficient Perfecter. Hallowed Standard.* The warm window against

my face, the orange glow as if the edge of the world is burning. Stars hanging as ornaments. I rub my eyes; the bandage smells. The croaking American accent calls through
the thickness of the walls, *Jehovah Nissi, our banner on the
battlefield.* Searching out for the man from my half-sleep,
for a shape on the lawn, in the trees that stripe the blackness,
the glinting horizon—a face I know from dreams before
in the tongue-in-groove wall of the shearer's quarters, as
a teenager waking with night terrors. Walker down in the
fields, rounding up the cattle in the night.

The triad of those dark horses canopied under the trees.
Their glossy eyes burning, keeping watch. Why are they
up near the house? The gilded distance from the highway
behind them, manes holding light. The sense of everything
shifting, as if I were truly to wake I'd not see these scenes,
horses with the heads of men and the hills that sway about,
but I need to turn off the radio.

I feel my way across the dark hall, a woman sings,
Elijah Rock, shout, shout, repeating. A slice of light seeps
through the crack into my mother's room. The door makes
its usual creak; the ill-fitting green curtains hang. Heading
for her old Panasonic, past her narrow bed, I turn on her
reading lamp. She's half-sitting up with pillows bunched
about her neck, her beaky face enveloped in a bonnet of
clouds. A faded blue sheet is pulled over her shoulders, one
limp arm raised with its fingers splayed about her nose. Her
specs still on. As I switch off the endless names of God, the
dawning creeps up through my chest. I reach to touch her
cheek. It's cool. No air from her nostrils against my fingers.

"Mum?" I remove her hand from her face and her fingers swipe her glasses from her eyes. She snuffles, drawing me back with a quick rattled breath. My eyes feel unnaturally dry, but a weight sinks inside my belly. Me and the night and my breath reignites as her arm reaches up to her nose of its own accord. The rise and fall of her chest returning like an afterthought. The moment I've always dreaded and occasionally prayed for passed, yet the guilt of it drags me down beside her, to her withered little frame. The body I somehow appeared from. Would she have wanted me to try to save her? Part her narrow lips and breathe into her coffee-stained mouth, pump her weather-beaten chest? My fisted hands would break her.

Placing her glasses down by the lamp, I slump into her bedside chair, unsure of what I've witnessed, another little aftershock? Unsure if there'll be fallout. A book underneath me in the folds of the cushions. I pull out the cup-stained cover. Snake art framing a wrinkled indigenous face carved in a red rock escarpment. *The Ropes of Time*. My Grade 6 English prize. *Haileybury* stamped on the inside and my name typed in: *Daniel Parkes Rawson*. Below it in my mother's hand: *Reggie Dumbalk*. My mother, innocent there, breathing again, giving my things away.

The book opens to a page where a worn red Staedtler pencil rests. *Aboriginal Spiritual Discipline. The details of bone-pointing and the cure for illness are taught to the novice Karadji by his elder.* Browned paper edged by the ring of a cup. Pictures of a corroboree, men dancing painted. Headdresses and chalk. How I was fascinated by this as a kid, spooking myself so I couldn't sleep.

I read in the lamplight. *The young Karadji can grow feathers on his arms, which, after a few days, develop into wings. Postulants see into the underworld, observe spirits of the dead all bunched together.* Did I underline that, or did the boy? *Karadji: One to whom the cleverness has been handed on, who has contact with the Dreaming. A magician who follows the aerial rope of time.*

The imaginary games I played in the paddocks, riding bareback in the night with no bridle or saddle, just wrapping my hands about Thunderfella's neck with my face in the smell of his crest as the ponies galloped in tandem in the wind then propped to a stop on the hill. Spying on Walker as he stole a calf from the yard, a bridle from the tack room, telling my father in the morning.

I start at a shadow in the hall; Reggie emerging silent in the doorway. A coppery green in his eyes—not just Sharen, but something wilder, of his father's making. Reggie who knows when to come and be near her.

"That's my book now," he says calmly, unfolds his fingers to reveal a small shape in his hand. The carved bird earring my father brought home from New Guinea, more ornate and delicate than I remember. "I found it in the garden," he says, places the carving between the open pages and quietly eases the book from my bandaged hand. He stands close beside my mother's bed, reaches and touches her blanketed foot.

"She's not well," I tell him. "Maybe it's time you went back with your father to Yarram."

But Reggie just reads from the book, mouthing shapes of words as though he's telling her a story in her sleep.

Maybe that's what he does when she's struggling. His eyes seem to shine. He says without taking his gaze from her: "I belong *here*," he says. "You think I don't but I do."

He may think I'm back because I have to be, but I dream of this place too, the way the sun is rising above the lip of the boundary, ready to eat up the day. The horses grazing, swishing tails, the early-morning sparrows prancing along their backs. I'm not just *from* but *of* here. The place belongs to me, or will.

"Ruthie taught me this," he says. He turns to the back of the book, reading aloud in a kind of fitful English. "'Moving through the dark . . . as if there are no farms or houses . . .'" He reads but his eyes strain on my mother. He's learned it by heart. "'Men in single file through the rough milk thistle field, under the white mouth of the moon.'" Familiar words, written longhand by me on the last blank pages in the book. About his age, fourteen, inspired and some plagiarized from the front. I won the essay prize at school. *Dreaming of Bones,* I called it. *A hum and rustle through the Dutchman's market gardens . . . land furrowed for the crops that haven't been picked . . . Horses always waiting at the fence.* As he reads it sounds more him than me. I stare at his dirty singlet, a shiny keloid scar on his upper arm, the way his chapped lips move. My mother laid out like a wrinkled queen, calmed by him, it's true. The intervals between her breaths slowed but regular now.

"She don't want no doctor," says Reggie, then reads on haltingly, ministering. "'The sound of men shifting up the lane . . . the Karadji in his possum cloak . . . his emu bone with hair and blood . . . It is amazing how the old men run . . . almost as if they are floating.'" He reads as though the words of two sons can be spoken at once.

The sound of a chainsaw and he stops. We both look out through the undulated window. The way his big eyes twitch, I can tell he's on edge. The chance of Walker.

"It's just Nev," he says. "Over the road."

We stare out as the sun creeps orange above the lavender distance. "What should we do about Walker?" I ask.

"Keep out of it," he says.

I look over at charred documents, feathered black in the embers of the fireplace. They've had their own burning ritual. I wonder if he knows I plowed his mother, that I'm no better than any of them, except perhaps him.

"He beats up Sharen," I say.

The kid nods as if that's not my concern. My mother's eyes half open. She frowns like a child, making us out, removes her blotched hands from her chest and places them down at her sides. A pink-orange drift of light dusts the room. "What are you two up to?" she asks; her voice hoarse but unslurred.

"Old Rags and Juniper have disappeared," Reggie tells her. They look at each other as if only they know what that means.

* * *

MONDAY

◆———◇———◆

In the morning I wait until there's movement over in Ruthie's room before I go in to check. She's in her jeans already, maybe she slept in them; her powder-blue nightie over the top. She studies the sleeves of a Fair Isle cardigan she's managed to wrangle over her head, but she looks confused about which arm should go where.

"How are you?" I ask, unsure if I should broach a visit to hospital.

"Feral," she says, twisting one side of her mouth as if the cardigan won't do what it's told. Her arms seem to have minds of their own so she doesn't complain as I move in to help, guide an errant freckled hand into a sleeve. If she remembers what transpired in the night she doesn't let on. Her body will do the telling. She relies on her usual fortitude to get to the dresser and leans, preparing for a move to the hall, but there's a banging on an outside door and she jerks.

"I called a carpenter from Clyde," I tell her, loud enough so she might hear over the noise. "He's putting slide bolts on the doors and windows."

My mother looks distraught, rubbing at the sore on her forehead. "Why on earth?"

"So we can at least lock ourselves in," I say. An odor, not unpleasant, just stale, like my grandmother's skin in the mornings, except my mother relies on the dog's tongue for moisture, not Pond's. But she doesn't seem different from yesterday.

"How will Pip get out to lift a leg?" she asks; her speech seems fine. She really means: *How will Reggie get in?* Will she wait until I'm gone and have Old Nev removing bolts, twenty-nine of them? I counted up the doors and windows before I rang the handyman.

My mother picks up a silver-plated hairbrush from the chest, tries to brush her hair but she seems to approach it backward, brushing her gray waves forward to create a kind of fringe. "Who's paying for it?" she asks.

"Me," I say. "He's also going to patch up the hole in my room."

"So you're staying," she says, a ripple of sarcasm from the side of her mouth. She replaces the brush on the matching silver-framed hand mirror, gives up on her hair. She takes the mirror and examines herself.

"I just wish it was the same as always," I say. "Without these people around." A drilling sound from Deneray the carpenter, making holes in a doorjamb. No sign of Reggie.

"You want *us* to be here," she says. "But *you* don't want to be." Her eyes bead as she turns; she knows she's landed on a truth. How my place in the world feels safer when this place exists as I want to remember it. My mother alone in the house and my father in Blind Bight, making his crumpled way over each day in the Camry to give Old Nev his orders and drive my mother to town.

"Did Walker steal those two ponies?" I ask. The truck without lights I saw on Tuesday, along Genoni's Road.

"Why don't you go take a look in the Lagoon Paddock?"

As I turn to leave, I notice her ancient tweed suitcase is open on the floor by the end of her bed. Years ago she asked me to reorganize it, her pile of old manila folders, Bendigo Bank statements, car insurance, shares. Now her will's on top, out of its envelope, torn free from its ribbon. *THE LAST WILL AND TESTAMENT OF RUTH BRAILSFORD RAWSON.* The version I arranged with the lawyers in Cranbourne, disinheriting Earley as she requested, *so no Elsie or any of his others could stake their claims.* Done as much for myself as her. All property, real and personal, her *hereditaments,* passing to me, but on the second page in the margin. Shaky blue pen. *No Doctor.* Her initials, and then, *Witness: Reggie Don,* scrawled in the same. More smudged writing in my mother's looping hand, below the original seal, a second codicil. *I, Ruthie, gift the bush block to Reginald Donald Dumbalk (Reggie Don), and all Broken Hill shares.* Her signature, he's the witness. Did it happen during the night? Did she leave the case open so I'd see it? Thoughts cascading. You can't witness a bequest if you get the benefit, but is this what she wants? And what does it leave? A few hundred acres and this open house; not the cottage out the back. Her current account if there's anything left and the acreage over the road. "And what's this?" I ask.

She eyes me evenly, her shoulders pulled back. "Reggie will take care of the land," she says. "You'll just sell it up." She's far too sharp to have had a new stroke.

"How do you know I won't get married and move here?"

"And live with Sharen?" she asks. The two of them out there picking up dung. Or maybe Reggie told her. I shouldn't have left him ministering in the night.

"You should be pleased I escaped from this," I say.

My mother breathes and closes her eyes as if to garner strength. "You left me with your father." What she means is: I left her.

I NEED TO be alone. A bath in the good bathroom that nobody uses, the tub cream-painted iron and narrow, almost four feet deep. Stains beneath the taps the shape of rusty tears. A window but not much of a curtain, so far from the boiler it was deemed a waste to run water this far. The giant showerhead I don't turn on because the tap is wrapped with red electrician's tape. It always poured rusty water and couldn't be turned off, dripping once every few minutes for twenty years. I'd lie here to escape, listening to the pipes groan and waiting for that moment.

The bath runs brown then clears as I wait for the water to warm, hoping no one finds me here. Undressed, I slowly remove the bandage from my hand, the red ridge along the stitches like an angry mouth. The scratch of a twig on the roof and the handyman drilling and banging echoes in here. Reminds me of LA and how they're always building in the canyon, the echo of each nail strike reverbing through the hills. I can't sleep through construction there. Here I can't stay awake, up half the night, the dreams that won't stop coming even when I'm only half asleep.

My grandmother washed me here when I was a boy, reaching in with soft soapy hands. Rinsing the farm from my hair and her thumb pressing a track along my brow to keep the soap from my eyes. She finger-painted in the suds on my tummy, shapes I had to guess. A horse and then a house I guessed was a pair of hats. "Wash up as far as possible, and down as far as possible," she'd say. "But for heaven's sake don't touch possible." She did her English laugh as though it was the first time anyone had ever said it.

I wash myself with the aged remains of glycerin soap, but *can't* make myself feel clean. The thought of Isabel on the beach at Sea Ranch, wherever that is, with her new girlfriend. She'd be swimming in the icy ocean, bodysurfing and collecting shells, conches, cones, baby's ears. Arranging them the way she does.

Back in the bedroom in just a towel, there's already a bolt on each window, shutting out the heat. The dog trots in then leaves so I shut the door and collapse on the bed in broad daylight, the altered will beside me on the sheet, as if custody makes a difference. Reggie has the book and now I am left with this. I'd planned to bring Isabel here on our honeymoon. Circle the Pacific—Tahiti, Fiji, New Zealand, Dunk Island . . . then the mysterious farm she's seen in pictures. She'd look up into these cobwebs, the blistered paint, and the hunting scene on the mantel that's just a print. She'd be disappointed. The place not how I'd rendered it. My father hitching past the dirty window, peering in. She'd be staring out the screen's ripped edges, flies buzzing against glass. Spritzing her face in the heat, the familiar waft of rosewater. I'd lift the soft linen of her skirt, her slightly musty traveling smell. I'd nuzzle the narrow elastic silk, kiss her there and she'd make a small sad sound and push down against my tongue, a quiet back and forth. Not like Sharen, but lovely still.

Isabel's grandmother said I'd be a betrayer, a *traidor*, because I resembled Isabel's Dutch father. *El Abandonador*. Now I resemble my own, dreaming of Isabel here.

WHEN I ROUSE myself the banging has stopped and all is quiet, but the day is already fading, pinks and purples hang like lips on the edge of the sky. All I can think of is Sharen, my body wanting more. Drunk with sleep and dressing without undies or socks, just a shirt and jeans and Blundstones. The comfort of dusty toes against leather, my feet reverting to dirt.

The silent Prius without lights feels as if it drives itself. No traffic, just an occasional reflector on a milepost, everything turned a ferocious purple, falling off the horizon. Avenues of poplars line the drives of hobby farms; sheds and treated rail turnout pens. Angora goats and llamas, Welsh Mountain ponies. I turn up Wedding Bush Road where the sand on the track beneath the tires is quiet as the trees. I park up near the open gate and wander down the eroded slope to the cottage, over the shallow gullies formed in years it rained, hungry for the heat and the smell of her. The chance of finding her naked in the rocking chair or lying in that bedroll in the bare sitting room sets my body humming. I can just make out the distant hump of Sharen's blackened car. Indifferent about the Munnings now, the rocking horse; all I want is to pump her stupid, stamp her rough into that burned-up grass.

But the porch light's off, the house dark as the carport. I head around to the back, to a silhouette near the garden fence. "Sharen?" The figure picks up a loose wooden slat and retreats beside the water tank.

"Not here." Walker not thirty feet away snarls from under his hat, *hoicks* phlegm and spits into the hibiscus. I tread closer. He must be in his mid-forties now, broader, heavier than I remember, stiff-necked. Ten years older than I am. He drops the narrow plank from his hand, as if he doesn't need it. "What you want here?" he asks, his stare barely visible under the brim of his Akubra, eyes that don't hold light.

"It's my place," I say, resting my gaze on him. I could take him if I really had to. Maybe. I was never a fighter but in LA I've been training, lessons I took with a guy called Kiwi Thunder at the boxing gym on Vine, it's all the rage now, fists up high, the uppercut and jab. "You know we're missing a couple of Ruthie's riding school ponies," I say. "Thought you might have seen them."

His grip seems to tighten near his pocket. The small flick-knife holstered on his belt; I saw it in the bathroom.

Even a good punch and my hand would be ripped right open, or worse. I eye the garden fork ten feet from me. Nice to know it's there. "Where do you take them?" I ask.

He makes a hissing sound, gestures with a flick of his head, and the night seems suddenly silent. Out past him over the bracken-covered rise, toward the housing tract, once sat the corrugated shed where Gracious birthed him; before his father fled. Gordie was a good man with sheep is all I remember.

I take another careful step nearer. Sweat on my back and neck. He once killed a rabbit with a slingshot in the dark.

"You don't come near me." He spits, raises his unshaven chin as he kneels, grabs the plank and beats the corrugated iron tank. So empty it echoes like a bell in the bush, has me jump back, the ant-eaten wood as it splinters about him. He picks up an old rope halter and drapes it on his arm, retreats into the night. "She's probably at the pub," he yells from the shadows. My hands trembly as my fists unclench.

I PULL INTO the gravel parking lot by the Tooradin Pub, the *Drive-Through Bottle-O* lit up like an all-night carwash. As I get out I listen to the cupping of the waves on the dense gray sand and the water birds squawk—ibis and blue cranes. The thrum of frogs from the eerie black inlet, the blood as it runs through my veins. The town's empty save the trucks that trundle through and I'm staring through the pub's new picture window into the gussied-up lounge.

Ted and Roxy McDonough sit on chrome stools at the bar. Mavis Pipes pulling beers as always, her hair swept back but silver now, red cylinder earrings, everything the same but different. This pub where I once watched my father work the girls. Now it's me leaving Isabel on the end of the phone, my mother alone in the house. Just as he used to.

Through a new glass door frosted with a colony of seagulls, I notice poker machines now light up the far wall, a row of miniature hot rods. What was almost historic converted to gauche. A multicolored all-occasion carpet, cheap blond wood for the bar. No Sharen perched at the bar, bare legs on show for the evening. Just Tony Genoni, who swivels on his stool and catches me, watching. I enter anyway.

"Earley's boy!" says Mavis as if I'm twelve. She gathers glasses. "We heard you were here." Her pale crystally irises. "What's your fancy?"

A television hangs from a metal perch, everyone glued to a game of night cricket at the MCG. "A Crown Lager," I say. "Thanks."

The McDonoughs ignore me, still nursing a spat they had with my father years ago, a missed appointment or cattle through a fence. Joe Madragona, the market gardener who lives over on Genoni's Road, tips back a bottle of Victoria Bitter. His rusted machinery and car chassis piling up in the gullies behind his house. "Joe," I say as if I'm here to see him. "We got a vehicle for you in the Back Paddock. A nice Mitsubishi."

Tony Genoni laughs. "It's a nice smoky black," he says. "Thanks to Sharen Wells."

Joe smiles in wry acknowledgement, he knows what goes on; then gets swallowed back up by the cricket on the screen.

Mavis slides my beer onto the counter; specs hang on the chain round her neck as if she has a second pair of eyes. "Be careful," she adds with a mascaraed wink from behind her pink and white frames. "She's a bit of a one."

I take a swig of cold ale and look down into the stitches scabbing on my hand, the vomit-colored carpet, as if I'm unsure what she's talking about.

"We went with wall to wall," she says and Tony yells "Fuckin' moron" at the television. Bessie Slaughter in her usual dark corner knitting gray socks for the hospital, staring at me. What did we do to her? Grumpy Unthank drinking on his own, just older, winks. Through the paneled glass into the other room, I catch sight of Bobby Genoni, leaning over the pokies, playing them alone. From behind he's pudgier than he used to be. Sharen speared him too. If only I'd known her back in the day, a girl a bit older who knew what to do. That's how it should have been. Not now, with Isabel waiting, me hunting Sharen along with my father and Bobby, Walker skulking around. The alarms in my head muted by animal craving.

Cloudy Gray lurches over with schooner in hand. "I like that Sharen," he says with a wet-eyed blink. "She's like a night at the drive-in, except you don't need a car."

"Fuck off, Cloudy," I say.

No one suggests otherwise.

"You must have a lot on your plate," whispers Mavis as if she understands. What the hell's she mean by that? "What with Ruthie and all." Ruthie, the least of my problems. She lifts her glasses and puts them on, grills me with aqueous eyes. "How's America treating you, since those planes ran into the buildings?"

I think of how a place can *treat* you. "Different and the same," I say. "Just like here."

"What's so bloody different about here?" Tony yells, spittle from his lips.

"Cloudy's drunk," I shout the obvious and even Ted McDonough laughs but Bobby's coming through the archway. "How're the pokies, Bobby?" I ask.

He tries to square his eyes, leans against his brother for support. I remember them as mean drunk teenagers, the Italian boys at the CFA parties at the local hall. They're both flabbier now, paunches, even Joe Madragona's balding. They've given up footie to watch cricket at the pub.

Bobby balances his hand on his brother's bready shoulders. "The apple doesn't fall far," he smiles. "How *is* your old man?"

He's not just meaning Earley but Sharen and me. I chug my beer with an illicit, edgy feeling as Bobby rollicks closer, gathering his thick hands into fists. A punch comes at me and I duck, pound him solid with my good hand right in his distended gut, courtesy of Kiwi Thunder. He crumples, winded, over the stool, and all is silent. Yes, I think, both hands burning, I've wanted to do that since I was kid.

Maybe this is why I went to the boxing gym. Bobby coughing and his brother's not moving toward me; his eyes are empty as plates. I leave a twenty for Mavis, claim my beer and take it with me out the frosted seagull door.

I should have asked Daniel if it was okay to let Lauren drive. But the way he was on the phone makes me want to yell out the car: Me cago en tu puta madre. *At least I'm not driving, in the dark, snaking along these cliffs. Lauren points at lights in the coastal trees and yaps about old timber cabins that are "architecturally significant." They look like boxes from here and the road makes me seasick. I haven't spoken for an hour, too busy staying awake in case she really does run off the road. She says we're nearly there but I could have flown to Australia by now, see what's really going on. The more I try not to think of him, the more I hear his phone voice.*

Gracias Cristo, *we finally turn up a track near a bridge. There's a waterfall up in the hills, she says, but I don't tell her I need a bed, not Iguassu. I have no idea what I'm doing. Just getting farther away from Daniel when all I really want is him. Despite his* familia de locos. *His stupid, steakhouse self.*

Darker still as I turn off the music and we bump along in silence, the car lights spraying yellow on enormous redwoods and the eyes of animals. Possums, she says, or deer. In the trees? The questions I'm too tired to ask. Too bushed, as Daniel calls it. Then a shape on the branch of a huge eucalyptus, this time a dress with bird wings, feathered and beaded, fringed arms that spread out like it's an eagle partly made from a skin. "My Christmas tree," she says as we crunch along the gravel. The apparition wafts in the breeze with green coruscated balls strung between branches. Osage oranges, she calls them, and I nod but I've only heard of Osage County, a play I saw in New York. For all I know, Daniel's family could be the Australian version of that one. Raro. Chiflada.

A dim porch light shows an open thatched carport, a rustic cabin with walls made from branches. Inside, a giant rusted sign strung along the wall. D'ASSU, *and below it,* ASSUR. *She says it's from a demolished insurance site in Paris but I don't know from insurance; that's Daniel's weird work world. I stretch out on a cool Danish sofa with a roll back and, from the pile of books on the side table, I pull a ragged copy of* Beowulf. *Undecipherable Middle English. I look up at Lauren in the lamplight and ask if she can read this.*

"I just like the shapes of words," *she says, and it's true that the language looks majestic. I just hope she doesn't cut it up for art. She throws a chalky firelighter into the potbelly stove and a flame goes whoosh, lights up the oversized black-and-white dairy cow on paper taped to the wall. A vintage wedding dress is suspended from the bannister above me, names on paper ribbons stuck to the hem.* Darius. Aaron 1. Victor. Cassius. The Monster. *I ask her who The Monster is and she tells me he was her deaf Buddhist.*

"Why are you single?" *I ask.*

"Because of guys like them," *she nods at the names that cascade from the dress, then asks what the deal is with my man.*

"He's gone walkabout, or bush, or whatever they call it." *I try not to sound so dejected but the anger has taken up residence as an ache in the pit of my stomach. Part of me wants to throw her books across the room but it's hardly her fault.*

"You could pin his name up there," *she says, points into the layered petticoats.*

I could but I won't.

Through the undraped window, I gaze out at the filmy appendages of the bird dress drifting about in the night as if nobody cares. It makes me want to climb up the tree and try it on, see if I can fly.

Lauren stands back from the fire. "Come upstairs," she says. "I have something to show you."

The steps wind up, treacherous as the road, bending to a loft with a big round bed she plops down on. It sloshes slightly. She watches up through a wide glass skylight, cantilevered open like a wing. I perch on the end on the wobbly duvet. The room is spare but for a row of pixie shoes, a pair of biker boots, and a tall plastic tubular lamp. She points out Orion's Belt and the Dog Star as if she just discovered them. As I collapse down, our arms graze and together we observe the silent vibrating sky. I wonder if I'm officially homeless, if I might just keep the Jeep and drive north through the night. Portland. Seattle. Vancouver. He said it was "our" Jeep. He said he wanted to see the Canadian Rockies. I wish I could drive to Cuba.

Soft footfalls on the roof and a narrow fur face appears through the gap between the skylight and ceiling. Black circles mask the small bright eyes. "That's my boyfriend," says Lauren. "He visits every night." The raccoon peers down at me and bares its teeth, a smile or a grimace, and Lauren takes my hand. We stare up at the shadow of the animal framed by stars, and then it pads off across the glass. In the gradual touch of her soft curled fingers, I cave into the realm of sleep.

* * *

TUESDAY

◆——————◆——————◆

I sit on the gate and watch magpies glide through the morning, the wooden earring Reggie dug up clutched in my hand like a charm. If I could just let Tooradin be Tooradin, let my mother die with Reggie mouthing Dreamtime stories, Sharen laying on hands, leave Earley to creep around the edges of his own home, let Walker steal the rest of Ruthie's ancient ponies. But now I've telephoned Isabel five times and she hasn't picked up, after all the times I didn't get up to answer her calls. I imagine returning to Laurel Canyon, the guesthouse stripped of her. Bookshelves without her Neruda or Lorca in Spanish, the photos of her in Japan, and her print of the famous gold and silver Klimt. The face of a fair-skinned Isabel dressed in threaded bullion. The time I first spotted her at the French bistro in Los Feliz. A dark leggy girl in white linen pants at the table beside me, both of us eating French onion soup. The way she smiled then lifted her sunglasses, her eyes crinkled up as if she already knew me. I drove her to a yoga class and thought it was odd that she'd traveled from New York with her mat. I didn't mean to wait but I couldn't help myself, loitering outside at the magazine stand. We walked round Hancock Park, the manicured lawns and California bungalows. Her dark unmade-up model's eyes, the way she moved so easily, willowy and tall. Her hair held up in a tangled updo, falling down. A beautiful girl trying hard to look ordinary, it pierced me through. I kissed her in the car in the bank parking lot; it felt inevitable. A feeling so far from this. Her voice soft and sultry. Yet here I am—Old Nev out there, digging at thistles. Old Thunderfella standing sunken-backed in the rust weed down by the pump shed, out here all these years, barely recognizable. This field that's been here all this time, waiting. The tinges of green in the cooch grass and kikuyu. The lone willow bereft of the branch I used to climb. My mother would hum as she handled the clippers, tracing the shape of a saddle and girth. Abandoning and being abandoned feel somehow interchangeable. A space forms between things. A body becomes bifurcated, struggles to sense where it can stand alone. This body, my hands, like hers, our separated yearnings. I stare up into a gaping sky streaked with cirrus. Mare's tails, my grandmother called them. I wish she were still alive, out in that fibro plank cottage instead of Sharen, it would be so much simpler. No blackened chassis smudging the horizon. Those three horses grazing around it as though it's always been there. Everything innocuous. I touch the scab between my fingers, feel the ragged stitches. Healing and now sore again, the ache for Sharen comes again like hunger pains. But what is this? It can't be just to show my father how it feels to lose. It's more a need for this gray earth, wanting to feel it ooze up through me, to bury my face in the soil, taste it in my teeth.

The sun gets high and I can feel my mother watching out her bedroom window, keeping an eye out as she used to. The grass fading into the stillness, almost green in patches underneath way out where it's been cut and baled. The oblong bales in rows, not yet carted, waiting to be stacked in the shed. A shorthorn heifer sniffs the air. What will it be when my mother is gone if I'm not here?

"Let's go," she shouts from her open window, playing life goes on. I want to toss the wooden earring down into the dry grass paddock, back into this bad-luck earth where I buried it as a kid, but my fingers won't let go.

I DRIVE HER to town in a hot airless silence, the snarl of the sun at the Station Road junction, the dog's front paws up on the console, panting between us. I concentrate hard on the gravelly sand, a surface designed for tailspins.

"Old Thunder foundered last spring," she says. "His soles dropped. Your father wants to put him down." My father's strange desire to put elderly horses to sleep. My mother reckons it's mostly to console their lady owners afterward.

"Perhaps you should before winter," I say, feel her spirit sag at my use of *you*.

"Perhaps *you* should while you're hanging about. Do something useful. Before he ends up in some dusty riding school in Scoresby."

"Is that where Walker sends them?"

"I don't know," she says. "That or the abattoir at Wont-haggi. Either way, Reggie's keeping lookout now."

I look over and try to assess how she's coping. She stares out at the back paddock where my father once wanted a polo field until she said he should first develop an eye for the ball. She seems so self-contained, determined as ever.

"You and Reggie seem to have everything under control," I say.

"Are you plotting your escape?" she asks but doesn't turn her gaze from the farm as we pass it by. The Sunday night seven years ago when I told her my plan to leave the law firm here and head to America, a short vacation from Hedderwicks in Melbourne when I had no desire to return. I told her how I could no longer wrap my head around my work, the thorny conveyance schemes and stamp duty, paper-ing the "Darwin Shuffle" to minimize taxes, so complex I couldn't keep the trail of transfers in my head. "I might have a chance to ride jumpers in the US," I told her. She'd once gone to Ireland to do the same, ride with Colonel Dudgeon. I didn't tell her I yearned to lose myself in faraway cities, to wash this place from me once and for all. "This is your home," was all she said, but when I flew from Tullamarine with my riding gear and a resumé in hand, letters of recom-mendation, I wondered if this was just where I was from.

Near the tree at the Tooradin Hall where my mother likes to park in the shade sits Walker, slouched on the steps with a paper-bagged bottle. "Don't stop here," warns my mother, the dog leash wrapped tight about her fingers. She knows better than to ask him things. I think of his coarse fingers on Sharen, his open hand against her face. Does she taunt him or is she just the object of his rage, pulling and repulsing different parts of her? Hungers of their own.

"Poor old Rags," my mother says and I remember the pony's show name: *Rags to Riches.*

"I'm going to call the Cranbourne cops."

"They have better things to do," she says. "Reggie won't let Walker catch any more."

"What if Walker catches Reggie?" I roll the Prius to the curb outside the new Food Mart, which my mother still won't enter.

"Then I'll be on my own," she says, reaches for the post box key looped over the indicator. Box 90 inscribed on the tag. The hundreds of postcards I've addressed to that box, from the show-jumping stadium at Conyers outside Atlanta. *Everything going swimmingly here. Watching the jumping finals.* The German stallion that won the grand prix was dead the next day from drugs or exhaustion; no one seemed surprised. Cards from Casa Grande, Arizona. *The horse van broke down and we've waited a week in the desert for engine parts, made makeshift stalls for a million dollars' worth of horses. Hope all is well on the farm.* Horses who didn't have health papers to cross state borders so I drove because I had no truck licence to lose, turned off the lights of the eighteen-wheeler to sneak across state lines.

"Reggie can look after himself," my mother assures me, gives me a quaint sort of smile as if trying to understand why I'm so quiet. Her age-spotted face and flyaway hair, smudges on her glasses. Then she hikes her shopping bag over her shoulder, her body a mix of tenacity and tremors. "C'mon, Mr. Pip," she says and the dog jumps through between the seats. "We'll go it alone."

Watching her get out, her tenuous limbs and the way she uses Pip for balance, I suddenly want to hightail it to Sydney. Why is it me who wants to run away? As if I'm trapped by something outside me. By this old woman who's stalking some unsuspecting farmer at the Ready Teller as if for sport, standing so close he shifts to block her from the screen. To cheer me up, she throws a coltish nod at me and proceeds inside, the dog at her heel, but the automatic doors seem to startle her, whooshing open. She leans to steady herself but the glass is sliding away, then she rights as if she's a dinghy on water, and proceeds. The way she pretends to be brave. Or maybe it's genuine courage. A thing she sees in Reggie. When I just have the itch to run away.

Silhouetted inside the neon supermarket, dwarfed by the height of the shelves, beneath the tube lights, she fishes a list from her dilly bag but she won't know where anything is. Pulling the keys from the ignition, I go to help but a familiar figure emerges from Coastal Clippers, the salon next door. Sharen, barely recognizable on the newly raised pavement, shaking out a haircut. Short and blown dry, streaked a softer blond. A fresh white miniskirt and espadrilles as if she's a prosperous young mother from Mount Eliza. She checks her makeup in the window, raises a sleeve to examine a bruise on her upper arm.

As I get out, she notices me, pushes at her new hair.

"What you reckon?" She sits on the metal bench, crosses her legs and pretends to show off her espadrilles, her newly waxed legs glisten. Having a turn at being who she isn't. Maybe that's who I am in LA. I know I should go to my mother but I'm walking up the steps to her. She lights a Virginia Slims. Her red and pink shirt already damp in the heat and slightly see-through. Her bra is red. "Just getting back in the game," she says and she touches the leathery tan on her legs and I notice a new bruise on her thigh she's hiding.

"Want one?" I'm nodding as she hands me a smoke and I kiss it alight from hers as she scoots over so I can sit. She twists a fine silver necklace around the forefinger of her free hand. I suck in the welcome hit of nicotine and her musky haystack scent, combined with a chemical waft from her hair, the sun strong as knives in our eyes. She's staring out across the highway to the bus shelter, a lone shaded figure. Walker, watching us. She holds my hand tight and I turn to her. This time I notice teeth marks red on her neck. "Why do you let him hurt you?"

"Got no choice," she says. "He always tracks me down."

"Maybe there's a part of you that likes it," I say. "Like the part of me that likes you."

"So you like me?" she asks.

"All I know is with you right here and Walker watching, I want you more."

A bus comes through and stops with a great rush of air brakes and then exhaust. High and maroon with shaded windows. We watch as if expecting something magic. The bus makes a hiss and accelerates, leaves the structure empty.

"Maybe love's like that," says Sharen.

We watch the dust and the bus as it heads out of town as if from a tunnel of its own making. I pull her hand up to my mouth, rest my lips on the silver chain that wraps her finger, but as the dust cloud settles we both light on Walker through the glare; he's heading back to the bridge.

"There's something wrong with him," says Sharen. "He wants what he wants and he don't care what happens."

"What's wrong with you?" I ask.

"I don't know how to stop him," she says and turns to me with her sapphire eyes. "So what's wrong with you, Daniel?"

"I don't know," I say. If I was Reggie, I could slide through the swill of the sluice gates, float with the tide out to sea and be emptied into nothing but mud, wait for the tide to refill me.

I watch out as semi-trailers rattle past on the highway stuffed to the gunnels with sheep. I want to get on the road and forget everything, Isabel, Ruthie, Rags to Riches, the taste of Sharen, and the smell of eucalyptus in the canyon.

I DRIVE MY mother home in silence, past Tooradin Primary kids wandering home early to the shops, brown canvas satchels and hats, zinc cream on their noses. Ruthie, with her crossword and milk from the usual source, rehashing how she *found not one bloody thing in that ghastly new self-service*. I wonder if she smells Sharen on me.

As I wait to turn from the highway back onto Station Road, the pale sky whitens, the blinker clicking just out of rhythm with the tap-drip sound as my mother opens and closes her nervous pursed lips. I stare across to the mudflats, wondering where I could be now, out the other side of the city, Donnybrook Road or Kalkallo, or maybe Trafalgar or Moe if I took the coast. Two semi-trailers rush past and the weight of them shifts us, my hands lifeless on the wheel. Genoni's yard of machinery behind the chain-link fence. Sharen in the distance, on the sandy service road gazing up at the pub or maybe the sky, as if she watches something rare in flight.

"Are you fifteen?" my mother asks. A memory of her finding me jerking off as a teenager behind the door in the bungalow, and how she told me to take it outside. As if I was playing with fireworks.

"What do you mean?"

"Holding hands with Sharen in the street," she says. "I've never seen anything so tragic."

The smack of her words from beside me starts the pinwheels inside my head. "Just trying to find out where Walker sells the ponies." Lying to her so easily as though she doesn't know the truth. I edge the car out an inch but the traffic keeps coming. Should tell her I'm like my father but worse; I have more choices than he ever did. We've always been alike. The part of me that used to escape all this, head up to the old cruising places, gutter crawling on Dalgety Street. Forty dollars for a young strung-out migrant girl I didn't respect, scouting the pavement for some oblique connection with my father whom I don't respect either, yet searching nonetheless. Not everyone's as relentlessly correct and respectable as Ruthie Brailsford Rawson.

A stream of vehicles pulling boats and sand bikes, trailers full of holiday gear.

"Do you love your Venezwegian?" my mother asks but I say nothing. The way this town, this farm, and family cave in on me makes Laurel Canyon feel as if it exists in a swirl of leaves.

"Interesting," my mother says in subtle condemnation. "Put a penny in it will you?"

As I accelerate, I turn on the radio to silence my mind. The beat of Cold Chisel staticky, familiar from decades ago. *The last plane out of Sydney's almost go-one.* The pub-rock fury that bubbles amongst us here, manifests in sharp wit and sarcasm. *And only seven flyin' hours, till I'll be landin' in Hong Kong.* I switch the dial to the ABC. A story of drought in the outback. I turn it off and just drive, don't want to hear about farmers whose land has sucked the dreams right out of them, who go out and shoot themselves at sunset in their trucks, leaving their families in distant houses with the awful moment of an echo. Trees on the horizon rippling like vegetables boiled in blood.

When my mother and I get back to the farm and park on the drive we don't get out, just stare at the stained-glass roses on the windows of the enclosed part of the veranda. Through the glass I make out my father chatting to the carpenter by the leggy wooden clotheshorse. My mother shakes her head as she focuses on him holding court as though he still runs the show.

"At least everything will lock now," I say.

My mother pretends to read the front page of the *Sun*

but it's mostly photos from the cricket at the MCG. *AUSSIES SLAUGHTER KIWIS IN FIRST TEST MATCH.* She looks up. "Hopefully we can keep *him* out too," she says. She folds the paper and I notice the tarnished gold band still on her wrinkled wedding finger.

"Why do you still wear your ring then?" I ask her.

She seems undaunted. "So nobody gets any big ideas. And because I can't get it off." The band embedded in the rolls of freckled skin, like the way she's folded into this soil and the soil folds into him. My father now motioning out through the leadlight, beckoning us in. He won't want to get sucked into paying for all the "ridiculous" locks and bolts.

"You could have it cut off," I tell her.

"Hold your horses," Ruthie shouts at my father, stuffing the newspaper into her dilly bag.

"Remind me, why did you marry him?" I ask.

She reaches over and rests her worn-out fingers on my knee, looks up from the ring, her deep-set burnished eyes creasing up more with a dry-lipped smile. "Because I wanted to have you."

I rest my hand on hers. "Why did you want me?"

She pretends to look puzzled. "I needed someone worth talking to."

Could that even be partially true? "That's a good reason to have a child," I say.

She grunts as she pushes the heavy door open. "Yes," she says. "Until they leave you." She raises a cupped hand and forces a halfhearted wave at my father, turning her wrist as if she's the Queen. "Or they end up like him anyway."

Now I'm hiding out on Lauren's pocked wooden toilet seat feeling queasy. Through the plywood wall, the sound of her humming in the kitchen where I left her stirring oatmeal. This washroom tucked under the stairs with the mirrored treads and risers inches above my head as I sit with this woozy, drifty feeling. A desire to get even farther from home. If I could stand up I'd take the Jeep and leave, but where to? I could fly out to that farm and surprise him, if I wasn't terrified of being stuck in a plane for more than a day. I could show up on a horse in front of that house if I wasn't terrified of horses. If he wanted me there.

Out the tiny window, the mule stands in its muddy pipe corral. Beyond it, the creek with the swimming hole where Lauren waited for me. She looked innocent without her mascara or a cigarette, standing with a careful smile. The touch of the water was silky and warm, fed from a spring, she said. A hint of sulfur as I lay out on the wide flat rock in the middle, felt my breasts loll above me like seaweed. She stepped through the water between us and draped her wet cloth on my shoulder, uninvited. "Maybe you're not used to being touched like this," she said when I flinched. She let the orange cloth hang there like a flag and the warmth of the water felt suddenly prickly. I was unsure if I'd go where she wanted, to be touched the way Daniel's rough hands don't know how. Daniel who I wash but he rarely washes me.

Without asking she soaped my arms. As I wondered what might come next, a dragonfly buzzed close to my face. "Look," she said. "A blue dancer." She let the cloth sink along the narrow ridge of my tummy. "Raccoon for curiosity," she

said. "Dragonflies for change." She massaged my belly, rocking me slightly from side to side and the tops of the mountains
brushed at the edges of my eyes as she kneaded and rocked
me. Then in a shot of morning light, the image of Daniel
doing this with someone else made my body jolt unexpectedly, a kind of spasm in my throat and belly and tears flooded
from my eyes, the taste of them salty in my mouth as she held
me in the water, quietly stroking my hair.

Another pang in my gut and I hope it's just dread. I strain
up to the image that hangs on the back of this bathroom door.
A collage of Lauren towering toe-out in a dress like a dancer.
Black pilgrim shoes with minstrel bells, striped leggings made
of scraps from torn prose and ribbons. The kinship I feel with
scrappers, or anyone who sticks things together from scratch.
The Christmas tree I left in Laurel Canyon on its own. What
a waste of time. I lean forward to read from the skirt: Come
my beloved before the beauty fades, and then on her arm: my
tears make a track to the water. Things Daniel would never
write, pasted in the shape of her calves, her stance almost
manly and the hem of her skirt frilling wide. Ring out a thousand songs of old. Maybe I should be with an artist. Her hair
and face up in the dark, formed from strips of fabric and
paper, dreadlocked purple and blue, a patchwork of pasted
BART tickets, words. DISAPPOINTMENT laid into the
strength of her jaw. A new twinge in my gut and the hope
that Daniel feels something like this, regret and panic and his
own disappointment. I just wish it wasn't coming over me in
the morning. When he talked of marriage, I tried to believe
he could commit to that, but we've never mentioned children.

"*Your oatmeal's ready,*" yells Lauren. *This troubled image of her looms in front of me. Ripped from books of poetry.* Ring out the grief that saps the mind . . . Ring out the false, ring in the true. *Daniel so caught up in his matter-of-fact world, he probably wouldn't recognize Tennyson. He'd never read Neruda, hadn't heard of Lorca until after we met. A curl in my belly and I wonder if I'd be ballsy enough to tear up Tennyson for art, but I know Daniel would if I asked him to. He doesn't have a fear of the sacred. I've never seen him afraid except of going back home to his mother, and maybe commitment. And answering the phone.*

"Oatmeal's for old people and children," I shout, and *white folks. The way Daniel cooks porridge in the morning and wonders why I won't share the milky, cream slush. The thought of it has me bending double, reeling down onto the floor and turning to the porcelain. A sudden retch of liquid from nowhere, vomiting all that's inside me, hugging this cold toilet as if it's all I have.*

THE BEDSIDE CLOCK shines 11:44 p.m. Still in my jeans, all doors and windows locked, woken by music from my mother's room. My hand aches so I reach for the painkillers, find a glass of milk beside the bed, flowers in a vase. I turn on the light. Black-eyed Susan, a rose, and pale hibiscus. Not from this garden. The chocolate purple center of the Susans, the vines my grandmother grew, the scent of the rose petals, Isabel, her fragrance Roses for Men. The one she always wants me to wear too, but the notion of men with perfume gives me that slithery feeling like when I see a husband carrying a purse for his wife. Phobias I live with from growing up here. I get up to check, find the phone in the sitting room to let Isabel know I was thinking of her smell, tell her something true, but as I tread down the dark the hall, I realize the music emerges from elsewhere, the main side-hall bathroom. My mother's old Frank Sinatra. *A very good year for small-town girls . . .* A voice sings along, throaty and maudlin. *And soft summer nights, we'd hide from the lights.* A smoky female voice. No need to have heard Sharen sing to know who it is. I open the door and she smiles up at me, half-innocent, sitting on the toilet seat sucking on a reefer in her short white skirt, bare legs dangling, innocent as a girl. A candle lit beside her on the marble stand, my old red vinyl portable turntable circling unevenly.

She lazily points at my mother in the wavery light, just in a nightie on the low antique folding chair at the bath end, the dog curled at her feet. Candlelit like something from *Oliver Twist*. She almost looks serene.

"Ruthie called me," says Sharen. "She was worried."

"Why didn't you wake me?" I ask my mother.

She opens her eyes reluctantly, scratches her hair with both hands and yawns. "We're waiting for Reggie to come home," she says as if she's not worried at all. Sharen sings on softly, pot smoke wafting through the open flywired window. *When I was twenty-one, it was a very good year. A very good year for city girls who lived up the stairs.* I feel as if I'm the intruder. This secret salon in the middle of the night. Outside, the warm gray lawn, the line of black cypresses. My mother dozing on the flimsy cloth chair, frail as a ghost in her nightie, hearing music she remembers with someone who's happy to share it or afraid if she goes to bed she might not wake. Her toenails have been painted dark blue. Sharen looks younger in the shifting light, the breeze from the window, her already messed-up hair.

"I can wait up for Reggie," I tell my mother, extend a hand to help her up. "Come on, alley-oop!"

"Cut it out," she says, shaking me off. "We weren't bothering you."

Sharen gives me a hard stoned stare then smiles. "We'll let Reggie in, Ruthie. Don't worry."

My mother regards us sleepily. "Well, if I'm not wanted," she says, struggling up with a hand on the lip of the bath, the dog scuttling from under her feet. She rests a hand on the windowsill for balance and stares at Sharen's arm, either at the doobie in her fingers or the bruise near her wrist that Sharen covers up with a hand.

"And look after her," says my mother and then I wonder

if she asked Sharen here for another reason, playing her cards to keep me. She wasn't a bridge whiz for nothing.

"Of course," I say as I usher my barefooted mother out into the hall. I watch as she touches the columns for balance, waves good night over her shoulder as she disappears around the turn.

SHAREN IN MY room with the candle and saucer, the spliff barely alive between fingers. She passes it to me and I take a drag like a pro between thumb and first finger, the end damp between my lips as I suck, the ease of the smoke down my throat till it tickles my lungs and I stifle a cough. I've forgotten how much I love this. Sharen amused as she sits on my bed. She places the candle on the side table. "Did you like the flowers?" she asks. The thought of her sneaking in while I dreamt of Isabel and I'm standing here pulling the last from her roach. How Isabel goes on about weed distorting time and memory, how she needs to be with someone who wants to be present, aware and whatever. Now I already feel the escape as I drag from the last of the blunt and Sharen collapses down on the bed. My mother's radio plays Harry Belafonte. *Brown-skin girl, stay home and mind baby.* The dog is in with us laid out by the open fireplace.

I ease the espadrilles off Sharen's dusty feet and I slide in behind her, my face in her already messed-up hair, her smell like an engine about to catch fire, the skunk and burnt sage smell of the smoke in her mixed with hairspray and dye, ether and ethanol, whatever is in them, paint and solvents.

Not a rose among them. I know this is crazy but I don't want to stop and the high is foggy and close to sublime.

"Pray for Reggie," she says. "I haven't seen him for days. I'm afraid Walker got to him for real this time." She turns her head and the sound of her breath makes it seem as if she's fading. My hand delving down under the skirt. No panties, not shaven or waxed like Isabel and her fancy Brazilians, but the full wiry bloom. I travel with my fingers to find Sharen's pinkness as the candle melts in on itself. Slip from my jeans and I'm pushing against her newly waxed thighs but her breath is a whistle. "Can I fuck you?" I whisper but she doesn't answer, nudges slightly toward me, opens and I make my way gently inside her, digging in softly. She moans her approval and I ply her deeply and even, keep watch out the uncovered window for her son.

"Can you take me away from here?" she whispers. "Take me to America?"

"Let's do it," I say as I rupture inside her, collapse down by her side.

* * *

WEDNESDAY

◆———◇———◆

We wake to the dog growling low in the gray light of morning. A mad kookaburra shriek then a deafening crash through the window, an echo on the headboard. Sharen grabs me by the arm, hauls me to the floor. We lie there wide-eyed, breathing into each other between the bed legs and the wall. The dog barks like crazy. Against the skirting lies a smooth stone the size of an egg. I reach for it, examine it in the faint light, an eye etched into the rock, the rough lines of the lids and a dug-out circle. Just a rock but I remember Walker stalking the sand hills in the bush, foxes and possums laid out in the night. It's heavy; the eye carved as if it's ancient, all-seeing, dug up from the land. Sharen with tears shining her eyes. She holds me, won't let me move, her lips warm against my rigid neck. "I brought this. It's my fault."

"I've brought it too," I say, this colliding. I brought it with me. But it doesn't mean Walker can watch between curtains then catapult rocks through the glass. "Lucky it wasn't a bullet."

"He's not normal," whispers Sharen.

"Really?" I feign surprise, listen for my mother to stir across the hall and realize her radio's off, no sound, only the dog who comes to sniff our faces. No morning birds in the trees, I pull the sheet down to cover her, crawl around shards like frosted leaves on the floor and look through the cracks that river from the hole in the glass like some distorted kaleidoscope flower. Nothing but morning. Horses grazing, a car passing along the road.

I go check on Ruthie, find her sitting alert in her bed, waiting. "It sounds like London in the Blitz."

"Walker," I tell her, hold the rock out as an exhibit in my hand and she reaches for it, looks right into the eye.

"The spoils of war," she says, strangely enlivened, the fire returned to her pupils.

Without asking permission, I close all the curtains, go to pick up the phone in the sitting room. The local police number's now been crossed out on the list on the wall, but it's in the front of the blue local phone book. A whiny receptionist transfers me to Sergeant Brent Gullikson, a name familiar from primary school.

"This is Daniel Rawson," I tell him. "Down at Tooradin."

"Yeah," he says gruffly. "I remember."

And I remember him, crying in a heap with a spider bite at school camp in Point Leo. When Mr. Stainer told him it was only a mosquito. "We've had some trouble out here on the farm," I say. "Someone threw a rock through a window." We speak as men, as if we don't remember.

"How big?" he asks.

"Big enough to kill somebody."

"Anyone dead or injured?" he asks.

"No."

"Bedroom window?"

Already I don't appreciate his tone. "Yes," I say reluctantly.

"Sleeping alone?"

"My mother's in her eighties," I say. "She lives here on her own. It could have done her in."

He clears his throat slowly. "Well I suggest you come in and make a statement or sort it out amongst yourselves." I can feel his smirk, this small-town mean shit. Standing in the dark room with everything already bright outside, the angry sound of Eazy-E, *Fuck de po-lice, fuck de po-lice*, runs through my mind.

"I'll do that, Bent," I say, his nickname from primary school after he showed some other kid his hard-on. I dial Deneray the carpenter, ask if he can come back and reglaze a broken window.

Then I am alone in a T-shirt and boxers wondering how the fuck I'm here, not in my office for a bit on the last day of the year, a conference call and then early lunch at the bar with a colleague at Chaya, heading to meet Isabel for dinner. The eye of vengeance on that rock.

Panicked, I try Isabel but it rings straight to the machine. "It's me. I'm all fucked up. Call me," I say and listen as it records me breathing. "Please."

I turn to find Sharen in the hallway watching, shrouded in the sex-soiled bedsheet. She stalks back up the hall, the sheet sagging behind her, getting caught on the arm of the pew. "Don't tread on the glass," I call behind her as she lets the sheet fall and walks nude to the room alone. I feel an awkward kinship with my father, caught mid-sentence on this phone. An early ingredient of his decline, his Gentleman's Guide to Losing Everything began with such small cruelties.

I check outside to be sure the rental car's undamaged, tempted to grab the key and jump in and drive. Track down my cousin Jenny near Great Western or Susie up in Kingaroy, let everything here return to its usual lunacy, an old woman quietly dying, grass in the autumn, horses weaving about the black skeleton of car. But now there's an angry nude woman in my bedroom to whom I made a mad orgasmic promise. I delay the inevitable for a minute, find a dustpan and brush and an old cork board behind the spare fridge, scoop up the sheet as I head up the hall. But back in the bedroom the unbroken window's wide open. Sharen's gone.

My mother appears, already dressed, as I clean up the floor. She examines the rent in the headboard, takes the catapulted stone from the bedside table then. "They seem to be breaching the walls," she says, looks up at the repair in the ceiling. "What did you do with Sharen?"

Now I see Sharen took back the flowers. "How come she was over here last night?" I ask.

"When I was on the loo she knocked on the bathroom window," my mother says. "Told me she was looking for Reggie." She sits on the bed and looks at the tumbler of murky flower water. "I'm a mother too," she says. "I know what it's like to lose a son."

I don't look up as I brush the last splinters of glass into the pan and toss them into the unlit fireplace.

"Don't put them there," she says. "Glass doesn't burn."

"That's the least of our problems," I say, lean the corkboard over the busted window and lie on the bed beside my mother in her Levi's, to wait until the carpenter comes. The ornate plaster molding, the headless cherub in the middle of the ceiling. I look over at this woman who delivered me, helped me learn to keep my anger deep.

She picks up the tumbler of flower water. "It's New Year's Eve," she says, drops the rock in the glass. Then she lies down on the bed beside me. "What should we do?"

"Wait for the return of the prodigal Reggie."

"At least he's loyal," she says, gets up to leave. "Poor unfortunate Miss Venezuela."

As I watch her leave, the magnified eye of the stone stares out at me from the green-tinged water.

A HALF-SLEEPING DREAM of a town, Poughkeepsie or Buffalo, somewhere it's cold, or maybe it's Russia? Dark Orlov horses galloping down through clusters of snow-covered trees, a provincial city on fire. A city where Isabel lives now, but she's nowhere in the streets. Just mongrel dogs that bay like wolves. Then I wake and it's Pip out on the veranda yelping, the thunder of hooves. Wary of stones, I jump to my feet and glance out the good window. The carpenter patiently waiting, leather-gloved, ready.

As I let him in he seems embarrassed that I'm only in

my jeans. "Sorry I'm so late," he says. "Had a job in Narre Warren. Took all damn day."

"What time is it?" I ask. All I hear is the television from the sitting room behind me, and before me, a large pane of glass in wooden casing in the back of Deneray's truck.

"Six," he says.

"Jesus!" On the floor half the night then fucking away the fear and confusion, sleeping through the day. Everything upside down. This outbackwards land.

"Jesus is real, Mr. Rawson," he says, observing me nervously; a half-naked unsaved lord of the manor, losing track of time. I precede him into the bedroom to pull up the Sharon-smeared sheets. Afraid he might suggest I read the scriptures or come along to Bible study in Beaconsfield, I leave him to it.

"This too shall pass," he says as I go.

I don't tell him his quote's not from the Bible. And, anyway, what if it doesn't pass? The eye still watching from the glass of water. "Once you get it cut and installed," I tell him, "can you board up both windows properly and add a bolt to this bedroom door?"

On my way to shower, the blast of the television draws closer from the living room. My mother, I surmise, glued to the cricket. India or Pakistan. I peek in to see her face in case it isn't. She's sound asleep, her sensible brown leather shoes and her pale blue socks on the floor, her blue-veined feet crossed on the pouf. Maybe she's waiting for Reggie to come in from the heat and bathe them. The rise and fall of her soft floral shirt, her breathing seems normal, her expression still fierce, even in sleep, both oblivious and knowing.

I let the water run warm, rinse myself of the night and
the morning, the stream running down my face until all
the hot water is gone, and still I stay, imagine being under
a waterfall up in the Whitsundays, Dunk or Lizard Island,
the places where Americans go when they visit. Drifting on
my own along some tropical river, no Sharen or civilized,
earnest Isabel. If it was just me on my own so I could see
life clearly, maybe even be someone new. But how do you
shed the skin of a family, really? These arms already peeling from this angry sun. The gay Beverly Hills dermatologist told me, as he froze off eleven moles, that most of the
damage was already done, growing up here as a boy on a
farm. No hat, no screen, no nothing. Maybe a shrink would
say the same, and then what? That I need to be back here
to change, not just swanning around LA pretending like
everyone else. Still, the idea of *processing* and *child of origin
issues,* or *working it through*, whatever they call it, makes
my skin itch.

When Deneray's finished, I pay him his hundred and
thirty dollars. In Laurel Canyon it would be three times
as much, even with the exchange rate. I count the bright
colored bills; they feel like play money, think of the dull
greenbacks that all look the same, how the ones look just
the same as fifties. Everything lost in the shuffle. I can't be
truly here or there.

"Happy New Year, son," says Deneray. But I'm not his
son. I am my father's, I've proven that. The three black
horses have survived the night, watching me over the fence,
judge and jury. I go down to consult with them and they

lean toward me, smell my neck, taking turns to nuzzle me, working in their unusual unison. No squeals or bites just the scent of them like nothing else, their cautious gentility. If I could just have been raised by these dark creatures with hooves, perhaps there'd have been dignity. I had my own great ponies, George and Paddy, the pair of grays, and Thunderfella, who won "best educated under saddle" at Sydney Royal, even though he'd eat you alive if you wanted to catch him in the paddock. I come from carnivores.

FROM THE CAR, I see the dog nosing the air from beside the camellia, its farewell silent as the flowers, trotting behind as I roll down the drive, through the open gate by the stables. Thunderfella and Patch down near the Pond Paddock fence, shadows under the trees. Waiting to be stolen. I hope Reggie's okay out there. Armed with stones of his own. He's more a David than his father. I just hope he knows what he's doing.

I turn onto Langdon's Road with a quiet desire for violence. The sun dips low in the sky, my eyes peeled on the fields, for Sharen or Reggie or Walker, haunting me each in his own way. On Station Road, I pass the rickety fence of the caravan park. Music bumping. Everyone celebrating the last red sunset of the year. Booze artists by a barbecue in shorts and wife beaters, the dull far-off thud from the band starting up at the pub and the first light of trucks on the highway, their headlights wipe my eyes. Down here, as I hunt alone for Sharen amid some country white men singing "Rolling on a River." Last year I visited Isabel in Manhattan in the snow in the dizzying crowds of the unexpectedly sanitized Times Square. The glittering ball dropped to a roar as Usher ushered in the New Year and then we walked back downtown to the W on Union Square. In the room we drank champagne, watched *Pan's Labyrinth* and made love.

In the Tooradin Pub, the noise of the some local grease-haired band spreads out over the crowd, over the bar and the rows of dark bottles, the beer-sweat smell of the people. *Welcome to the Hotel California.* Really? Nothing changed since 1977, as if punk and hip-hop never existed. Cloudy collapsing over his pint, the only one not dancing. I take a flute of touted Tasmanian champagne from a tray that's waiting, swallow it fast, and lean up to the bar. It's so sweet it's almost undrinkable, the fizz running high in my throat as Mavis appears in a red hip-hugging Christmas dress, re-ties her plastic apron.

"Howdy," she says, clearing glasses from the bar. "Having fun yet?"

The sound of these people pretending it's midnight already, two girls dance as they play pinball, the low stench of beer in the carpet and the walls. The old fisherman's photos seem kind of lonely. Lonnie Ridges from the fire brigade moving against the rhythm of his dowdy Norwegian wife. Cloudy crouched beside me keeping watch over his beer and chips. I order a vodka martini, "Grey Goose, if you have it."

Don Barlee, his face so red he looks like a furious sheep, dancing with a girl I hope is his daughter, Jimmy

Saddler swinging around his wife who was always nice. No sign of Sharen when she said she'd be here. "Smirnoff, I'm afraid, love," says Mavis. She hands me the martini glass and I take a good gulp, feel the sweet fire of vodka in my throat. "That should cheer you up," she says. "The band's from down Warragul way." Her accent with that nasal barbed-wire twang.

"What are they called, Cold Storage?"

Behind the bar an ancient photo slipping sideways in its frame, a cow or an ox pulling a cart from a swamp. The beast being beaten with a branch. Now I remember the way vodka lowers that line between me and sadness, leaves a vague, unpredictable starkness. I think of my mother locked up in her mansion, the saddle of guilt, but I'm still relieved to be here.

Mavis gives me a wink with a blue-shadowed eye. "Let old acquaintance be forgot," she says.

"*Should* old acquaintance be forgot," says Cloudy, correcting her without looking up from his drink, and the band plays a version of Stephen Stills's "Love the One You're With." Maybe proximity is my problem. I feel myself getting restless, cruisy, the girl who leaned over the pinball machine is making her way to the floor. "How's it working out?" asks Cloudy. I look over as he runs his fingers through his sweaty hair, his bulbous beetroot nose. More couples dancing, the pinball girl joins a group of young single women doing faux mod moves in a group, raucously singing the lyrics. *Well there's a rose in a fisted glove, and the eagle flies with the dove.* The vodka is strong.

"Oh Sharen," says Cloudy, looks over with a wet-eyed blink, his bottom rims like bloody rivers. Everyone knows bloody everything. I look up at the fly strip hanging from a hook in the ceiling covered with tiny brown bodies, like a dead snake, then down to the purple veins of a plump woman dancing, flipping her cork sandals across the floor to slide her bare feet.

Concentration slip away . . . because your baby is so far away. I order a second martini and search through the crowd. Maybe Sharen was really upset. I resist the impulse to leave, why shouldn't I be here? I went to primary school with half these idiots. Bobby Genoni cheek to cheek with his wife Vicki, from a dairy farm down near Drouin. We used to call her Vicki Verka, as in vice versa. Elegant here in what looks like a swirling vintage Pucci dress, paisleys of blues and lime green, her hair "done up" for the occasion. I wonder what she'd look like nude. Long-legged, quiet, biding her time.

"Haven't seen your mother in here since we had that Back to Tooradin," says Cloudy.

"What's that?" I ask.

"She wore that pretty blue dress and her hair all permed up." He coughs into his sleeve. "How is the old girl?"

"Stubborn as a mule still kicking," I say. Left alone on her last new year on earth. I scold myself but tonight I'm not playing. I'm not who I was, the last boy on earth. Those shoes feel way too small. I finish the drink and order another.

Through the fray of bodies dancing, I catch sight of my father sitting down at a table on the far side where the jukebox was. He looks crumpled and sad, his dicky hips have him anchored to the chair. Poor old bugger. He used to get up and dance with anyone. He had his moves. Now all he has are his eyes out on sticks, alive with longing. A wife in one house and a girlfriend in the other. Still not enough. There are breeds of men who want more than they're entitled to and end up getting less. I fooled myself that I wasn't like them.

With the second martini flaming in my head, I weave through the group of carousing surfer girls beneath the red and purple disco ball, their tan legs and breasts made even darker, objects of my father's helpless stare. They boogie around me as I move with my drink held up in the air. The short one with beach-dyed hair smiles as I glance down at her cutoff jeans and Billabong sandals. "Hey," I whisper to her, head past to sit with my father. *Hey sister, go sister, soul sister, go sister.*

"G'day, son," says my father, toasts with his Pimm's as if he's glad I'm here. Two men alone while the whole world dances, our eyes hooked on the sight of three surfer girls threading their bodies, wheeling arms in the air and laughing, singing along. *Voulez-vous couchez avec moi ce soir?* Still in the seventies, the bass so loud the speakers drum the floor, no room for conversation. My father who still believes he's in with a chance, and I can't help checking out the Minogue-looking girl who noticed me. This is what we have in common. Flesh as an escape. *Coochi, coochi, yaya.* Sharen emerges from nowhere into the throng, shaking her tits, a pink bikini top under a short see-through blouse, a blue turquoise pendant that matches her eyes swings about dangerously, the same white mini that now has a gold-link belt, stamping her bare feet into the floor with the beat, joining the swirling surfer girls. Her nasty grind says she clocks me but she won't look, only at my father, sliding her feet across the sweat-and-beer-damp floor. *Voulez-vous couchez avec moi ce soir?* She tries to get my father up to dance and I feel the panic rise in me. Fucking Sharen. She knows he can barely stand, but he struggles up, eager to take her hand. I throw her a hard look but she pours all her goddamn into her grin bearing down on starstruck Earley. *Don't, Dad,* I want to warn him but he wouldn't want to hear as she drags him doddery and dangerous to the floor. He tries to keep balance as she pulls him, then he's out there trying hard to make his old moves, his smile seems false and otherworldly, his hips about to fail him, a body kept upright by the need in his eyes. Sharen swings about him, thrusts at him from behind, mocking, her gaze on me all hot and mean and what you gonna do about it? Braiding hope and hate and lust like a charm, then she leaves him out there on his own. She latches onto someone else who kisses her. My father puts on his silver-tooth smile, pretends it's funny as she moves on to yet another, makes my heart scramble up.

I weave through the smell of booze and armpits to retrieve him, put my arm around his bony shoulders and sit him back down as Mavis, who misses nothing, delivers us each a drink. As he raises the glass my father's hand is shaky in the purple light, he's pale and heaving, out of breath. "Dad, what if you went home?" I ask. "Spend the New Year with Elsie." I try to spot Sharen among the thrashing bogans.

He throws his head back, an attempt at a laugh. "You don't like the competition?"

I take a swig of fresh vodka. "Sharen was fucking with us," I tell him but the words don't even compute. For him attention is attention, however fleeting. An infusion of blood even though he looks totally drained of it. He waves like some tragic celebrity at English Dick the painter. The hotel thumping like a disembodied heart. *American woman, listen what I say-ay.* The canyon I can barely remember, the Christmas I could have had.

"I can't bear to watch you gawking at those girls," I say.

"You sound like your mother," he says.

If only I wasn't like you. Too drunk to get into it with him, I should go outside into the warm salt air, but the band begins a rendition of Prince's "1999" and I make out Sharen in the crowd, above it, lifted high and swung about by a tall city guy in a black polo shirt and a square shovel beard. I lurch through flinging arms, weave past the surfer girls to grab Sharen by the wrist. Her bracelet stabs my sore hand. "How dare you do that to my father," I shout and her face goes mean with disgust.

"You did it to me," she says, her blue eyes and red-smudged lips. Disgust at ourselves and each other, reeling away I let her hand go and she throws her arms around the guy, then turns. "Fucking Rawsons, think you can have everything," she spits at me, kisses his big beard mouth.

Hazy with Smirnoff and loose on my feet with the beating guitar. "What are you even doing here?" I yell. "Fucking Ned Kelly wannabe." But he's puffing up for a fight and I almost fall as I try to slug first, catch sight of Bobby Genoni bursting through, florid eyes and sunburned nose. It's his fist from the side that sends me to the floor.

BEING CARRIED THROUGH the parking lot, the thrum of frogs, Lonnie Ridges at my feet, the red sheep eyes of Don Barlee above me, surrounded by stars. My father limps along beside, reaches to touch my arm. "I'm okay, Dad," I tell him, my head as if it has nails inside it, the stitches seeping in my hand. I close my eyes. My skull seems to throb beneath my skin.

"I'll look after him," a woman's voice. "Earley, you go home."

Shoved in the front of a plush leather seat, someone getting in with keys on a chain with a silver tractor. Vicki Genoni with the kindness in her made-up eyes. "You boys are like children!" she says. I want to tell her I haven't been plastered in years, haven't been in a fight since I left here, since I punched her husband just the other day. She fishes past me into the glovebox, pulls purple Handi Wipes from a container. "That Sharen Wells." She shakes her head in disbelief.

I try to apologize for ruining her New Year's but I can't seem to speak. The car clock says it's only 11:11. It smells of orange oil and sanitizer. A Lexus with a burled

wood interior. I dab my oozing hand with the moist tow-
elette, think of Isabel trying to keep things clean. Where
she might be now—if she witnessed this she'd be gone for
good and ever.

As we cross the highway, past the eerie black inlet, I
wonder if I'd have married a woman like Vicki would I have
stayed? Been comfortable or miserable or even happy. "That
Sharen Wells," I repeat like a retard, who turned on my
father and me. Who wouldn't blame her?

"Poor woman," she says with strange compassion. Does
she have no idea? Bobby inviting Sharen to stay with them
after she lit the car on fire. Bobby probably poking her in
the spare room. I pat the side of my head for signs of blood;
examine the wipe for evidence in my hand. The tiniest spot.

"Are you a Christian?" I ask.

"I try to be," she says and I wonder if there's something
in it. A road to generosity, this kind of heartfelt samaritan-
ism. If one can't be like that anyway. She makes me feel so
obsessed with myself, slumped here like a carcass. Rising bile
that makes me think I might need to open the door. The sight
of the crowd still at the caravan park, their fire now in a drum.
It makes me nauseous, Ruthie left alone. "Poor devils," says
Vicki, seeing the shadows. I don't ask if her belief stretches
to the devil or hell. That's when it all gets crazy. I just hope
Walker's there on a stump with a beer among his fellow itin-
erants. When I'm drunk on my ass, beat on the head by this
woman's old man. Trying not to lose it on her fancy dashboard.

"How are you faring?" asks Vicki and I appreciate her
choice of words. We pass the half-fallen sign for Wedding

Bush Road, the turn to that godforsaken cottage, and I wonder where Reggie is now.

"Bobby got me this time," I tell her, try to make light of it, my croaking voice precarious, the tender spot on the side of my head. I feel for swelling under my hair.

"He just envies you," says Vicki, turning into the drive, the big house barely lit on the hill. "The one who got away."

She parks her Lexus by the dome of the underground tank. Water saved for fires when there's none to keep the garden alive. "Would you like to have gotten away?" I ask.

"It's good for me here," she says and I feel an unusual contentment. People who live without the restless need for elsewhere, different, more.

"Will you be all right?" she asks as I climb out in pieces, like my father does, but I'm half his age. Standing as if my blood runs weak.

"Thanks, Vicki, I'll manage," pat the top of her shiny roof. The moon a gold cradle low in the sky beyond it. A shape on one of the slated gables above the house, a tall, pale bird, a heron come inland, spreads its wings and flies off, coalesces with the night. Unsure if I'm imagining, I kneel in what could be confused with prayer and vomit in a rosebush.

Wait up in this casuarina to keep watch out for Walker. Close my eyes and ask for Uncle Worry dead for years but I still see him. Watery eyes all deep and droopy, I seen him in photos years back. On this farm. Shut my eyes and imagine him coming down with old lawmen from Gundagai, their chests chalked white and red with clay, they'll leave their trucks and piss their fire, come looking for me when the moon gets up. Amazing how the old men run, almost as if they are floating. No one even notice them in the windbreaks, the old ones coming. Karadji in his coat. Won't let Walker hurt Ruthie or drag me back to Yarram stealing horses, ride for miles at night with just a bridle through farms and up into the hills until he has enough to send to the killers, disguise them all by cutting manes and paint them Appaloosa with my dots. And I feel Worry whisper, Move Reggie. They come run cross-country, old men. Makes Reggie wanna lie down in the clearing and cover himself in feed sacks. But Worry in the wattles whooping as if he's some extinct bird to warn me how Walker comes wild to brute me, tie me in the back of a truck. Hear the three black horses canter through the ground and make my run as they do to protect me. Worry sing me past, make me shoes so soft all covered in feathers and leave no trace like a stone into the hollow of a neck. Just hope they get here in time.

RUTHIE SLEEPS AND I'm still shit-faced. Curl up on something soft, the dog's sheepskin beside her bed. I collapse into sleep, dream of a lightning storm and horses plowing through barbed wire, their chests ripped open, running through the halls, a wind that drags up the giant pine at its roots and makes a huge cave that swallows all the cattle. Then I wake to a rattling wind on the glass and the rumble of hooves. Struggle up with a foul taste in my mouth and the side of my face already swollen. In the front hall, I lean and peer through the pain in my eyes, out the leadlight on the door. A figure with a stick? In the darkness I can't tell. I sway to the door and the moon comes out from behind the sky, a dark silhouette staring out at the shadows. "Fuck off," I yell, squinting to see. "All of you."

A quick knock on the door. "Daniel, it's me, Reggie." Pleading.

He's never said my name before. I open the door to turn on the porch lamp but he stops me. All I make out are the long-shanked cypresses roiling in a crazy wind, and the boy—shirtless, standing on one leg as if he's guarding the house. "What is it?"

As though he sees what I can only hear: the horses snorting, bumping up along the post and rail, the thud of cattle, the earth reverberant. As if the paddocks might rise up and explode. I grab for some boots.

"Stay here," says Reggie. His hand on my arm, warm and light and the hot moist air feels heavy against me; I try to crawl back into my skin. The call of a bird almost human. I feel him strain to see. A clacking like horses trotting on cement.

"We should check the stock," I hiss.

"No."

Normally, the word would scorch me silent, being ordered about like that, but tonight the blackness seems too weird and alive, the horses and trees all coupled together. Then I notice his leg is wrapped in a shirt. "Are you all right?" I ask. The back of his neck glistens with sweat in the moonlight.

"Got cut," he says, "but I got away." As he turns he wrinkles up as though whatever happened really scared him.

A loose branch sweeps across the lawn then a white flash. A white pony canters past, out on the drive. Is it one of the missing? Gates must be open. I feel as though I'm losing my bearings or haven't quite woken. Passed out somewhere in a ditch. But Reggie doesn't shift from the steps, half in and half out, beneath the lip of the veranda, and something rolls close by, behind the trees. A birdcall then the shadows half-open and the mouth of the wind bears a thing in the air that glints and Reggie buckles. He cups his stomach as I crouch beside him. The pungent smell of his sweat and the fear in it, blood vessels burst in his eyes. "Slingshot," he says, his voice has a quaver. "I'm okay," he says but I can tell he isn't. He reaches out for the small rounded rock in the dirt and tries to stand. "He's trying to . . . " wiping his eyes on the back of his hand. I herd him back into the house as another stone ricochets off a veranda post, the sound of a tuning fork, the hollow iron column.

Reggie limps up into the hall where the light from Ruthie's room drapes out on the shape of her standing in her nightgown, squinting and disoriented. He turns away, not wanting her to see him crying and now I can see his leg, blood seeping through his shirt. I close the door and lock it. He tries to stand straighter but he's clearly unable, his young skin scalloped about his eyes, cradling his bare ribs. "We been checking on things, me and Daniel."

She searches our faces, looks down at the whittled piece of wood Reggie leans on, the one she threw in the water. He covers the stain on his leg with a narrow hand. "You both look pale as ghouls," she says. I take her brittle fingers in my hand and they feel cold and bony, and I feel as if everything's swaying. Through the leadlight window, the shadows play games in the wind; a branch chafes at the corrugated roof. "Horses are loose; it's gone wild out there."

My mother straightens a picture of herself on the drop-side table. She's in the past, as a girl, jumping high over a wide triple bar at the old Ranelagh Club. "You two can sort him out," she says. She puts the book, *The Ropes of Time,* facedown on the chair in the hall.

"I'm calling the cops," I say and Reggie's face falls.

"Family business," my mother says. "Anyway, it's New Year's. They wouldn't get here for a week." She heads back to her room, a hand on the doorjamb for balance.

"You should'na done my mother," says Reggie, sweat in his eyes. "He don't like it was you."

I try not to nod as I move down the hall; the house seems to roll like a ship.

"The police will take me," says Reggie.

"And what will Walker do?"

"Wants me to catch the horses. Ride them to the hiding yards. Truck comes. Takes them off." I imagine Bobby Genoni's Cousin Angel from Meeniyan in some old green Bedford, the loading ramp on the side.

"Can't you just run away?"

We jump at the sight of a skewbald pony in the main dining room. Reggie looks at me doe-eyed, as if it isn't his fault. A pony and a piano. I touch the new swelling on the side of my head; try to get my eyes to focus. What world is this I've fallen into? I find the number for the Pakenham police on the list, the new one I added. As I pick up the receiver to dial, Reggie limps toward me.

"We're under threat." I tell the operator, but a sound, a shot or a stone, comes crashing through the stained-glass window. I kneel for cover as Reggie reaches and places the stick across the switch hook. "We're at Tooradin Estate," I say but the line's gone dead.

"Ruthie said no police," he says, collapses in my mother's chair, nursing his stomach, and Patch, my mother's pony, now stands in the hall, come out from the dining room to see what's happened.

"Pip's gone," my mother says, appearing down the hall with what at first looks like a large cane but as she enters the room I see it's the Winchester. "Under my bed for fifteen years, waiting for nights like this." She sits on a stool by the fire and leans the gun against the bookcase, studies Reggie. I don't know if the rifle's even loaded and I'm not exactly sure where Reggie's hurt, but he grimaces in a stab of pain. "He needs a doctor," I say.

"I heal myself," he says and he turns, motions instinctively into the kitchen. Out the window a red light flashes in the bush, then two. Taillights. Somehow he sensed the movement way out there.

"I'll guard Reggie," my mother says in her nightgown. "He's done nothing wrong. You go see what they're up to."

The pain returns to my head. "So I'm to be sent out to the slaughter." I don't admit my condition. "We need an ambulance," I tell her. "And police protection."

"You're not in America now," says my mother.

"I'll go, Ruthie," says Reggie, wincing as he tries to get up. Blood seeps through a knife tear in his jeans.

"No you won't," she says. She shifts the gun around so the barrel passes the dark television toward me. "If Daniel wants this land, he'll go out and protect it."

Reggie passes me the walking stick as if it might bring luck.

OUTSIDE, THE BLACKNESS drapes me. Ibis squawk from their roosts in the trees in a wind that's turgid again, laced with a soft whinny, and I can just make out the vague outlines of the big horses, ears pricked on high alert along the fence, watching the red lights in the distance. Not as drunk as I was but it's a strange, potent feeling as I walk toward the black horses. Walker's truck arriving, maybe a group of them corralled out in the bush. I could at least get the license number of the lorry, track them down that way.

I traverse the garden, trip over a bucket by the clothes-line, the carved stick and a hooked carpet knife I managed to grab on my way through the boot room, imagining yonnies being slung at me through the night. The rabbit burrows in the earth are traps, but I remember these pad-docks like the fingers of gloves. The three horses braid into the sable air behind me, as an oddly festive entourage—following me as they did Reggie. They won't let themselves be taken easily. Silence, save for the sounds of their hooves in the grass and snuffling, an odd humming in the Center Paddock wind, the faint shapes of skittish cattle. The stick in my hand, useless as a tennis racket, but adrenaline drives me now, clearing out my head. Running, imagin-ing a whistling spear in the wind behind me as I used to, running as a kid from *The Red Chief*, the book from school with the clever chief Gunnerah, the Red Kangaroo. And still the silent red lights.

At the windmill gate, two of the black horses stop short together behind me; the bigger gelding disappeared. The tin vanes whine in the windmill above the brick tank as I strain at a shadow high up on its edge where Reggie had tracked me the first night. Now a figure appears, poised up on that thin line of bricks, there for a second, then gone. I'm still as the fence posts, training my eyes, unsure what's real and what's drunk. The stick clenched two-fisted like a bat at the ready, the remaining two horses, my guardians, not spooked at all now the image has gone, then I hear a clacking sound—a few wary heifers down near the trough, the rattle of their hooves and another red-orange flicker in the bush. A shape's up ahead in the dark and I blink through the sweat that curtains my eyes as I remember riding a train on the Nullarbor, mesmerized by the row of giant emus crossing the horizon, discovering later it was just tumbleweeds, a mirage. Sleights of the wind, shimmerings. But something here feels uncanny, my breathing too loud in my ears.

The horses move forward, inquisitive now, and the figures shift too, half-seen then unseen, playing with me. I sway, try not to betray myself, steady. Another vision, a trunk and a star-flowered wedding bush, the sound of whining. Pip chained up, pawing at a rope harness tied round his face. Happy to see me as I dash to him, slowly use the hook knife, cut electrician's tape acting as muzzle, careful not to stab him. Why would the leave him like that? A shrill whistle and the whoosh of something, maybe a stone, a figure moving through the field and I don't care if it's real or dreamed. I sprint after the dog as he races to the cottage, leaping over fallen logs and rotted posts. Running to scramble the rail into Sharen's garden. Banging on the door, I kick it wide, heaving for air and standing in a living room still bare save a chair and the lamp and Reggie's graffiti. Surprised to see Sharen here on the bedroll alone, in shorts and T-shirt, no longer in bikini and see-through, but she has a sling about her shoulder, as if she's fractured an arm. She holds a baby bottle and in the sling a tiny wallaby cradled in sheepskin, its brown eyes staring at the panting dog that tries to sniff about its narrow face. "What are you doing here?" Sharen asks.

"Reggie," I gasp, my head pounding, I can hardly hear my voice. "He's hurt," I say. "Taillights . . . he shot him. Slingshot." Hands on my knees as I struggle for air. "His own son."

Her mouth tightens, she won't look at me. She puts down the bottle, walks to the window, balancing the animal, the dog jumping up at it. The floorboards stained with wallaby piss and engine grease. She parts the curtains and glances outside. "Where is he?"

"With Ruthie," I say. "Up in the big house. She has a gun."

She unfolds the creature from her homemade pouch and puts it down quickly, as though it was another woman I was yelling at on the dance floor. Her naked legs shine from her frayed shorts. The dog stalks the joey as it hops in slow motion, unevenly, long back legs and tail, hare-like face. Sharen looks out into the night, at the hill of stringy eucalyptus, presses her lips together as though deciding something. "Sometimes he imagines things," she says. "That Aboriginal stuff about pointing the bone." She reaches for the mantel, finds her cigarettes but doesn't take one. Instead she hugs herself. I notice there's a shake in her hand and it makes me want to comfort her as she leans down for her boots. "He gets paranoid sometimes," she says. A ripple in her voice and the way she won't look at me, I can't be sure what's real. She was worried enough the other night, or was that just a ploy? Her savory scent and the wallaby smell, I hug Pip to me. "One time he was up north with Walker and wanted to visit Gracious's grave. Somewhere near Junee. But Reggie said these Abos drove through and took him prisoner, drove to a place way up near Wilcannia." I think of the map on the wall in school. A long way, on the road to Menindee. Burke and Wills. "He just disappeared."

I think of my own imaginings, running around this farm as a boy, and now. "Well he didn't imagine being hit by a slingshot," I say. "I saw it happen and then I found Pip tied up with his mouth taped."

She grabs the baby animal and launches it quietly outside, into the open carport and lets it hop away. I keep hold of the dog so it doesn't follow. "I thought Reggie'd be safe here," says Sharen, tying laces.

The gnarl of a truck changing gears, its lights through the trees, low red stars. Is this some game they're playing to scare us away, some settling of scores? But Sharen seems panicked now too as I head out into the blackness and reach for an old Queensland bridle from its hook beside the outdoor fridge. "How bad is he?" she asks.

I comb the dark for those black horses. "I have no idea." One horse alone by the garden fence, the mare with the white on her face. It unnerves me how they're not together, how she's way back out here. She doesn't shy away as I pull the bridle over her crown, the familiar feel of dry leather and my thumb in her wet mouth to open it, the jingle of the bit against her teeth. Quickly, I adjust it to fit then buckle the throat latch, hoist myself up. Sharen looks up at me, wanting to come.

"Climb the fence," I tell her, sidle the mare's haunches over. "Grab my arm." I help her straddle up in front of me, holding mane, and feel her heart beat against my chest.

"Thank you," she says. Finally her frailty, weary and scared in my arms, as we jig through the darkness, up to the Lagoon Paddock hill in a wide black windy silence.

"We're being watched," she whispers, her hair in my face. And I can feel it too. The other horses just behind us now, falling in line and all I see is the quivering grass and the dog up ahead, as if I'm riding into a kind of vanishing time. Shadows seem to fling above us and Sharen clings to me as the ibis, like slow-flying planes, flap off their perches in the trees beyond the house and the missing black horse gallops in from nowhere. Both the big geldings now flanking in triangle formation. The mare's head is high, her mouth hard as iron, as Ruthie with the gun. I raise my hands above the level of her jaw and check her, calm her, and then I smell smoke. It could be a campfire, some illegal New Year's party over the road.

I click the mare forward, up to the fence line. One gelding rears and the other one spooks from behind. "We'd have heard if a fire was headed this way," says Sharen. It's true; we'd have smelt it, there'd have been smoke coming down through Tynong North, across the flats at Nar Nar Goon, this region dry as straw. "It's got to be him," she says.

"Jesus fuck me," I say, slide us both down from the horse.

As I round the servants' quarters, the horses set loose, I see flames rising high from the cypress trees, streaks of them purple and red, the row of old papery trunks that climb straight to the sky then plume. The fire whips up them just lengths from the house. Then I see my eighty-three-year-old mother in a nightgown and gumboots on the lawn, brandishing the hose. "Call the fire brigade. You can't fight this on your own, are you crazy?"

"Well, you weren't bloody here." She doesn't want to give up the hose.

"Where's Reggie?"

"Told him to stay inside."

I find the rickety extension ladder from the veranda, lean it up against the spouting, and climb, yelling at Ruthie: "Pass me the hose." My mother looks up at me almost as if this is thrilling, fighting a fire together. As if she doesn't care if she's incinerated. "Then fill the buckets from the tap," I yell, but as I climb the ladder it pitches, shifting in the wind, the rungs seem too narrow. A limb cracks loud as it falls, the trees exploding. I look down and it's Sharen steadying the ladder's base.

"I got you," she yells. I hook my elbow through the ladder frame as my mother lifts the hose toward me. The water bubbles in spasms, dry air smarting in my eyes. The high limbs are catching, the flames lick the bark. If the wrong branches break, they'll fall and be blown on the house like matches. Maybe Walker wants to flush Reggie out of the house. I irrigate the roof as best I can, hoping my mother's gone inside to make the call or someone smells smoke soon. Water blowing back, spitting in my face, the ladder not well enough moored in the dirt. It feels shaky but Sharen holds it down with all her might, the flames curl up the trunks like snakes. She can't look up.

"Go check on Reggie," I yell as I climb even higher, crawl over the gutter and onto the uneven bullnose of the roof. "I'm okay now." The hollow of the tin veranda beneath me, where I teetered as a kid. The taste of burning on my breath and mushrooming smoke stings my eyes. These trees my father's wanted to fell for twenty years, my father who's not here, the upper branches crackling, embers fanned by a quick vicious wind. The sudden snap of a limb sounds like another shot and I scream down at my mother but she can't hear. "Call the fucking fire brigade." With a sack, she slaps at a branch burning on the lawn, the roof so slick with water I have to kneel on the slant to get to the ladder, wanting to climb down and help her, but a high flame from the trees has me standing again. Dousing all I can to save the roof. Sharen is still out there, pointing up past me. "Find Reggie," I shout but the wind has subsided all of a sudden and an ember floats past me as a silent guided moth. I moor myself and spray at the eaves where the ember nestles, and then I glimpse another phosphorous hint of orange.

"Come down," shouts Sharen.

"Call Bobby," I yell back, my lungs stinging, pull my shirt up over my nose and mouth. I make out shapes through the smoke—cattle? The old dome tank left full of stagnant water waiting for a night like this, but where is my father and where's the pump? Just like him to forget the essentials. My mother down there in just her nightie, smudging the ground with her sack, losing her balance and then going back at it. Now Reggie appears from out in the night and the smoke like a wraith. His hands slack by his sides. He wasn't inside at all.

THE SIREN BAWLS along Langdon's Road toward us. Sharen dragging Reggie back inside; doubled over, that slashed leg not holding weight. Wish I hadn't left his stick at the cottage. The red light whirs up the drive. Men jump from the wagon—Lonnie Ridges and the Saddler boy. They scurry across the fire-lit lawn with extinguishers on their backs, lights from their helmets, self-important, when the night is bright with fire.

Bobby Genoni appears, suited up and meaty, along with another, their hoses unspooling. Great cascades of water blast the flame-ridden trees. Bobby doing what we couldn't. We did need him, dammit. I just wonder who called—not Ruthie, that's for sure. She sits on the top veranda steps, her nightdress sooty and her hair all out at angles and watches. First one tree doused black and then another; the force of the hose shoots a wet branch to the ground. I climb down and sit aching and breathless on the brick arms of the steps, useless, my throat a furnace from the smoke, my head and hand throbbing. We should have just let it burn, opened the gates and let the place go to the devil. Not let the town rescue us like this. Two old codgers and an absent son with lawyers' hands and product in his hair.

A patch of my mother's sparrow face is lit by a last surge of flame. Alive in her eyes. "Look," she says as Pip appears, skulking along the wall. He sidles to her, crouches low as she pats him, the dull shapes of firemen moving through the smoke, their yellow jackets grayed by ash as they drench branches, soak the charcoaled trunks.

My hand and head pulse in unison. I rub my watering eyes. "What was Reggie doing out here?"

My mother picks at dry grass that's grown through cracks by her feet. I imagine the house a blackened ruin, smoking for days. Relief mixed with horror, the thought of it gone. These mosaic veranda tiles in the rubble. Ornaments igniting on the dried-out Christmas tree, the dining room portraits in flames. Aunt Emma Charlotte melting down the wall. I picture seven chimneys remaining, a charred labyrinth. Ashes sprouting weeds and ants returning with the rain. But the opposite is happening, there will be no relief. Bobby Genoni, his fist still alive in the swelling under my hair, irrigates the last of the fleshy orange branches. Saving us from ourselves. "Did you really not call them?" I ask my mother.

She looks over at me as if she had more important things to do. "They came, didn't they?" she says. Where would she go if we were burned out of here? I can't imagine her anywhere but here. Then I notice the kerosene canister from the laundry, by the side door. My mother sees it too.

"That's mine," she says, she pushes herself up and wanders over, holds the wall for a second, leans to grab the can. She doesn't look back as she tucks it under her arm, takes the dog inside. Did she light the trees, or is she covering for Reggie? It doesn't make sense, unless she's gone loopy. She once told me that when she was a girl at Carbrook she lit a grass fire as an experiment, to see if she could put it out with a sack. How the wind came up and the flames nearly got away. The look of fervor in her eyes as she sat on the step tonight. I don't know how to read her anymore.

THE HOLLOW SOUND of high-pressure water on the roof right above me, Bobby posturing on the dark night lawn in triumph, almost wetting me from the gutters. I get up and nod my appreciation at him, wish I could give him the finger. "I'll get you guys some beer," I shout to the ghosts of them in the thinning smoke.

Sharen kneels over Reggie, now lying on the couch. She sings softly in his ear. One hand cups his tight sunken belly; the other rests on his narrow chest where there's some illegible tattoo. The gamey smell of him mingles with smoke and the resinous Christmas tree drying out in the corner. She's wrapped his thigh in a towel packed with iced peas. *Choku Ray, Honshu Say,* she sings, or something like it. Her shorter-cut hair as it falls about her ears, the way she concentrates. I've never seen her with Reggie, as attentive and worried, as mother, her boy unnervingly frail.

The boot room fridge is empty so I take two jugs of lime cordial out as the guys take off their hats and sit down on the wagon's running board, sooty-faced, exhausted. The fire engine running. "Sorry, fellas, we're out of beer."

"No worries," says the Saddler boy, guzzles straight from a jug then toasts. "Tooradin, Tooradin, oi, oi, oi."

I raise the other jug and hand it to Bobby. "Thanks for getting out here."

"That's what we do," he says and chugs.

"Deliberately lit, it looks like," says Lonnie gazing out at the remains with a quiet authority.

"Walker Dumbalk, most likely," says Bobby Genoni, wiping dirty water from his mouth. "Settling his dues."

"It's a miracle none of us is dead," I say. This place of old feuds. Reggie inside being cradled back to life.

"Not yet," says Bobby and laughs, pours the rest of the cordial over his face. That same thick-set hand that met my skull just hours ago.

"This place makes LA seem peaceful," I say and they laugh as if that's praise.

Bobby offers back the empty jugs. "See you in the soup," he says.

"Happy fucked-up New Year," I say in a glib kind of truce, the way we country people pave over the fury and yet it still hovers in our eyes. Minimized, in waiting. I hate who I am when I'm here.

I wash my own face in the kitchen, listen to the fire-truck leaving and wonder where Walker is now. In the living room, Reggie doesn't look good. Rivulets of sweat on his brow, down the side of his small flat nose, the tendons taut on his neck. Sharen's hand where it was on his chest, on this very couch where I lay as a boy, with mumps and measles. The same moth-eaten red and purple blanket that was supposed to protect the sofa from the dog now over Reggie's unshod feet.

"The stone could have ruptured his liver," I say. Firemen are not trained as paramedics here or else I'd have granted them entry. "He needs to be in hospital."

Sharen doesn't show she heard me, doesn't open her eyes, keeps on with her humming, gripping Reggie's arm as if to hold him conscious. "His body is processing things," she says. His breathing is labored, pushing up shallow against his bony sternum. The amount of his sweat seems unnatural.

"We need a doctor." I say it too loud, lift the frozen peas and examine his thigh. A shallow knife wound where the skin has broken, a livid pink strip against brown skin. A new river of sweat runs down his cheek and I think of that rock appearing from the moonlessness.

"This isn't doctor stuff," she says. "This is bad magic. Doctor can't do nothing about this."

"But—he's got a fever. Let's at least get him a tetanus shot." In America we'd all be in hospital by now. But Sharen's here tracing symbols in the air, jagged boxes and zigzags, my mother shakily emerging with a new saucepan of water and a facecloth, places them down on the magazine table.

I know I should call the ambulance but there'd only be a struggle, Sharen fighting for the boy. "Why would his own father do this?" I ask, think of the time my father threw a hammer at me but that was just blind fury, he wasn't hunting me down.

"Walker," says my mother. "Doesn't like him here with us." She leans with an elbow on the mantel, among the figures of the drab wood-carved nativity, rubbing her index finger against her thumb the way she does.

I think of Walker out there. "So who actually lit the fire?"

"What difference does that make now?" she says.

I wonder if all fathers secretly hate their sons just a little. "Where's the Winchester?" I ask.

Sharen shushes me. "You're safe," she whispers to her son. "All's over." She scoops air from the top of his head and his throat, as if clearing him of something, and there are tears in the corners of his bloodshot eyes. I want to comfort him too, he looks so scared, but I know it's more important to get him to Emergency than let him die here bathed in prayer and hoodoo.

"Tell him he's all right," says Sharen, smoothing his matted hair. He opens his eyes for a second, groans slightly, and Sharen searches my face. "Tell him he can have the land."

"I beg your pardon?" I ask. When he's already tried to finagle a chunk of it. The self-witnessed codicil.

"Look at him," she says. "You can give him this."

His skin so dull, a slatey gray, and he's squinting up at me from under the cloth on his forehead. I don't know what's real, if I'm being set up. To what lengths would these people go? Am I supposed to offer something then take it back, the way my father did to Walker twenty years ago, that started this whole thing?

"I won't do that," I say, feel myself close up into a fist. Yet I remember the relief that flooded me as I pictured the place burnt down to the chimneys.

Sharen fixes on me, a blue-green agitation bright in her eyes. "You don't understand about healing," she says. Reggie getting better by getting what he wants? What *she* wants? When I thought she wanted to come away with me.

Reggie's hair is wet with sweat, his eyes fallen shut, the lids shine: he's folding into himself.

"For Christ's sake let me drive him to the hospital," I say, lean down to pick him up but Sharen swipes my arm away with a ferocity that matches her eyes.

"You don't understand anything," she says, stabs me with a mean stare.

I think of the Lancaster girl at the Cranbourne gymkhana whose parents were Christian Scientists, how they refused treatment and the daughter died right there in the tent. I plead with Sharen to let me. "Don't let him die," I tell her. *Not here.*

"I'm his mother," she says. "I'm the one who says."

"Leave him," says Ruthie and I turn at the clarity and reason in her voice. A reasoning I don't understand.

"I did what I had to," whispers the boy and there's a tingling on the roof; this time it's not the hoses but the unlikely sound of rain. First it sizzles in the trees, then tumbles on the slate. My mother heads to the window. No one mentions it in case it stops. The old superstitions. Even Sharen knows.

"What were you going to say?" whispers Sharen. "About the land." She caresses Reggie's woody hand and maybe she truly wants for her son. I think of the disingenuous promise I made to take her away as I fucked her, that lit up her body and made me come. I look to Ruthie, it's her house; she's not dead yet. She nods at me, scratches dry skin on the top of her hand.

"Reggie, you can have the cottage." I look over at my mother and think about the will she tried to change. What she wanted. "And the bush block."

"The whole place, Daniel," my mother says. "Unless you're going to stay."

The chimneys, the portraits, the burnt car, the black horses. "It's too much for him," I say. "This way he can live in the roof or wherever he wants, paint all the pictures with dots." Stand outside with a stick, if he has to. "But the farm is too much for him, Walker would take it away."

"Don't worry about Walker," she says.

Reggie breathing more easily and I feel my own breath rest in my throat. The fire gone and now there's rain.

"We'd make it work," says Sharen, reaches out to touch my hand, the anger turned to yearning in her blue-green eyes.

"The cottage, Reggie," I say. "Ruthie lives here as long as she can. You can rent out the land but not sell and I won't sell unless you say so. We'll write a proper codicil. It's as much as I can do."

Sharen grabs Reggie's wrist, feels it desperately. "Reggie?" Pleading. "Sweetie?" His eyes closed and I feel a sound travel through me, a primitive call that doesn't find voice. He smiles and takes my hand as he falls into sleep or loses consciousness. Sharen's head pressed to his chest, listening to her young boy's heart. A last smell of smoke from outside as if it whispers him away.

Uncle Worry coming as a darkness at the window, calling me back into his creased-up eyes. Wants to take me with him, out there deep into that dark smoke, with him and those lawmen, drive me back. Pointed the bone and I got fevers and pain in my own bones and my belly is a fire started and the inside throbbing, Worry waiting through that cobweb glass because of what I done to Walker, I see you, he says, tries to have me travel on the snake's tail. Come away with me. That world where Worry lives, just a spirit comes and goes as some old ghost. But I got a place here, got the bush for real. Make you the ghost boy, he says. Uncle on the chimney roof, in the trees when I needed, showing me how. Saved us all. Reggie Don gone and done it, protecting, end him proper with the gun. Left the gun out there beside the bastard, left the bastard in the dark. Reggie made it back on this old couch with his mumbo-jumbo mother over him, Ruthie watching from out her old bandicoot eyes, she try not to cry, even Danny all chalky and sad as if he'll miss me in the Dreaming. But I ain't gonna go so easy, not now. Gonna teach me those black horses on my own.

* * *

THURSDAY

◆────◇────◆

4:44 a.m., almost morning. The skewbald pony standing in the kitchen, keeping watch out the window. Ruthie snoring gently from her recliner, the dog snuggled up at her side, snoring too. Reggie silent but breathing again, asleep in his mother's arms. This vigil for his return to life, the way my mother did the other night. I wonder where they go, down a well that's deep inside them, telling them to stay. That still-small voice I've never heard. Perhaps I've never listened.

The shrill ring of the phone and Sharen glares at me, daring me to answer. As if she already knows who it must be. At this hour.

I get up from the couch and reach over for the receiver. The international wind-tunnel sound. "Are you back in LA yet?" asks Isabel.

"Not exactly."

"It's New Year's Eve." She sounds exhausted too. "You promised."

Still yesterday there, seventeen hours behind. "If I could be," I say and there's silence as my eyes meet Sharen's. "Where are you?" I ask.

"Santa Rosa Airport."

"Wine country," I say, Sharen staring me down through the lamplight, stroking Reggie's forehead and humming some kind of prayer. Her aqueous, marbled eyes.

"I thought I'd be back by now but things have gone apeshit here," I say. Sharen squints as if fearing I might make light of what's happening.

"You don't even sound like you," says Isabel through the hollow airport noises.

"There's a boy fighting for his life right here," I say. "I'm not sure how I'm supposed to sound."

Sharen nods approval, as though at least that's real.

"I don't know what to believe," says Isabel. Maybe she thinks it's me fighting for *my* life, and why wouldn't she? But I don't sense her empathy now. The softness has gone from her voice, and it feels as if I'm drifting down another river.

"I don't know what to believe myself," I say. I look out through the curtains. The rain has stopped, the burned-up trunks straight and mute as blackened teeth. Walker still out there, maybe, or the chance of him gone. My mother and her kerosene. A faint wisp of crimson on the horizon. It could be a wisp of hope but it's a peek of red sky and it's morning. Delight doesn't rhyme with morning.

"I thought I was pregnant," says Isabel. My stomach turns tighter, as if tied in two. I glance back at Sharen and listen. "I confirmed that I wasn't in the bathroom at a Walmart," says Isabel. I can't tell if she's happy with that result.

"Would it have been mine?" It slips out too quickly, I'm blurring, the line gone quiet as the room. Mascara-smudged Sharen looks over; she knows what that question means, and my mother's no longer snoring, maybe she listens too, the dog with its legs up in the air. Just Isabel's breath.

"My grandmother warned me how men only accuse you when they're guilty themselves," she says.

I want to make light of it, but I'm too worn down for that. "I haven't been perfect," I say, wait for her to ask more but she doesn't. Maybe she knows anyway, hears it in my voice, the erosion of what a heart holds. The brutality of distance.

"Then I'm going to New York to party with Doug and Bennie," she says, her gay friends with the Schnauzers, the swank penthouse in Chelsea where I always feel not quite "up with people." The idea of Isabel there drains the life from me. Then I remember.

"What about my Jeep?"

"Is that what you care about?"

She can't just abandon it. "Then what about Laurel Canyon?" My sudden desire to salvage things garners a shrewd glance from Sharen.

"What would be the point?" asks Isabel and I'm not sure. The thought of her in some drugstore bathroom peeing on a strip and waiting for the color, flying into LAX on New Year's Eve to spend the night alone.

"I'll be there soon," I say.

"What if I had been pregnant? What would you do then?"

An ache returns behind my eyes. "I would come home," I say.

"Don't insult me with your promises!" she says, then a fax beep in my ear; she's disconnected. I stand there stunned as Sharen searches down at Reggie. The words she spat at me on the dance floor, how we Rawsons think we can have everything. *Everything and nothing at all.*

THE DOG BARKS as car lights appear up the drive, make shadows in the room. I glance at Reggie sleeping in his mother's arms. Her nurturing is unlikely but somehow hopeful, her belief in her ability to save him, or for him to heal himself.

I watch my father limp across the lawn, the red dawn opening its lips through the trees. My mother stirring in her chair as the screen door slams and my father stands lop-sided in the sitting room doorway, his shoulders hunched about his ears. "Couldn't sleep," he says, surveys the room.

"Daniel's given your mother's cottage to Reggie," Ruthie announces. Has he not smelled the fire?

"That's the least of it," I tell him.

"That house is mine," he says, his eyes alight and Sharen observes him with quiet disgust. He slides a plastic reindeer off the desk onto the floor and frightens the dog.

"Then why don't you live in it?" my mother says, puts her legs down from the ottoman.

"It *was* yours, Dad," I say. "A long time ago. Before you screwed yourself out of it."

He fossicks furiously through a desk drawer. "I worked my whole bloody life for this farm," he says. "And I did it for you." He presses a faded Polaroid in my face.

This picture of him windblown in his forties beside his diminutive mother, Hilma, standing on the cottage steps. She shades her glasses from the sun, her soft gray perm and rosy skin. "For absolution," I say, as if he knows what that means. "To assuage your guilt."

The pink sag of my father's eyes meets mine. "I've been more loyal to this land than you could ever be."

I angle the image in the light, knowing what he says is true—the fancy little English woman who rocked me on her childhood horse from Coventry, then died in the bed beside me. And here we are. The cottage emptied of its history by this woman on the couch. "You promised Walker he could have the twenty-five acres where he was born," I tell my father.

My father grabs the photo out of my hand. "That was before he started stealing horses," he says. "Before your mother demanded I get him off the place."

"You could have given him something." I feel Reggie's eyes on me, a compass searching. Gauging every word. "Otherwise he mightn't have come back to haunt us."

"He was always wrong in the head," says Ruthie in her own defense. "And the town didn't want him."

"As if you care what the town thinks," I say and she winces at the chord of my disloyalty.

"I gave him calves and instead of letting them fatten into heifers he took them straight to market," my father says.

"They were *his*," I tell him.

Sharen squints at my father and me the way we talk about the man who tracked her down, who she had to escape.

"He didn't listen to me," he says and I can feel his energy waning, knowing he was wrong. "And neither do you." He tosses the picture down on the desk. How must it feel, being a man no one listens to? "This is the place we belong," he says. "You don't just give it away."

The eerie exhilaration of just a row of black chimneys. "Unless you want to," I say but my words just hang in the air as my father focuses on Reggie as he stirs. Sharen curls an arm about him as he sips from a cup of water.

"What happened to you?" my father asks the boy.

"His father," says Sharen, cradling the boy how she'd held the wallaby. It seems like days ago my father tried to dance with her. But it was only a matter of hours. Last year. A decade older than I am, she's made a bed here, earned it in a strange way. Now her son is sneaking back to life. His eyes open, seeking her comfort. Making choices. Time for me to make mine.

My father limps to the window. Outside it's on the verge of daylight. The reds turning into purples and grays. "The trees!"

My mother blows out a candle on the mantelpiece. "Walker," she says, catches Reggie's eye in a quick complicity I recognize. She did set the trees up as a decoy for Reggie. A ruffle of wings sounds in the chimney and the dog is poised and ready. My mother catches me, stares back in an old communion.

"Where is he?" my father asks, his face burning with what my mother used to call his *agitatus.*

"Let's go see," I tell him, Reggie catching my eye, looking for a sign. He and Ruthie running things the old way. I nod, *yes, I meant it. You can trust me.*

My father prods the skewbald pony out the back door. "Bloody horses inside," he says. He should realize Ruthie was just keeping her favorite safe, Patch or Patchouli, whatever his name is these days. He stands on the bluestone path, munching on plants. "Get out of here, little blaggard," my father yells but the pony doesn't budge, just looks at him as we pass. The clouds seem to move against the morning breeze.

"You better round up the stock," my father tells me. "See what's left." The notion of rounding up stock feels beyond me. Out here I feel even more sleepless and hungover. The morning birds silent after the fire.

"I'm giving the land to Reggie," I tell him. "Not to sell, but to keep or rent."

My father gimps along in disgust, the vague scent of damp smoke in the air as we round the veranda, the sprawl of the cotoneaster, the ground emerging before us, a carpet of charred twigs and branches, the trunks giant black legs going up into a layer of mist.

My father, speechless, peruses the damage. A fireman's shovel left in the crisped sand. A memento. "Bloody lucky the house didn't burn," he says.

"Is it?" I ask but he just examines the burned cypress leaves like fine black feathers and beyond, the black horses sniff at something down near a small cross-country jump, the fallen log where there used to be an explosion of calla lilies in spring. I head through the sooty garden gate. Bile rises at the sight of a body, half on its side, one leg bent and folded under the other. Walker, his face fallen into his beard. I try to breathe, try to hold myself to the facts of it, but my imagination runs to an injured boy desperate, killing his father. My elderly mother in cahoots. And I feel as naive and useless as my approaching father. One of the geldings sniffs the top of Walker's half-bald head, the hair fallen sideways. Blood blooming dark through the blue plaid of his shirt, wounds from belly and chest. The rifle planted by his side. More than one shot concealed by the sound of the branches cracking, the siren, my father beside me now, and the horses circling at our backs as the day spreads light around us.

"Who did this?" he asks, strangely calm. "Walker Dumbalk wouldn't do himself in for love or money." He kneels to reach for the stock of his own dead father's trench gun.

"Don't touch it," I tell him, his fingers already on the wood stem. Fresh prints mingled with the others. I recall how rain doesn't erase fingerprints as you'd imagine. Reggie's and Ruthie's probably still evident, now my father's too. I think to wipe it down and bury it, but hiding a weapon that clearly matches the bullets never bodes well. Both of us staring, sinking into the ramifications. I look back at the eerie trees still scarfed in mist. My mother no doubt watching, opening the curtains further, scraping the rings along the rod. No wonder they didn't want police. Even without the gun, Sharen would be the primary suspect. Two casings here in the damp gray sand, her bruiser ex-lover gone. I imagine that cop Gullikson from Cranbourne crouching before this and smiling, knowing the Winchester's placed too carefully, that the angle of the bullets won't jive with a rifle suicide. My father looks at me in general disbelief.

"Go get some feed sacks," I tell him.

He blanches at me, stunned. "Are you barmy?"

"Yes," I say. "Let's put this to bed."

His whole body sags as if he's a child been given orders as he gimps away to the stables. I grab the abandoned shovel and dig before the sky clears its throat. The cutting edge sharp, the sand digs deep and easy, softened by that downpour from nowhere sharp as nails, as if from the Bible. My hand that was healing hurts again, the wooden shaft of the spade against it plying this soil as I haven't in years. The horses line up as undertakers, witnesses; my head aching still and this shot-up body behind me. As I dig, an image of the front page of the *Pakenham Gazette*. *One Unfortunate New Year*. A photo of the house and trees. *Walker Dumbalk recently of Yarram found dead in the paddock at Tooradin Estate. Alleged he lit a fire then shot himself.* The story of how Walker was born here and taken away. Then, the suggestion: *Foul play not ruled out.*

I square off an end and keep shoveling, try not to glance at Walker, the first dead body I've seen up close. I think of the word "slain." Sweat through my shirt and my father returning with a wheelbarrow's worth of hessian sacking.

I take a break and catch my breath, stare past him into the distance, the rows of hay bales that have been rained on. Next he'll want them stacked damp in the shed. The way moist bales build heat and smolder all year. My father was born taking risks, the Massey Ferguson chugging on its own through the grass in first gear, alongside us. The baling wire dug into my fingers as this shovel digs now. He went off to talk to Annabell Lipman who rode up on a buckskin, left me with the unmanned tractor, the stick locking its steering wheel. And I just let the tractor go on ahead. The Fergie got right to the fence, the posts so rotten they snapped to the ground as it rolled right over the wires, churning into Royal Genoni's rented paddock.

Now he looks fearful, all the years he walked through these paddocks, checking on troughs and fences, wearing out his hips, treating yearlings caught in barbed wire, lighting the boiler each morning to keep the water hot. All of it penance. Along with the sense that sags heavy in the air between us—that this will not make anything easier. My mother out on the veranda, shading her eyes, guarding the house in case of reprisals, surveying through the black cypress trunks as they cast their narrow morning shadows. Pleased at how we finish what she's wrought.

I line the grave with hessian, my father trying to help, grunting beside me. Ants already pour over the bloody flannel-covered wounds. To avoid the weight we both kneel and roll him, his limbs stiffer than I imagine. His eyes unblinking, glare, his neck and jaw bulge with fury, the last moment of his face as he flops into the sandy hole I hope is deep enough. We stand there with him half-facedown, turn him, the rifle in his arms like a scepter—*rest in peace, you crazy bastard*—and begin to fill him in.

"There was once a rumor," my father says. "That he was your grandfather's son." Then he talks about how we should put an old bath here, make it a trough, be sure these horses don't start digging around. I shovel till my hands are bleeding. Knowing I will leave.

* * *

FRIDAY

◆————◆————◆

I watch the familiar trees go by. Winding up the canyon in this grubby Los Angeles cab turning onto Lookout Mountain, past the fallen-down stone mansion where Houdini was supposed to have lived. This canyon I envisioned as a boy, singing myself to sleep in the shearer's quarters beneath the festooned horse show ribbons pinned to the tongue-in-groove walls, listening to the sound of Bob Seger from a dusty tape deck. *Those Hollywood nights in those Hollywood Hills.* It was *this* winding road umbrellaed by eucalyptus, these perched wooden houses. I saw them then, rocking my head on a pillow eight thousand miles away, my dreams reaching out. *This* road, *these* trees, *these* bends, the weatherboard cottages, California bungalows, colored Cape Cods, envisioned without any frame of reference, just the words of a song. The same as unfolded before me as I drove up here the first time. Seven years ago. The same as unfolds now. And it feels as though I buried a man in a dream. How I want to pretend there's no way that rumor could be true, he couldn't have been my cousin; he didn't look anything like us. Still, the notion of my grandfather even fondling Gracious hollows me out with sorrow.

Usually I chat to Ethiopian taxi drivers, talk about Eritrea and war, and what life is for them here, but I've been awake too long to talk, trying to sleep on the plane, watching foreign movies. Isabelle Huppert as a sado-sexual piano teacher, just to cheer me up. A documentary called *Sun Come Up* about the ocean rising on an island called Carteret near Bougainville. Then I dreamed the farm was under the sea, Walker's body rising through the water and the stone with the eye floating up beside him from his grave, the undressed Christmas tree I laid to rot on top of the sand that covered him.

My father stood there with his hands cupped in front of him, reverent. "May the roads rise up to meet him," he said and I wondered if there was space inside my father where he might blame himself. For legacies and tendencies, the possessed and denied, himself and others. And if there's a space inside of me. "If anyone asks," I said to him as I smoothed the sand. "Tell them it was me." I stared out to the hills over past Cardinia, to Bunyip, as far as Labertouche as the sun roped up to fill the sky and the black mare walked over to nuzzle me, her hoofprints on the grave. With her warm breath I found words I did not say. *May his son take over and let the place run wild.*

When I said good-bye to my mother this time, she'd gone deaf again. I held her to me then drove away, leaving her and her dog and my stooped little father striped by the shadows of those burned-up trees. As I turned through the gate near the stables, the skewbald pony Patch looked up from the grass in the pond paddock and it was then I began to cry.

It was only when I saw the electric vastness of this city painted on the earth below; I fastened my seatbelt and began to feel my heart both alive and still. Energized by the frequency here, the absence of a past and the chance of Isabel. The prospect of the cab pushing through the early traffic on the trek up La Cienega, all the way to the morning-lit hills. The winter air crisp and everything vivid as though the winds of climate change have been a gift for this unbecoming, dirt-aired city. The ugliness strangely comfortable, the surprise of bougainvillea and lawns pretending it's not a desert, fancy cars shining as if water to wash them is as available as money to pay off the loans. Drivers staring each other down at the lights, hungry for something—attention or connection. Random things feel possible. The best and the worst. The thought of Reggie running that farm like a menagerie, Sharen keeping an eye on Ruthie, my father as fringe dweller, until Ruthie dies. And then what will he do?

On Wonderland Avenue, the blacktop becomes slick as always. It's good to be back in the shade. Water rolls down the hill where the stream is forced to make the road its bed, and a new knot in my stomach begins again. My fear of where I'll end up if Isabel's gone. I hear the echo of hammers. New construction on the hill face and a fear that she'll not be here, or here. Her books and paintings, her photos from the top of Angel Falls. The chance to tread lighter, learn integrity.

"Eighty-seven twenty-nine," I say through the hand-smutched plastic that divides me and the back of the driver's Yankees cap. The strange house numbering scheme; short streets numbered in the thousands. "Leave me at the bridge," I add, fishing for my wallet, searching for signs of Isabel. The meter's reached sixty-four dollars.

The pair of retrievers from next door greets me, wagging their fat golden bodies on the damp maple leaves that carpet the driveway at this time of year. Golden as the dogs and the day. The rattle of my bag rolling up the bricks behind me. The same bag I rolled to the curb at LAX just a fortnight ago, her reluctant hug good-bye. It feels like a minute and a year. If a story could be retold: a boy in a sandpit, his watchful parents on veranda chaises, the mother reading something light, maybe *Mapp and Lucia*, the father drinking a beer in the afternoon, reaching over for the mother's hand. The boy waves at them, smiling. Who grew up and drove like a normal person, kissed his girlfriend good-bye at the airport, telephoned her every day.

The big stucco house where my landlady actress chants. Her *Namu Myōhō Renge Kyō* and old white-tired Mercedes left in the garage. My red Jeep is parked beside it. I pass the big shuttered windows and turn up the path to the guesthouse, its ledge of geraniums and louvered windows opening into the vines and chaparral, cottonwood. Succulents in their pots, here all along, watered by the rain. My eyes are dry, sore from stale air and uncertainty, but the top of the stable door is slightly open, and in the breeze a dress hangs from a sycamore, the cream linen one she'd have worn at Esalen, pinned with old-fashioned cardboard luggage tags. Like the dresses clipped with prayers in the tree above Big Sur. A prayer of my own as I lay my bags down and reach for the door.